BITTERSWEET HERBS

A POTTING SHED MYSTERY

MARTY WINGATE

BOG OAK PRESS

ALSO BY MARTY WINGATE

The Potting Shed Mysteries

The Garden Plot

The Red Book of Primrose House

Between a Rock and a Hard Place

The Skeleton Garden

The Bluebonnet Betryal

Best-Laid Plants

Midsummer Mayhem

Bittersweet Herbs

The Birds of a Feather Mysteries

The Rhyme of the Magpie

Empty Nest

Every Trick in the Rook

Farewell, My Cuckoo

The First Edition Library Mysteries

The Bodies in the Library

Murder Is a Must

The Librarian Always Rings Twice

Historical fiction

Glamour Girls

Bittersweet Herbs is a work of fiction. Names, characters, places, and incidents are the products of the author's imagination or are used fictitiously. Any resemblance to actual events, locales, or persons, living or dead, is entirely coincidental.

Published by Bog Oak Press

Cover design by: Phillips Covers (phillipscovers.com)

To Leighton with love

CHAPTER 1

The Winchester Medieval Garden Society
Cordially invites you and a guest to an evening lecture

The Medieval Herb Garden:
All Things to All People
by renowned scholar Acantha Morris

Hundred Men's Hall
Hospital of St. Cross and Almshouse of Noble Poverty

21 January
7 p.m.

You will be greeted with mead and ale,
and after the lecture, enjoy a buffet menu of:

Tart in Ymber Day
Compost
Payn Puff
Frumenty
Gingerbrede

The evening in support of the Society's garden project

Pru turned her phone on speaker and set it on her desk in the library so she could continue typing into her laptop.

"No, I really don't think we'll be eating garden compost," she said. "It must've meant something else in medieval times. I'm looking it up now. Wait, here it is—an old English recipe with roasted fruits and vegetables pickled in vinegar and wine. They used parsnips and cabbages and turnips and raisins—that sort of thing."

"Hmmm." Her sister-in-law's response was less than enthusiastic. "Well, as long as there's wine."

"We'll be drinking mead," Pru said. "I tasted mead once—at an organic farm just south of Dallas."

"They make mead in Texas?" Polly asked.

"It's a thing," Pru explained. "A medieval thing, but still popular in some circles." Possibly not her favorite drink—she remembered it being a bit heavy and sweet with honey.

"I'm beginning to see why you weren't able to talk your husband into going to the lecture," Polly said.

"Christopher has a community policing meet-and-greet in Dunbridge that evening, or he'd be delighted."

"Ha!"

Pru leaned back in her chair and took the alligator clip out of her hair. Its texture, midway between slightly frizzy and barely wavy, resisted control, but still, she combed through and reclipped. "We could ask Bernadette," she offered. "This group is raising funds to create a garden near the medieval Hospital in Winchester." After living in Britain for several years, it still amazed Pru that something that old could be just down the road. "I'm sure they'd allow me two guests if we make a donation. It'll be fun!"

"Do you know any of these people in the—"

"Winchester Medieval Garden Society," Pru filled in. "No, but perhaps it's a mass mailing to all of Hampshire."

"Perhaps they've heard of you."

By the end of their phone conversation, Polly had agreed to go to the medieval evening and said she would ring Bernadette, the vicar at St. Mary's—the three women enjoyed the occasional night out together. Pru emailed her response to the invitation and then sat back, wondering about the group and its garden, which she had never seen or heard of. An online search brought up a single web page framed by ancient figures at war. "Vignette from the Bayeaux tapestry," the photo credit read, accompanied by a brief message: *Our mission is to re-create a medieval herb garden to accompany the Hospital of St. Cross, that venerable institution in existence since the twelfth century.* Other than that explanation, there was only a note to say that the website was under construction. Pru had never visited the Hospital of St. Cross, but Winchester was a short drive. Perhaps she'd dash over for a recce before the evening event.

Polly's comment "Perhaps they've heard of you" stayed with Pru, who was half-pleased and half-mortified that her name could be recognizable in the world of British gardening. But if pressed, she might admit its likelihood.

It was how she'd landed a recent writing assignment for a new magazine, *Designs On Your Garden*. The editor, a man named Nate Crispin who sounded too young to be editor of anything but his school newspaper, had contacted her, saying he'd read her account of renovating an eighteenth-century landscape. Would she be interested in working up an article for him? Initially flattered—it was her hope to do more writing—she was then blindsided when he'd mentioned the article's title, "Death in the Garden."

She knew what he meant, but long ago had had her fill of such veiled references to events in her life. Biting back the urge to tell him what she thought of his idea—Pru avoided confrontation whenever possible—she offered a subdued response, and declined his offer. He must've sensed her ire, because he followed hard on by saying the title was expendable and what he truly wanted was a scholarly but readable approach that would be an "inspirational synthesis explaining the enduring appeal of gardens in the historical context of both ornament and use."

Mollified, she had agreed, but regretted it almost immediately and rang Nate Crispin back. He'd given her a pep talk, told her that the article's direction was completely up to her, and asked for two thousand words by the end of the month.

That had been a week ago, just after New Year's, and since then, each morning Pru had retreated to the library to stare at her blank computer screen before eventually giving up for the day. She would then make her way to the kitchen, where Evelyn, their housekeeper and cook, asked how the writing was coming along.

"Good. Fine."

Each day so far, she had managed a plausible excuse to quit early, but her imagination had run dry at last, and at this time when Evelyn asked, Pru grasped at straws. "It occurred to me that I'd promised Simon I would clean and oil the spades, and so I'd better get to it before he arrives for coffee at eleven. Don't you think?"

Evelyn made no reply to that, and so Pru slipped out the door, waiting until she stood on the stone threshold outside the mudroom before buttoning up her heavy coat. Perhaps a walk round the terrace. It was a fine, bright winter morning and the perfect time to admire the gardens at Greenoak—from the hardy cyclamen blooming under the hornbeam hedge to the shredded ribbon flowers of witch hazel hanging from bare branches.

Pru and Christopher had lived at Greenoak—a small manor house in the village of Ratley, and just outside the town of

Romsey—since they'd married not quite three years earlier. It was where she gardened with her brother, Simon, Polly's husband, who lived the other side of the village. The gardener siblings worked fewer hours in winter, but Simon usually appeared just in time for elevenses—coffee and one of Evelyn's pastries always went down a treat.

Not that January was a slouch time in the garden, and the cold weather didn't deter Pru and Simon from necessary tasks. At least it was dry. Unusually dry, causing the rhododendrons to droop and curl their leaves to protect against moisture loss. But as for work—she and Simon had already dug the remaining leeks, checked the dahlia tubers stored in sand, and salvaged a few lengths of guttering for starting the first crop of peas later.

Better get to those spades. Pru made her way to the potting shed, where she discovered all the tools already cleaned and oiled. But instead of going back inside to start on the article, she spent a few minutes rearranging seed packets until she heard Simon's car in the drive. All the while, a tiny voice in the back of her head told her that in order to be a writer, actual writing was necessary. She ignored it. Apparently, Pru had found a new skill she was quite good at —procrastination.

"The Hospital of St. Cross and Almshouse of Noble Poverty is such a commanding name for the place," Pru said to Christopher. "And, it lives up to it. It's a lovely setting by the river with ornamental gardens on the grounds. There must've been an herb garden all those centuries ago—it makes sense to put one in again."

She pulled on her decent pair of wool trousers and a blue sweater with a high neckline. Having taken a look at the large stone rooms at the Hospital—ancient and unheated—she knew layering was a must, and stuck her head into the wardrobe, searching for a scarf.

She turned to catch Christopher straightening the epaulets on the shoulders of his uniform. He made a dashing figure—short dark-brown hair with perhaps the suggestion of gray at his temples, that penetrating gaze, those shiny brass buttons.

"Well, Detective Inspector Pearse, you don't wear that often," she commented.

Christopher acknowledged the fact with a nod. "It's the Women's Institute—they asked if I'd come formal."

"You're a big hit with the WI."

He sighed. "I'm not sure I wouldn't rather be drinking ale with you this evening in Winchester."

"Didn't I read somewhere that you had to chew medieval ale before swallowing?" she asked and saw that ghost of a smile round his lips. "I tell you what, I'll bring you home a slice of tart in ymber day. I looked it up—it's a sort of onion pie concoction with currants and spices."

"I believe Evelyn's chicken and leek will do me fine," he said, kissing her forehead and then the tip of her nose and then her lips. "Take care on the roads—as dry as it's been, there are still icy patches."

Pru had chosen mead from the server's tray that passed by just after they arrived for the lecture. Polly took mead, too, but Pru persuaded Bernadette to try the ale. It came in a small taster glass and was dark and smelled malty—but at least there were no bits. The vicar sipped carefully.

"How is it?" Pru asked.

"Sort of yeasty—like bread. Do you want some?"

"No, thanks."

But it couldn't be that bad. As Pru drank her mead, she saw

several men round the hall throwing back glasses of ale. They had a sort of determined look on their faces that reminded Pru of the tequila-drinking contests from her college days at Texas A&M—except those took place in bars full of cowboys and loud country music.

Polly pushed up her glasses with the back of her hand and surveyed the scene. "It's a good crowd, don't you think? There must be close to seventy people here. See anyone you know?"

"No one," Pru replied. "I really should get out more. The least I can do is meet a few people this evening."

Only one new person, as it turned out. The three women split up, and Pru found herself talking with a fellow who, upon learning she was a gardener, engaged her in a discussion of using paper collars on brassica seedlings to keep cabbage moths away. Across the hall, Polly perused a table with drawings and books and what might have been a three-dimensional mock-up of a walled garden. Bernadette, who was not tall and would be difficult to spot in a crowd if it weren't for her bright-purple tunic and dog collar, stood nearby chatting with another priest.

Twenty minutes later, when a bell called them to take their seats, Pru fetched her companions and led them to the front row.

"It's ambitious, I'll say that," Polly reported. "There's a field not far from the Porter's Lodge they want to buy—it's outside the Hospital grounds, but close enough to be associated. The cost for the first phase alone is a million pounds. That's without putting a shovel in the ground, but it would at least let them make an offer on the land."

Pru hoped the society didn't expect to raise that much this evening. But she put the money out of her mind as a short, well-dressed man stepped onto the podium and stood behind the lectern, his round head just barely clearing it. He introduced himself—Rollo Westcott, chairman of the Winchester Medieval Garden Society. He spoke of the Hospital, its creation in the twelfth century, and its founder, Henry of Blois, bishop of Winchester and a grandson of William the Conqueror. He described the fifteenth-century addition of the almshouse and how the institutions were secular good works, and perhaps that was why they had been left alone during Henry VIII's Dissolution of the Monasteries.

"And now, we have a real treat this evening," Rollo said. He turned to a woman standing at the bottom of the podium steps. She had dark skin, her black hair was pulled up into a tight bun on the top of her head, and she wore a suit of deep mulberry. "Here is scholar and member of the board Acantha Morris to discuss the importance of herbs in health and well-being in medieval England."

Rollo departed the podium, and Acantha took his place. She scanned her audience and then began.

"Look now," she said, "I want you to put your hands in your pockets."

There was a titter through the crowd, and she smiled. "No, I'm not asking for money—not yet, at least." A bigger laugh. "I want you to put a hand in your pocket and tell me—do you have something in there that could save your life?"

A general stir, followed by an offer of "Four pound twenty—would that save me?"

"You couldn't even buy a round in the pub for that, now could you?" Acantha responded, and her audience chuckled and settled back in their chairs. "But look what I have." She pulled a handful of dried plant material from her jacket pocket, and Pru leaned forward. She saw delicate, ferny foliage with the remains of daisylike flowers attached. If Acantha crushed it, Pru thought for certain she could catch the scent of apples. It was chamomile.

"Chamomile," Acantha said. "A tea with chamomile, dittany, scabious, and pennyroyal—our medieval brothers believed—could save you from poisoning. So, in this instance chamomile means life. But it's also used as a comfort—a calming tea or tincture. Herbs often have more than one application. Just as rosemary can season meat, it can be combined with other strong-smelling herbs and spices, such as lavender, and exotic frankincense and myrrh to disguise unpleasant odors. To hide the smell of death. You see, medieval herb gardens had to be all things."

~

"She's sold me on the project," Polly said at the end of Acantha's talk as the crowd made its way into the Brethren's Hall, where food awaited. "Doesn't she have a wonderful way of making the past come alive?"

"I'm going to volunteer," Pru said with a zealous rush. "What am I doing with myself—the gardens at Greenoak practically take care of themselves, and when Simon and I hire a new assistant, there'll be even less to do."

She didn't mention the other decision she'd come to—that the perfect topic for the magazine article in *Designs On Your Garden* was, of course, the medieval herb garden. She needed to get into the reception and have a word with Acantha.

In the Brethren's Hall, servers circled the room offering not mead or medieval ale, but glasses of wine. Polly grabbed a white as a tray passed, but Pru was driver and so chose fizzy water instead. A long table just inside the door was spread with a variety of foods, each with an accompanying label. The women —along with a handful of others—circled the table, reading and inspecting before choosing. Pru played it safe and took a payn puff – boiled fruit in pastry.

"It's like a little hand pie," she told Polly and Bernadette. The two abandoned what they'd chosen and each nabbed one.

Pru spotted Acantha across the room with a small crowd

gathered round her, made her way over, and, when the others had drifted off, introduced herself.

"A gardener from America," Acantha said, "wonderful. Are you on holiday?"

"No, my husband and I live near Romsey—he's English. I so enjoyed your talk. Is your degree in garden history or medieval studies?"

Acantha shook her head. "I have no letters after my name. It was generous of Rollo to describe me as a scholar, because I was a bookkeeper for my working life. I am, as you would say, 'self-taught.' But I learned that just because I have no university degree, I needn't stop learning, and now that I'm retired, I can indulge in my secret passion—the past. The long past. Medieval times, how people lived, what they grew, and how growing herbs helped not only their health, but made life more pleasant, from flavoring their food to making their houses smell better."

"This is fascinating, and I'm interested in helping."

"And we'd love to have you!" Acantha exclaimed.

They exchanged contact details, and then Pru said, "I wonder if I might—"

She was about to explain the article she was writing—would write—when someone tapped a spoon on a glass, calling for attention. The room quieted, and everyone looked to a tall woman with blond hair cascading over her shoulders. She wore a short black dress and a long red scarf that swept round her neck and hung to her knees. Her smile was broad and engaging, and Pru, along with others in the crowd, automatically smiled back.

"Please forgive me for interrupting the fun. Thank you all so much for being here. Wasn't that a wonderful lecture?" She swept her arm toward Acantha as if introducing a new car on the showroom floor. "I certainly don't want to take anything away from the outstanding talk this evening—"

Acantha smiled back, but under her breath said, "Oh, yes, you do."

Pru's eyes darted between the two women, as the blonde continued.

"For those of you who don't know me, let me introduce myself—I'm Claudia Temple. It's been only six months ago that I joined the society, and since then, I've learned a tremendous amount about medieval times. We have such high hopes for establishing the garden and everyone has been working so very hard, but as you all know, fundraising can be an uphill battle, and costs for the project are high."

Pru saw many in the crowd nod sadly, and a few shrugged shoulders at one another.

"And so," Claudia continued, "I wondered, what could *I* do? What part could I play in moving us forward to our goal? A donation? Of course. But if I encourage you to give according to your means, then so should I. And so"—she took a deep breath and threw out her arms—"it is my pleasure to pledge one million pounds."

The silence in the hall was deafening, as if all the air had been sucked out of the room. Then, a second later, came a crash from somewhere in the crowd—a wineglass dropping to the floor—and the silence broke with an uproar of cheers and clapping.

CHAPTER 2

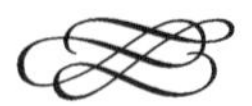

"Claudia Temple certainly took care of that first level of funding," Polly commented in the car on the way back. "She must be worth a considerable amount to promise a million pounds in one go."

"Did you notice how she glowed with pleasure at the cheers and applause?" Bernadette asked thoughtfully. "As if she needed the approval."

"I'd say the society will put in an offer for that field immediately," Pru said. "I'm going back day after tomorrow to meet Acantha and find out more. I got the idea Claudia took them all by surprise—either they didn't know about the money or didn't realize she would announce it this evening. Did you see the look on Rollo's face? There were a few others that looked stunned first and happy second. Expected or no, it is remarkable. Think how hard some organizations have to campaign for funds."

"And she's been a part of the group for only six months," Polly added. "But, of course, the tax break will be significant. I wonder if that's part of it."

"If they don't have anyone in charge of finances on the board, maybe you could help out?" Pru suggested. Polly worked as an accountant for a handful of small businesses and volunteered her services for several nonprofits. "And Bernadette"—Pru glanced in her rearview mirror at the vicar in the back seat—"weren't you talking with the reverend what's-his-name from the church on the grounds? We should have a combined coffee morning—his church and St. Mary's. It would help spread the word."

"Well," Bernadette replied, "that is my job, after all. Spreading the Word to my flock—on Sundays and throughout the week."

Pru's blush went unseen in the dark car. Bernadette had managed to get her on St. Mary's flower guild and Christopher volunteered with the church-sponsored Scout troop, but their Sunday attendance was spotty, at best.

"You know what I mean," Pru said, and she caught Bernadette's smile.

"Yes, I do," the vicar said.

Polly pointed to the windshield and out into the darkness ahead. "You don't want to go too fast on the bends along the Straight Mile," she said. "Could be a bit of ice."

Pru rolled her eyes. Her sister-in-law drove—as Pru's dad would've said—like a bat out of hell, which in Pru's mind made any curve dicey. Still, as she drove along the Straight Mile, she slowed her Mini to a crawl.

Smoke curled from one of the chimneys at Greenoak when Pru arrived. It didn't take her long to shed her coat and seek the warmth. Christopher had a fire going in the library. He had changed out of his uniform, had his sock feet up on an ottoman, and an open book resting on his chest. On the coffee table sat a bottle of wine and a plate of cheese and crackers.

His eyes popped open when Pru leaned over the sofa and put her cheek against his.

"You're freezing," he said.

"It was my dash from the car into the house—doesn't take long in this weather. I checked the thermometer on the way in. It's minus three." She scooted up close to him on the sofa. "Let's see, what's that in Fahrenheit—about twenty-six degrees, I think. Brrr."

He poured her a glass and handed it over. "I thought you might want something when you arrived—I wasn't sure if they would be serving you an actual meal. Or how it would taste."

"We gave the frumenty mixed reviews. Wheat boiled in broth, I think. But there were a few high spots." She took a sip of wine. "How were the WI and their families?"

"I believe the PC's uniform impressed them more than I did," he replied. "And the lecture?"

"Enlightening. Inspiring. It's an ambitious project and they need volunteers, and so I've signed on. I've set up a meeting with Acantha Morris on site to talk with her about it. Not only that, but I've decided the medieval herb garden will be the subject for my magazine article. There." She heaved a sigh of relief. "Now that I've landed on a topic, I'm sure the writing will take care of itself. The whole thing will be as easy as … payn puff."

Pru had lost track of Acantha amid the celebration that broke out after Claudia Temple's announcement, and so hadn't actually mentioned the magazine article, but what nonprofit organization wouldn't love to have its mission splashed across the glossy pages of an upscale periodical? But first, Pru needed to be familiar with the subject herself, and so spent the first half of the next morning seeking knowledge. She began online and, when her brother arrived for elevenses, decided he should know more, too.

"I can't believe you don't have any books on medieval gardens," she said to him, pouring their coffees as Evelyn handed over a plate of warm raisin buns before returning to her work at the kitchen sink.

"I can't believe the university graduate in our midst doesn't have a full library on every gardening subject."

Pru, with a quick glance to make sure Evelyn wasn't watching, flicked a raisin at her brother.

Although Simon and Pru might easily be identified as siblings—something about the slight frizz to their hair and a certain look about their brown eyes—they had not grown up together and so had not worked through that sibling stage during which the older brother tormented his annoying little sister. Since meeting, only a few years ago, they had tried to make up for lost time, ignoring the fact that Simon, fifteen years Pru's senior, was nearing seventy.

"Polly used to watch those Brother Cadfael television programs," Simon replied, retrieving the bit of dried fruit from the floor. "They're medieval and it's about gardens. Ask her. She probably knows more than the two of us put together."

Pru had found the program online and watched one episode before bed, but had became distracted by the murder mystery and how young Derek Jacobi looked, and had forgotten to inspect the garden in the background.

"Did she tell you what we ate at the reception?" Pru asked. "It was all quite interesting. I might try cooking a medieval recipe."

Her brother laughed.

A massive potato slipped out of Evelyn's hands and *thunked* into the sink. She muttered something Pru couldn't make out.

"What did you say, Ev?"

The cook whirled round and braced herself against the counter, her face flushed and firm with determination.

"No lavender," she announced in a voice that bounced off the walls of the kitchen, and then added, in a conciliatory tone, "You won't cook with lavender—will you?"

"I hadn't actually thought that far ahead."

"Lavender scones, lavender pies, lavender crème brûlée"—Evelyn waved her paring knife in the air—"pretty soon the entire kitchen will smell like a soap factory."

"Well, then, of course I won't cook with lavender," Pru said. "Absolutely not. Don't worry."

When it came to the kitchen, Pru did what she was told. She had grown up gardening, not cooking, and so had never been able to do much more than scramble eggs. Now, in her midfifties, she had embraced the world of cookery and, under Evelyn's tutelage, had recently made it through the shortcrust pastry lesson, which had culminated in quite an adequate treacle tart. She could see a vast new world ahead of her, one filled with sauces and soufflés and crisp yet chewy meringues.

Simon stood and headed for the door. "Right. I'd say those black currant bushes won't prune themselves—we'd better get cracking."

They were halfway across the gravel yard heading for the potting shed when Simon added, "Next time she makes a pan of shortbread, sneak a bit of lavender in and see if she can even tell."

Pru stopped in her tracks. "I would never do that to Evelyn," she said. "It wouldn't be fair." And because she'd seen Evelyn angry.

A sly grin crept across her brother's face. "Afraid of the cook, are you? Go on, I dare you."

The following morning, Pru dressed for her meeting with Acantha as if preparing for battle. Working out in the garden in below-freezing weather was one thing—at least you could gin up some inner heat—but to stand and discuss garden design in the cold was asking to be chilled to the bone. Layers were the answer, and so she laid out each piece of her outfit on the bed—camisole, long-sleeved T-shirt, thin pullover sweater and, to cover it all, a woolly cardigan. She stood wrapped tightly in her tartan robe with her back to the cold fireplace getting up her nerve. Then, she counted to three, threw off her covering, and pulled on each layer, gasping when cold fabric hit her warm skin. She struggled into tights, a thick pair of socks, and heavy corduroy trousers and headed downstairs, where her boots and coat waited.

"It's on-the-ground research for my article," she explained to Evelyn as she buttoned her coat and added a red beret, forcing it over the large clip that held her hair at bay. She gave herself a quick check at the mirror in the mudroom loo and saw that her head had taken on the shape of a lopsided mushroom. Comfort over fashion—it was any gardener's first rule.

Evelyn paused from her task of cutting up chickens and turned, meat cleaver in hand. "This article—is it the one you've been writing for the past fortnight? And it's on medieval gardens?"

"Yes, that article. Now that you mention it, this is a change of topic—" from nothing to something "—and so, I suppose I'd better run it by Nate Crispin. He's the editor, you know." As if mentioning the man's name meant they were the best of friends. "I'll give him a ring tomorrow."

Or the next day, Pru thought as she motored over to Winchester under leaden skies. Nate didn't seem to care what she wrote about, only that he would be able to publish an article by her. Again, that niggling thought surfaced briefly that her name meant more to him than her talents. She would prove him wrong.

Pru parked along St. Cross Back Street, got out of her Mini, and pulled on mittens. Across the road, Acantha emerged from an old plum-colored VW Polo, turned up the collar on a deep-purple wool coat, and tucked a large, thin portfolio under her arm.

"Good morning," she called. "Ready for your tour?"

"I am," Pru replied. "Can I carry that for you?"

"No, dear, I'm fine." But when she opened the oversize folder, several colored-pencil drawings slid out and drifted to the ground.

Pru pulled off a mitten, retrieved the sheets, and held them out to get a better look. A few were plan views—showing the layout of beds and paths from above—and the others were elevation drawings, seen from eye level. Those gave a sense of the scope of the garden, including trees and fruiting plants trained against high brick walls. Details of herbs in flower had been included as a border around several pages, and in the corner of each sheet, the boxed legend read "Winchester Medieval Garden Society." It had been written in what she assumed was script from the Middle Ages, but what she would call calligraphy.

"These are quite good. I believe my sister-in-law saw them at the lecture." Pru hadn't had the time that evening. "Did you have them professionally done?"

"No, Rollo drew them up," Acatha replied. "He trained as a landscape architect before he went into the family business. You see, we each of us on the board have our own talents to bring to the endeavor."

She led Pru out into the empty field across from the Hospital, their feet crunching on the frozen ground. There, Acantha took an elevation drawing, held it up, and swept her arm across the empty landscape. "Here it is—or will be. Our medieval herb garden."

Acantha launched into what sounded very much like a lecture on the definition of a walled garden and how the structure protected plants from wind and extreme temperatures. Pru squinted into the distance, comparing the bare expanse to the landscape in the drawing. It was always an exciting and hopeful time in garden-making, but she could not ignore the cold seeping through her many layers.

"We'll have the traditional square beds, naturally," Acantha said, "with wild areas nearer the walls. Of course, we'll include not only infirmary plants, but also there will be a small orchard and a kitchen garden." The description abruptly halted, as Acantha's eyes widened and she laughed.

"How silly of me," she said. "You know all about medieval gardens, don't you? Wasn't your degree in garden history? You see—I looked you up."

"I'm certainly no expert on this time period," Pru replied, pulling her mitten back on. "I fashioned my own degree at university and concentrated mostly on the eighteenth century and on. But, I'm eager to learn."

"Horehound rock?" Acantha secured the portfolio under an arm, rummaged in her handbag, and came up with a small, crumpled paper bag filled with dark-brown chunks of what did, indeed, look like rocks. "Most people know it only as a boiled sweet today—and an old-fashioned one at that. Horehound—the plant—grows wild throughout much of Britain, so no one would think of including it in a modern garden. But in medieval times, it was indispensable. Made into a tea, it would loosen phlegm, you know, so that you could cough up all that thick mucus and be rid of it. We've forgotten that today."

Pru would like to forget it now. "Yes, I'd love one, thanks."

She pulled off the mitten again, and—not wanting to look finicky—put her hand in the bag and grabbed the first piece she touched, which turned out to be the size of a jawbreaker.

"Oh," Acantha said with a smile. "You've got a gobstopper there."

Pru popped it in her mouth politely, at the precise moment

Acantha asked, "How do you feel about the Doctrine of Signatures?"

Her response—more gargle than words—sent Acantha into peals of laughter. "Don't I have the worst timing?" She looked over Pru's shoulder and added, "Oh look, here are Rollo and Finley. I asked them to come along to meet you today."

"Ahglee," Pru replied, aiming for "lovely." A bit of sticky drool escaped out the corner of her mouth.

Acantha gave the two arriving cars a wave. "You'd better spit that out. Go on, I don't mind. I don't really care for it, myself—I'm more of a rhubarb-and-custard girl. Just chuck it into the grass."

Pru did as she was told, and then dug in her pocket for a tissue, looking up to see Rollo Westcott standing behind a navy Renault. Only his head was visible until he walked round the front of the car. Then she saw he wore a plaid hunting jacket adorned with an array of straps, buckles, and pockets. He paused to pull on a fleece-lined trapper hat with earflaps that hung down to his shoulders.

A little cornflower-blue sports car with a black convertible top had nosed up behind the Renault, and a man Pru did not recognize emerged. He secured a Cossack hat over his bald head and buttoned up a gray coat, then leaned over and—with a sleeve of his coat—dusted off the car's bumper. Meanwhile, Claudia Temple climbed out of the passenger seat. She wore a gold puffy coat that swept to the ground. Another woman wearing such a thing—Pru counted herself foremost—would look as if she'd crawled inside a sleeping bag. On Claudia the coat accentuated her height and her elegance and made her look like the angel atop a Christmas tree.

Claudia threw one end of her long red scarf over a shoulder, where it dangled to her knees, and waved enthusiastically at them. Acantha dropped her hand and said, "Oh, of course—wouldn't you know it?"

When the trio reached them, introductions were made. Board members Rollo Westcott and solicitor Finley Martin gave Pru single, businesslike handshakes. Claudia Temple grasped both Pru's hands—one mittened, one bare—in hers.

"We're so very happy to meet you," she said, flashing that wide, engaging smile Pru had seen at the lecture. "Isn't this a thrilling project?"

From a distance, Pru had guessed Claudia to be in her midthirties, but on closer inspection, she saw fine lines at the corners of her eyes and noticed the long blond hair had a few streaks of gray in it. Pru adjusted her guess to nearer fifty.

"Has Acantha shown you round?" Rollo asked Pru. "Have you seen the plans?"

"I've had only a glance. You did a fine job on them, I can tell that." Rollo bobbed his head in acknowledgment, and Pru continued. "This is a wonderful space, and what a great addition to the medieval Hospital and Almshouse across the road."

"Too bad we can't put a shovel in the ground today," Rollo said, stomping a foot on the hard surface.

"Yes," Pru replied, "digging would certainly be tough going in these conditions."

Therein began a brief exchange about the unusual weather, during which a few tiny crumbs of snow drifted down from the glowering skies like dandruff brushed from a cloud's shoulder.

"An anomaly, to be sure," Rollo said, gazing upward. "It was so hot last summer, and now we can't get above freezing."

Claudia shivered and stuck her hands in her pockets. Finley glanced at her and said, "Rollo, can't we adjourn to the pub and carry on with this?"

Everyone deemed that a grand idea and they started off to the Bell Inn, just up ahead at a bend in the road. The two men walked on discussing administrative issues, and Pru joined the women.

"Acantha," Claudia said, "what was it that you had in your hand the other night at the lecture?"

"Chamomile—remember, that was one of the first herbs we studied." Acantha's voice was a mix of patience and exasperation.

"Oh yes, of course," Claudia replied with good humor. She turned to Pru. "Acantha is teaching me all about herbs, but I'm a terrible student."

"You wouldn't be if you studied," Acantha replied, in a voice that reminded Pru of her mother.

Claudia accepted the admonition without offense. "Acantha says I don't know mint from … oh dear, what's the other one? It starts with an *m*, I'm sure it does."

"Mandrake," Acantha offered with a sigh.

"That's it—I don't know mint from mandrake." Claudia laughed. "My husband says I can't keep anything in my head longer than it takes the kettle to boil, but I'm ever so keen on learning."

They were the first customers of the day in the pub, and took a large table at one end of the room. Rollo went up to the bar to order the drinks—three teas and two coffees—while everyone peeled off layers of coats, sweaters, and gloves, and chatted among themselves. Pru noticed a man who had come in after them. He was tall with brown hair that was parted in the middle and fell to his shoulders, and he wore faded denims and a fisherman's sweater. He gave them a quick glance and then abruptly turned the other way and took one of the wingback chairs by the fireplace at the opposite end of the room. Its tall back hid him from sight, apart from his long legs that stretched toward the fire, and his brown dress boots with pointed toes. Those had seen better days.

Hot drinks in hand, Rollo took the lead, beginning with what sounded like a prepared statement. He thanked Claudia once again for her generosity and made reference to the offer on the land already in the works. He moved from there to describing—for Pru's benefit—the planning and execution of the garden, with Finley supplying the business details. Acantha chimed in often, but Claudia remained quiet, although engrossed, with her hands wrapped round her coffee mug.

"We have located a source for bricks for the walls," Finley said proudly. "Medieval bricks, as you may know "—Pru knew nothing about medieval bricks and hoped the solicitor wouldn't quiz her—"were thin and long. Not the sort of thing you find lying round an old farmyard these days."

"But fast-forward eight hundred years or so," Rollo cut in with enthusiasm, "and we see that the Edwardians had quite a fondness for the medieval brick, and began making reproductions. Those bricks are not nearly so difficult to find. So, our walls will be medieval in intent, although early twentieth century in fact."

"You can find enough for all four walls of the garden?" Pru asked. "How many bricks is that?"

"A massive number," Finley said.

"We've located quite a large lot this morning," Rollo said, "and we've also hired the excavation company. These first steps are huge and, of course, costly, and only made possible through Claudia's generosity."

They beamed at her. She responded with a wide smile, and said, "I surprised them, Pru—I surprised everyone at the lecture."

After a general lighthearted titter, Finley patted her hand and said, "Only with your timing, Claudia. But what does that matter?"

Rollo continued.

"As you can imagine, the Winchester Medieval Garden Society has a long road ahead, and we are eager to find others who share our dream and want to see it become a reality. And to that end, Pru"—Rollo glanced at the others and they leaned forward—"because of your deep knowledge of horticulture, as well as your great interest in garden history, we would like you to join us on the board."

Pru had been thinking more along the lines of being a volunteer—helping to dig the beds, to plant and prune. A member of the board? Did they want her to be merely a name on the letterhead, or did this offer carry responsibility?

Claudia, her eyes sparkling, reached across the table—a large rock of a diamond bobbing on her ring finger—and squeezed Pru's arm. "Oh do say you'll join us. It's such fun."

"I'm honored that you would ask me," Pru began, attempting to sort out her thoughts. "And—"

Acantha glanced at her watch and shot out of her chair. "Oh dear, look at the time. Sorry, but I must be on my way—my daughter will be dropping the baby off in twenty minutes." She turned to Pru. "Granny on call three days a week."

"I'll see you tomorrow morning, won't I?" Claudia asked. "Our usual time?"

"Of course," Acantha replied, throwing on her coat and heading for the door. "And please do look over your notes before we get started."

With Acantha gone, Rollo said, "It seems as if our impromptu board meeting is breaking up. Pru, perhaps you'd like time to consider our offer?"

A reprieve. "Yes, thanks," she said. "I would like to think it through. You don't mind?"

"Only right," Finley replied. "Well, that's me away. Ready, Claudia?"

They stood, gathering coats, sweaters, and hats.

"Lovely to meet you all," Pru said.

"We hope to be seeing a great deal more of you, of course," Finley said.

"We'd be ever so grateful if you accepted the offer," Claudia said. As she walked out with Finley, she added, "Your expertise is much needed. Bye!"

Rollo donned his trapper hat and tugged on the earflaps.

"Your drawings are good," Pru said. "I admire your ability to translate ideas onto paper so that they can be brought to life. And your details of herbs all round the edges of the plans are lovely. Have you ever thought about going back into landscape architecture?"

Rollo blushed. "Thank you. It was a dream of mine, but I'm afraid I had to give it up long ago, when I went to work for Westcott Plumbing—the business my dad started. I had responsibilities, and they certainly haven't let up over the years. I've two sons at public school—you'd faint if I told you the fees. You have them in America, do you—public schools?"

"Yes, but they're called private schools in the States."

"Are they?" Rollo asked in wonder. "How odd."

Back at you, Pru thought.

"I suppose I should confess," Rollo said with a sheepish smile, "that in addition to the historical significance of our great undertaking—the medieval garden—I do harbor half a hope that my work will catch someone's eye. Now that we have Claudia's generous donation in hand, we're really going to call attention to ourselves, and perhaps, after the boys are through school, I could make a second career in design."

Rollo's phone rang. He sat down again at the table to answer and Pru stood nearby relayering clothes, trying not to look as if she were listening in.

"Hello," Rollo said. "Yes, thanks for getting back to me. Finley has it all in order—he's the one who has been working on the necessary requirements for the donation. So, I'm happy to tell you that the PR package you quoted us is a 'go.' Also, we'd like to have a full color plan of the garden printed out, mounted, and framed as soon as possible." He glanced at Pru as she adjusted her beret. "And, we're hoping to have another board member to sign off on it—Pru Parke." He raised his eyebrows at Pru.

She offered a noncommittal smile before walking out of the pub in time to see Finley's sports car coming toward her down the lane. It turned at the bend and stopped in front of the pub. Claudia climbed out of the passenger seat on the opposite side while Finley waited in the driver's seat, engine idling.

"Oh, Pru," she called, flashing a giant smile and throwing her arms open wide, "wouldn't it be fun if both you and Acantha could be my herb teachers?"

"Yes, well, I'm sure—" Pru called back, but the pub door behind her opened and Claudia's gaze shifted. Her eyes widened, her smile melted away, and her face lost all color. She dropped back into the sports car, and it sped off.

CHAPTER 3

Pru turned, thinking Rollo had come out of the pub behind her, but instead, it was the man with the pointed-toe boots. He gave the sports car a hard look, then turned his gaze on Pru and seemed about to speak when Rollo himself emerged. The stranger shot him a backward glance before retreating into the pub.

"Do you know that man?" Pru asked.

Rollo looked at the empty space round them. "Who?"

"He just went … oh, never mind."

Pru's phone rang—it was Evelyn.

"I'll leave you now, Pru," Rollo said. "But not without a last word to say you'd be a great addition to the board. I'd go so far as to say that you are the missing piece. No pressure, of course. Cheers."

No, no pressure.

As Rollo walked to his car, Pru remained in front of the pub and answered her call.

"You aren't anywhere near the shops, are you?" Evelyn asked straightaway. "It's only that Peachey's up in Stockbridge tending to a flat car battery, with two calls waiting after that, and I'm in need of a few things."

"I'll stop on my way home," Pru said.

"You're a lifesaver. Would you bring back a bottle of Fairy liquid, some madras curry powder, five oranges, and three smoked haddock fillets?"

In Romsey and on her way to the grocery, Pru walked past the statue of Lord Palmerston in Market Place but held up inside the coachway at the White Horse Hotel. An item had gone missing from her mental list—Fairy liquid, madras curry powder, smoked haddock and … what? She would text Evelyn. As she gazed down at her phone screen, a pair of worn, brown boots with pointed toes came into view and stopped in front of her.

She looked up to find the man with the fisherman's sweater and shoulder-length hair blocking her way.

"Oh, hello," he said. "I just saw you at the Bell, didn't I? I wonder if I could have a word."

This close, Pru took note of a nervous tic at the corner of his eye, and his stubbly beard. She looked past him at people hurrying by, bundled up against the cold.

"Do I know you?" she asked.

"You're Pru Parke, is that right?" He smiled, revealing one of his front teeth sat at a jaunty angle. It was a friendly smile, so different from the hard look he'd shot Claudia.

"Are you following me?" Pru demanded.

"Following you?" he echoed.

"Excuse me," Pru said, sliding past him to join the crowd on the pavement.

He caught her elbow. She jerked it away, and he put both hands up in surrender.

"Sorry, sorry," he said. "It's only that, I thought I'd better warn you about something. You'll thank me for it, really you will."

"I don't know who you are." Pru made the statement in a voice loud enough to be heard ten feet away, and it caught the attention of a few passersby.

He reddened and took a step back. "I don't mean to—look, I'm Terry Reed. I'm with the PHDHN." She stared at him blankly, trying to make sense of the letters as he continued. "Your group—you've just had Claudia Temple promise you a million pounds for your medieval garden project. Haven't you?"

Her group? Did Pru want to be involved with a group if it meant she would be accosted on the street by dodgy-looking characters?

"How do you know Claudia?" she asked, hanging on tightly to the strap of her shoulder bag. She edged to the right, so that she could duck into the lobby of the hotel if need be. "How do you know me? I don't know you. You're being very mysterious, Mr. Reed. You're acting suspicious."

"I *am* suspicious," was Reed's heated reply. "I'm suspicious of Claudia, and you should be, too. You aren't the first, you know. As it turns out, neither were we—there are the field cow-wheat people before us. I tried to do our lot a favor by warning them. They wouldn't listen to me, but you're new, so maybe you will. You should, if you know what's good for you. That million pounds—I wouldn't go spending it any too soon, not until you have the cash in hand."

"Are you saying Claudia's offer is a scam?"

"I'm saying she promised us the same thing—one million pounds for habitat restoration. And then she scarpered."

~

His message delivered, Terry Reed turned on his heels and Pru watched him disappear up Church Street, leaving her with a headful of questions. He said he'd already warned "her lot" about Claudia. Whom did he tell—Rollo? No, Rollo hadn't given Terry Reed a second glance at the Bell Inn. Had he talked with Finley or Acantha? Pru remembered the look on Claudia's face when she spotted Reed—fright? Panic?

Pru contemplated her next move. She could march right over to the Romsey police station—Christopher's station, just on the other side of the shops—and report the incident. But that idea had no more entered her head than she dismissed it. The word "incident" to her detective inspector husband would imply criminal activity, and this had been—what? Pru had been startled, but not necessarily intimidated.

Before she could come up with a better word to describe the encounter, Reed came hurtling back round the corner, scanning the faces until he spotted her. He waved wildly as he approached.

"Sorry," he wheezed, and stuffed a business card in her hand. "There." And he was gone again.

Pru took the card and her pounding heart into the hotel bar.

By the time she had arrived home with Evelyn's groceries, Pru had calmed down considerably. Now, sitting at the old pine table in the kitchen at Greenoak over a lunch so late that it could be considered tea, she took out Terry Reed's card and told the story of her morning.

Evelyn, who had taken a break from packing up the twelve meals-to-go she cooked every weekday for pensioners in the village, studied the business card carefully, examining both sides as well as its edges. But it held no secret message, only Terry

Reed's name, contact details, and the name of his organization, PHDHN, which stood for Protect Hazel Dormouse Habitat Now.

"He was threatening you over a dormouse?"

"Warning—he was warning me about Claudia Temple." Pru slathered a bit more mustard on her ham sandwich. "He told me Claudia had told his group she would give them a million pounds, but never actually donated the money." Taking the card back, Pru tapped it on the table. "I'm not arguing who needs the money more—of course dormice habitat needs saving."

"Poor wee things," Evelyn murmured.

"He mentioned something about cow-wheat. I don't know what that is, but I wonder does that have something to do with the dormice." Pru shook her head. "Reed said he'd tried to warn the others, but they hadn't listened. Still"—her shoulders drooped—"I don't see why he had to come to me."

"Now, then," Evelyn said, "I've something to take your mind off dormice and cows. If it's too cold to dig in the garden, you can make a Bakewell tart."

The finished tart cooled in the pantry and a comforting scent of almonds and raspberry jam lingered in the kitchen by the time Evelyn had gone and Christopher arrived. Pru put their dinner, a fish pie, in to bake. Later, once settled with their meals, she went over the events of her day—even meeting Terry Reed who, in the retelling, lost any suggestion of dodginess and turned into a quirky character. Christopher took the practical approach.

"Did Reed and his group actually have an agreement with Claudia Temple? Does the medieval garden society have her donation in hand? Because they wouldn't start spending money unless everything was in place, would they?"

Pru seized upon this suggestion as good news. "Of course they wouldn't. Claudia might've been searching for the right place to donate her money, and when she found us, she knew we were a good fit." Pru pushed aside any thoughts of how little Claudia actually knew of medieval herbs. "And there's a solicitor on the board—Finley Martin—so we would have legal issues covered. And I believe we have several costly projects already set in motion. The dormice people must've misunderstood her."

"Still," Christopher said, reaching for the bottle of wine, "it might be best to ask a few questions to make sure your society knows the whole story."

"*My* society? Hang on, now—"

"You didn't hear yourself?" He smiled. " 'We have several costly projects.' 'She knew we were a good fit.' "

"Have I already made up my mind and I didn't realize it?" Pru asked. "I am drawn to the idea, but I need to find out what my responsibilities would be as a board member. I hope they don't think I'm good at fundraising."

On Friday morning, Simon stayed home with a bad head cold, which left Pru with no one to distract her either from writing her magazine article or brooding over medieval herbs, dormice, and Claudia Temple's alleged history of empty promises to donate enormous amounts of money.

She found her outlet in a myriad of tasks. The paraffin heater in the potting shed needed more fuel, so she made a trip into Romsey, after which she replaced the desiccant in the drawers of the seed cabinet and then walked into the village and stopped by St. Mary's to chat with Bernadette about flower arrangements.

Pru didn't actually do the arranging for the altar and windows, but much of the material came from the gardens at

Greenoak. In winter the broadleaf evergreens were vital—wax myrtle, winter-flowering garrya with its blooms that hung like pale-gray icicles, and fragrant daphne for the windowsills. Bernadette broke away from writing her sermon for Sunday, and the two of them held an impromptu flower guild meeting.

Afterward, Pru walked down the road to the local pub, the Robber Blackbird. Polly volunteered at the post office window in the shop adjacent, and so Pru's arrival gave her an excuse for a break. They sat in the quiet pub over coffee, until someone needed to buy stamps and Polly went back to work. All in all, a busy morning, followed by a bowl of parsnip and apple soup for lunch.

"How is that magazine article coming along?" Evelyn asked, smoothing the mashed potato layer on top of each of a dozen individual cottage pies.

"I've had a lot to do this morning," Pru said.

"You aren't skiving off, are you?" Evelyn asked, as if Pru were twelve and trying to avoid math homework.

"Did you know that chives were used in medieval times to treat insect bites?" Pru asked, grabbing the first factoid off the shelf of her mind, and then, remembering another, added, "And leeks were hugely popular."

"Well, of course they were," Evelyn commented.

"The Doctrine of Signatures figured into medicine, too."

The cook paused in her work. "Is that where the medieval doctors signed their names?"

Evelyn, it turned out, was much easier to distract than Pru's mother had been over the math homework.

"No, it means they thought if a plant looked like a particular part of the body, then it must be medicine for that part. For example, wild strawberry was thought to cure heart problems, because the fruit looks like a tiny red heart."

A frown spread over Evelyn's forehead. "That's a bit daft, isn't it?"

"Well, I suppose I'd better get back to it, hadn't I?" Pru had made it to the swing door, but turned back to give the cook a smile. "Thanks for the nudge. Oh, and I mentioned to Polly and Bernadette that I'd made a Bakewell tart yesterday—they'll be by later for tea."

After a good hour on the article, Pru had written three different beginnings and liked none of them. Staring at the computer screen, her mind began to wander. As much as she'd like to join the board of the Winchester Medieval Garden Society and be a part of such a large venture, she could not agree to it before knowing more. The board members had looked into her background—at least Acantha had admitted to the research—and so, Pru should carry out her due diligence as well. Wouldn't they expect it? She would chat with each of them about their experience, their attachment to medieval gardens, and their hopes for the society. Who knows, perhaps those conversations would yield a few quotes for the magazine article.

She would start with Rollo. He seemed in charge—perhaps he was board president. *See now,* she chastised herself, *you don't even know the officers.*

Should she add Claudia to the list? Because how could a casual interview with any board member not involve the exciting details of what would now be possible with Claudia's million pounds? Had the money—pledged to the dormouse people but never realized—actually landed in the coffers of the medieval garden society? It must've. She'd overheard Rollo putting in an order for publicity material. Hadn't they already bought those bricks?

With her phone in hand and Rollo's number keyed in, Pru hesitated. *No, this isn't fair. I can't tattle on Claudia without asking her straight out if what Terry Reed said is true.* And so instead, Pru rang Claudia's number, which went straight to voice mail.

"Hello, Claudia, this is Pru Parke. It was lovely to meet you yesterday, and I wonder if the two of us could have a chat. Please give me a call when you can."

And with that one message, Pru had given herself a slight reprieve—there would be no telling tales of dormouse habitat until she'd sorted out the particulars with the big donor. Wasn't it almost teatime?

The doorbell rang. It couldn't be her sister-in-law or the vicar—they always came in through the mudroom. Pru looked into the kitchen to see Evelyn—her hands stained with beetroot juice as she carved up a mountain of them to roast.

"I'll get it," Pru said.

She opened the door to Acantha, in her deep-purple wool coat, its collar turned up. Her face looked drawn, and her eyes were puffy and red.

"Oh, hello, good afternoon." Acantha took a quick breath followed by a shudder. "You invited me to stop by—do you remember?"

Pru caught herself before she said, "Did I?" and substituted it with, "Yes, lovely to see you. Come in."

Acantha didn't move. "You didn't say today, of course—'any time' is what you said. I remembered you were in Ratley, but I had to stop at the pub to ask where I could find Greenoak. Fortunately, they knew exactly who you were."

"Well, you'll want to come in from the cold, won't you?"

The woman seemed frozen to the doorstep, and so Pru took hold of her bare hand, and felt as if she'd plunged her own into a bucket of ice water. "Acantha, what's wrong?"

At that human touch, tears sparkled in Acantha's eyes. Her chin trembled, and she gripped Pru's hand with surprising strength, took a deep breath, and said, "I don't think you will have heard, but—"

A sob went through her like a tremor, and she shook her head so violently a shiny tress of black hair came loose from her bun and draped itself over one eye.

"Claudia is dead," Acantha whispered. "She hanged herself."

CHAPTER 4

Pru tugged on Acantha's arm to get her over the threshold and inside so that she could close the door.

"How dreadful about Claudia," she said, shivering. "I'm so sorry." But the terrible news took second place to wondering why Acantha had come to her. "You should sit down, don't you think? Why don't we go to the kitchen for a cup of tea? All right?"

After a whispered yes in response, Pru still had a job of it to get the woman moving. They shuffled through the entry slowly, Acantha barely looking at her surroundings, until at last Pru pushed open the door to the warmth and brightness of the kitchen. Evelyn, at the sink drying her hands, looked round at them, and Acantha balked. Pru put a firm arm round her shoulders and, in a quiet voice, said, "Ev, this is Acantha Morris. I'm afraid she's had a bit of a shock, and I thought we could use a cup of tea." She turned to the woman to finish the introduction. "Evelyn Peachey is my good friend and an excellent cook. Don't you want to sit down?"

Once she'd settled Acantha in a chair, Pru sank into her own, unaccountably drained from such little effort.

Evelyn asked no questions. "You're in good time," she said. "I've just poured up the pot."

The cook set the tea on the table and took cups and saucers from the Welsh dresser. When she set these down, Acantha reached over to pull a set closer, but her hands shook so badly the cup toppled over and skittered dangerously close to the edge.

Pru caught it and said, "Perhaps mugs?"

Evelyn didn't care for serving tea in mugs—she thought it too common—but she seemed to see the logic of it in this instance, and quickly exchanged drinking vessels before setting the milk pitcher out and pushing the sugar bowl across the table.

"No sugar," Acantha managed.

But Pru said, "Perhaps just a bit," and when the woman made no further objection, added two spoonfuls along with milk.

Evelyn put a box of tissues on the table, and the three of them sat without speaking for a few minutes. Acantha leaned over her tea as if the rising steam offered comfort, and the loosened tress fell across her face and dangled above the mug. She tucked the escapee behind an ear, and it promptly fell back again. That happened three times until exasperation overtook sorrow, and she wrapped the lock round a finger, located a hairpin from within her bun, and reestablished order. With that act—and a deep breath—a bit of animation returned to Acantha's face.

"She seemed so happy yesterday," she said, and Pru took this as permission to talk about what had happened. She turned to Evelyn.

"Acantha's just learned that one of the board members of the medieval garden society has died."

"Suicide." The word had no sound apart from its sibilants.

"Dreadful," Ev murmured. "I'm sorry for your loss."

"I had gone over this morning for our lesson."

Pru continued to fill in the blanks for Evelyn. "Acantha was teaching Claudia—the woman who died—about medieval herbs and medicine." She turned back and asked, "Do they live in Winchester?"

Acantha nodded. "Sleepers Hill. Only the two of them in that cold, echoing house. I offered to have us meet in my flat in Worthy Lane, but Claudia insisted, and well, you know how she could be."

Did she? Pru had spoken with Claudia only once and didn't think that qualified her to know much about the deceased. Then she recalled the evening of the lecture, when Claudia had smiled at the crowd, and every single person had smiled back.

"When I turned the corner into their street," Acantha said, "there were police cars, and an ambulance was leaving. I went to the door, but they wouldn't let me in at first. I told them who I was and what I was doing there. I have nothing to hide!" she declared as if Pru had suggested otherwise. "Then, I noticed Ellis staring at me through the window. He looked hollow. They were talking with him, and then they let me in, but only to the side room where the laundry is."

Pru asked, "Is Ellis Claudia's husband?"

"Yes. He had found her—that's what the detective told me. But he would say little else." She frowned.

They were quiet for a moment. Pru thought she might ask how Claudia's interest in medieval herbs came about, but heard a car skid into the yard outside the mudroom.

"Ah!" Acantha cried. "Who is it?"

"It's all right—it's Bernadette." Pru could identify the vicar by the sound of her Smartcar kicking up gravel in the drive. "Reverend Freemantle. And probably my sister-in-law, Polly. They were at your lecture on Tuesday when Claudia announced her donation."

The new arrivals entered through the mudroom laughing. When they reached the kitchen, Polly spotted Acantha and said,

"Oh my, you've brought a guest to tea today. What a lovely surprise."

But it took only a moment for them to detect the sorrow in the atmosphere.

"Shall we come back later?" Polly asked quietly.

"Or would you prefer that we stay and have a cup of tea?" Bernadette offered. "And perhaps a chat?"

Pru told them what had happened as briefly as possible, and then set about to distributing slices of the Bakewell tart—its filling a bit more wobbly than Pru would've liked—as Evelyn made a fresh pot of tea. Meanwhile, Bernadette gleaned what she could from Acantha—the vicar had an unparalleled skill for combining comfort with prodding. When Acantha had arrived at the Temple house, the body had been out of sight or taken away, and she had learned only the bare facts that Claudia had hanged herself from the railings on the first-floor landing, fifteen feet off the ground floor. Acantha may not have seen Claudia's body, but there had been one thing she recognized.

"Her scarf," Acantha said. "That long red one—she always wore it. I saw one of the police carrying it out in a plastic bag. I think that must be what she used."

"She was wearing it at the lecture," Polly said, shaking her head. "She looked so lovely that evening. So ... vibrant."

That gave them all pause. Pru imagined Claudia's tall and elegant, but lifeless, body and the scarlet scarf wrapped round its neck.

The tea, the tart, and the company seemed to revive Acantha, who next sounded peeved. "The detective asked me a great many questions. Why was I there? When had I last seen Claudia? What sort of teaching did I do? I told him about the society, and he wanted to know who else was involved. They asked more questions than they answered. Why was that? Why were they even there when she killed herself?"

"The police must be called in if the death isn't from natural causes," Pru explained. "I suppose Claudia's husband—Ellis—was accustomed to seeing you there?"

"No, I went over mornings when he was at work. I'd met him only once before. And I've never met Danny, the son, although Claudia talked about him all the time."

A sedate set of tires crunched into the gravel yard. Evelyn stood, reached over, and patted Acantha's hand.

"That'll be Albert," she said. "My husband. We've deliveries to make."

A moment later, Albert Peachey strolled in. He was a string bean of a man, dressed in the coveralls he wore for his work—mobile auto repair—and sporting a toothy smile as he swept off his flat cap. " 'Afternoon, ladies." He spotted the one he didn't know and nodded.

After a swift introduction, Peachey added, "How d'ya do?"

Acantha smiled faintly.

"Evelyn, my love." Peachey gave his wife a peck on the cheek and she blushed. "Your chariot awaits."

The cook started to clear dishes off the table, but Pru put a hand out to stop her. "You go on," she said.

Evelyn gave in. She pulled on her coat and buttoned up. Once the pensioners' dinners had been packed up in Peachey's van, the two of them left on their delivery route. That signaled an end to the afternoon. Polly and Bernadette offered another round of condolences and then departed.

Acantha took a deep breath and looked round the kitchen as if seeing it for the first time.

"You've a lovely home," she said.

"Oh, it isn't ours," Pru replied. "My husband and I are caretakers of sorts, and my brother and I tend the gardens. The owners live abroad." It wasn't the easiest arrangement to explain

—why is it difficult to put generosity into words? The Wilsons owned Greenoak, but they were on an extended archaeological dig in Tuscany—something to do with the Etruscans—and had entrusted the house and grounds to Pru and Christopher. It had all started with that Roman mosaic in a London garden, but Pru didn't believe Acantha would be up for the entire story.

"And your cook, Evelyn, also cooks for the old-age pensioners?"

"The owners asked her to stay on—they started the program of meals for the pensioners. Evelyn's become a good friend." Pru and Christopher were always looking for ways to give back—they'd only recently been able to persuade the Wilsons to let them pay Evelyn's wages.

"Such kindness," Acantha said, and her voice caught. "I was not terribly kind. To Claudia. She was an enthusiastic but rather flighty woman, and she exhausted me. But she always seemed happy." Acantha reached for a tissue, blew her nose, and continued. "I wanted to come and tell you what happened, Pru, but also thought I should deliver a warning—the detective said he will want to talk with you, too."

After Acantha left, Pru sat back down at the table and absentmindedly brushed a few errant flakes of pastry into a small heap as she thought about life and death. Eventually, she heard another familiar arrival in the yard—this one brought her great comfort. Christopher walked in through the mudroom. They exchanged greetings as he unbuttoned his coat, hung it on a peg, and took in the kitchen scene. His gaze landed on Pru last.

"Did I frighten everyone away?" he asked lightly, his brown eyes seeing through her.

"No, they left a bit ago, and I didn't have the energy to move. It's lovely and warm in here."

"I'll go and start the library fire," Christopher suggested.

"Not yet, sit down." She nodded to the last slice of Bakewell tart. "There's your reward for reaching the end of the week. I'll put the kettle on."

"Let me." He moved behind Pru, put his arms round her, and kissed her hair before turning to set the kettle to boil. He took the chair at the corner and reached for her hand. "So."

She sighed. "I've had some sad news this afternoon."

Christopher listened as Pru told him about Claudia. She finished with "I had phoned her this morning to talk about the medieval garden. She was already dead then."

A melancholy lingered round Pru during the rest of the evening, and her conversation kept circling back to Claudia's suicide.

"Acantha said the police want to talk with me," she said.

"Routine, I expect," Christopher replied. "They heard the phone message you left and will want to know if you have any insight into her state of mind."

A bright Saturday morning did wonders to clear Pru's head. After Christopher left for a Scout meeting at St. Mary's, she took herself outdoors and, standing in the gravel yard, she inhaled deeply. The temperature had nudged up to just above freezing, and her spirits lifted with it. She pruned the step-over apple trees that formed a low fence down the middle path through their kitchen garden, tied the trimmings with twine, and stacked them up to use for kindling. She stood quietly by the compost piles and thought about the hedgehogs that had made a nest under a loose board at the back. She hoped they were warm enough in their hibernation.

"Sleep tight," she murmured.

Pru and Christopher ended the day by meeting Polly and

Simon at the Robber Blackbird for a meal. Sunday she slept late, and Monday, Simon returned to work and the two of them set up shop in the warm kitchen. They spent most of the morning squabbling over how to describe the qualities needed in a new garden assistant—they were hoping to hire someone before spring hit. Then, in the afternoon, they dived into a stack of seed catalogs to shop for annuals they would sow directly in the garden. Working their way through the alphabet, they soon lost themselves in dreaming of summer.

"This nasturtium," Pru said, tapping on a photo. "Alaska mixed."

"It's got spotted leaves," Simon complained.

"Variegated," Pru said, defending the old favorite. "Foliage splashed with cream."

"Looks diseased to me. This one. Peach Melba."

"Yeah," she agreed, "all right, both. Now, for nigella it has to be Miss Jekyll."

"It certainly does."

They had rounded out their order with three different zinnia selections that each claimed to be mildew resistant, and Simon left just before Peachey arrived for the pensioners' dinners. Christopher followed him in.

"You're early," Pru said. "That's a welcome change. You don't have a police-community meeting this evening, do you?"

"No," Christopher replied with a quick smile. "It's only that —here, Evelyn, I'll take those out."

He loaded his arms with boxes and followed Peachey to his van. Pru stared after them. She'd seen a guarded look on her husband's face.

"I've not left you any dinner," Evelyn said as she donned her coat. "As it's Monday."

That jerked Pru's attention back to the kitchen. "Oh yes, it is, isn't it? Well, not to worry—everything's under control."

As part of her in-house cookery school, Evelyn had decided

Pru should take over preparing the evening meal on Mondays. In the three weeks since that policy had been instituted, the nascent chef had managed a passable beef stew, soupy chicken cacciatore, and scrambled eggs. This fourth Monday looked to be a repeat of the previous week.

"But just in case," Evelyn added, taking her handbag off a peg, "I've left a chicken goulash in the freezer."

By the time Christopher came back in, Pru had set the kettle on to boil, cleared the pine table of seed catalogs, and set out two mugs. He hung up his coat, kissed her, and took a seat while Pru gave him a preview of the summer floral display at Greenoak. He listened and asked questions about cosmos and cleome—he'd picked up a good few plant names from her—until, at last, tea ready, she sat across the corner from him.

"So," she said.

That ghost of a smile crossed his lips and eased the creases in his forehead. He took a swig of tea, stretched his legs out under the table, and said, "I've been seconded to Winchester—at the request of the detective superintendent."

"Have you? For how long?"

"For the length of a particular enquiry."

"And out of all the Hampshire Constabulary and the Thames Valley Police and the Crimes Investigation Department, the superintendent chose you. Well, it's only logical." Christopher had an exemplary record as detective chief inspector at the Met in London. When he and Pru had married and moved to Hampshire, he'd said he wanted to get away from that sort of pressure, but they hadn't been at Greenoak long before he agreed to take a DI post with the local police.

"The detective superintendent who asked for me," Christopher said, a shadow passing over his brow. "It's John Upstone."

Pru let this information sink in. "John Upstone? Your first boss? But doesn't he live up north—York?"

Christopher's first job as a detective sergeant was more than twenty years before they had met, but she'd heard plenty of stories and knew how much he had admired Upstone—an admiration that edged quite close to idol worship.

"He moved from York last year, getting on in Winchester. I'm surprised he hasn't retired. I certainly had no idea he was here."

"Well, this is a happy coincidence," Pru said. But Christopher's sigh told her it might not be that happy, after all. "What's wrong?"

Christopher shifted in his chair. "He's old."

Pru squeezed his hand. "Old*er*—there's no escaping that. He must've wondered where that fresh-faced DS Pearse from twenty-five years ago had gone."

Christopher grinned. "Sometimes I wonder where he's gone, too."

"And it has been awhile since you've seen John."

"Nearly eleven years ago, when I went up for Molly's funeral."

Pru had heard of Molly, too—Upstone's much beloved and greatly mourned late wife.

"He sent us a lovely card and a wedding present," Pru said. "The antique rosewood tea caddy on our mantel upstairs." It had been her only contact with the man.

"That was one of the few times I've heard from him. His work became his life after Molly was gone and he was alone," Christopher said. "But seeing him today, he seemed … unsettled, uneasy. He didn't explain why he moved south. Perhaps it got too cold for him in York."

"He must feel right at home at the moment, what with Hampshire in the middle of the coldest January in thirty years. Does he have family nearby?"

"None that I know of."

"Let's invite him to dinner," Pru said. "How about this weekend?"

"He's beaten us to it on that account—he's asked us to dinner this evening."

Pru felt herself lifted off the hook of meal preparation. "That's lovely of him. In that case, I'm off to have a bath." She picked up their mugs and took them to the sink. "Oh wait. What's the enquiry you'll be working on?"

Christopher reached for her hand and pulled her back. "I want to tell you something."

He didn't speak for a moment. Instead, he watched her. She knew that look, and it did not bode well.

"It's a murder enquiry," he said at last. "The murder of Claudia Temple."

CHAPTER 5

Pru dropped back into her chair.

"Claudia—murdered? But Acantha said she hanged herself." Upon hearing the news, an image had sprung up in Pru's mind, and now it returned full force—the sight of the woman's body hanging from a first-floor landing by her own red scarf. "Someone did that to her?"

"The autopsy results are expected tomorrow," Christopher said, "so, at the moment it's still uncertain. But John heard the callout Friday morning and decided to take a look. He suspects something, and he'll push for the coroner to keep the inquest open so that the enquiry can go forward. He hasn't carried out much more than preliminary interviews as yet."

Pru realized John Upstone must have been the one to talk with Acantha when she had arrived at the Temple house.

"Acantha told me to expect a call from a detective. She must've meant John. I suppose the two of you will be talking with anyone associated with the society who knew Claudia. Well"—Pru attempted a lighthearted tone—"am I to be interviewed this evening? He doesn't think I know anything, does he?"

"He asked after you, although not in relation to the case. But, let's just say I have a strong suspicion that this will be more than dinner."

~

It never took Pru long to dress for any occasion—gardeners aren't known for the breadth of their wardrobe. She had pulled out her best wool trousers and the other of her two best sweaters. This one was a deep burgundy with a neckline that showed off the art-deco necklace she always wore. It was a fan pendant shape, gold and black—a lovely piece that Christopher had given her not long after they'd met. She checked herself in the mirror, put a hand up to touch the necklace, and saw him standing behind her. He straightened his tie and gave her a wink.

She threw on a pink pashmina and, once downstairs, her heavy coat. She decided to forgo the beret, as she'd put her hair up with a dressier clip than usual—a French barrette with a floral design made from tiny seed pearls. She wasn't entirely sure it would hold.

In the car, Pru quizzed Christopher about his detective-sergeant days and his first "guv'nor"—a sort of refresher course on stories she'd already heard.

"And that time with the missing shipment of French perfume. How did he know it was the fellow in the white Ford transit van who'd planned the heist?"

"Firstly," Christopher replied, "he would be suspicious of anyone driving a white Ford transit van. And secondly, the fellow had dropped one of the cartons while he was shifting them into his garage for safekeeping before he could sell them on. A couple of bottles broke, and the suspect's dog had rolled in it. He had the dog in the bath when John nicked him. He said the place reeked of Chanel Number Five."

Pru turned to her husband. "And now, I can ask John for stories about you. This'll be fun."

Christopher muttered something under his breath.

They were driving down lanes of houses now, nearing Winchester, and Pru's thoughts shifted. "Did he say why he suspects Claudia's death is murder?"

"We didn't talk details about the enquiry. Not yet."

"Did he say why he wanted you in particular on the case?"

"He's an officer short—or that was the reason he gave me. Right, here's Milverton Road." Christopher turned down a street of comfortably lived-in detached brick houses.

"I've seen your old photo of John, but tell me about Molly," Pru said. "What did she look like?"

"She was not as tall as you. Had a round face. And dark hair she kept swept back. A quick smile." He nodded. "Here we are."

The houses all had low brick walls at the street and small front gardens. John's was mostly paved over for parking, but there was a side gate.

"Orchard House," Pru said, reading the brass plaque at the drive. On the way to the door, she voiced one last thought. "All these years without her. Do you think he's lonely?"

Christopher grinned as he raised the knocker and let it fall. "It isn't a question a man often asks himself about a male coworker. Especially his superior."

A form appeared through the glazed glass panels. The door swept open, and there stood John Upstone.

Pru would know him in a minute, although the only photo she'd seen of him was more than two decades old and he'd put on a few pounds since then. He'd had quite a head of ginger hair, which had now faded to the color of sand. His pencil mustache, slightly darker, reminded Pru of David Niven. He stood a head above her—quite as tall as Christopher—and broke out in a wide smile at the sight of them.

"Well now, Pearse, you're at last letting the old man meet the love of your life, are you?"

He ushered them into the front hall, shook Christopher's hand, and then Pru's, followed by giving her a peck on the cheek. They exclaimed over never having met but feeling as if they had. Once coats had been shed, he took them into the sitting room.

Such a comfortable house—well furnished with a fire going and a painting above the mantel that captured Pru's attention so totally she almost didn't hear when John asked her what she'd like to drink.

"Oh, vodka and tonic? Yes, lovely. Thanks."

It was a landscape painting in oil or acrylic—Pru didn't know how to tell the difference. A glassy body of water filled the foreground, and beyond, craggy, rocky hills rose to several points in the distance, one of them looking as if it had a topknot. The painting's style seemed to fall somewhere between abstract and realistic. It was so evocative that Pru felt as if she had become a part of the scene itself.

She squinted at the artist's signature in the corner, but could not make it out. Then a tinkling sound at her side brought her back to the moment, and she noticed John holding out her drink.

"That's Molly," he said, nodding to the mantel. Pru was one second away from exclaiming she had no idea Molly had been an artist when she saw the small framed photo of a smiling, round-faced woman with her dark hair pulled back.

"Oh yes, she's lovely. I'm sorry we never met."

John gestured to the sofa. Pru settled beside Christopher and admired the rest of the room—sparsely furnished, but with good, solid pieces. She became aware of pleasant sounds of clanking and chinking drifting from the kitchen and realized that John must've hired a caterer for their dinner—or perhaps he had a cook come in regularly. A good cook, Pru suspected from the mingled aromas of roast chicken and cooked fruit.

"Christopher has told you about the enquiry?" Upstone asked.

Oh dear, perhaps this evening was to be a police interview after all.

"Yes. It's dreadful what happened to Claudia. I'd met her only once, the day before, and so I don't know what she was like as a rule. That afternoon she seemed … full of life." Pru cringed at the trite phrase. "Acantha told me what happened—that is, she said Claudia committed suicide."

"When did Ms. Morris give you this news?" Upstone asked.

"She came to Greenoak Friday afternoon."

"Why?"

Out the corner of her eye, Pru saw Christopher following the exchange.

"To tell me about Claudia," she responded. "And to say that the police knew of my involvement in the medieval garden society." She shook her head. "No, 'involvement' is too strong a word."

Upstone sat forward. "She warned you about me?"

Christopher sat forward, too, but Pru put a hand on his knee and said to John, "Why do you suspect it's murder?"

"What about this society?" Upstone countered. "Do they use herbs as medicine on a regular basis?"

"Much of modern medicine is plant based," Pru replied. "Aspirin, quinine, digitalis for heart problems."

"Of course, but—"

"Taxol for breast cancer," Pru added, wishing she could think of more, and then rushed in with "camphor."

"Yes, yes," Upstone said. "But do you know these people to use any concoctions they make themselves?"

"Did you find something at Claudia's house?" Pru asked.

"Answer my question," John said.

Christopher snorted behind his raised glass. Upstone let out an exasperated sigh, leaned back, and said, "This is what comes of marrying a police officer."

"Good evening."

A woman stood in the arched doorway to the corridor. Tall and lithe, she looked to be a bit older than Pru—her bobbed hair was mostly white, but her face, although flushed, was strong and firm.

"I couldn't come out earlier," she explained with a tentative smile as she wiped her hands on her well-stained pinny. "The hollandaise sauce was at a delicate stage."

The cook. Pru took this announcement as a signal that dinner was ready, and stood along with Christopher.

John rose, too, and cleared his throat. His easygoing manner had vanished, and he sounded out of breath as he said, "This is Sabine."

Sabine glanced at him and then at Pru and Christopher. She held out her hand to Pru.

"Hello," she said. "I'm John's wife."

CHAPTER 6

John's wife? Stunned at this pronouncement, Pru stumbled through a greeting and shook hands. At least, she thought she had put her hand out, but a million thoughts whirled round inside her head like so many dust devils that she couldn't've said for sure what she'd done.

John had remarried and he had said nothing—not to Christopher earlier in the day, not to Pru when they'd arrived. Not even when Sabine came in the room. Pru cut her eyes at Upstone, who had remained near his chair. She caught an expression of both pain and chagrin, and such discomfort that he looked as if he'd rather be anywhere else in the world at that moment.

And so he should, Pru thought.

Christopher, meanwhile, had introduced himself to Sabine, shaken her hand, and offered the bottle of wine Pru had carried in. Sabine admired it, commenting it would go perfectly with their meal, and held it out to her husband.

"Would you open it for us? And we can all go through to the dining room."

They sat at the table and began with the first course—little crab and avocado tarts with hollandaise sauce. Conversation had a noticeable veneer of politeness about it. Pru avoided Christopher's gaze lest she blurt out her frustration. They stuck with safe topics, starting with the safest possible: the weather.

"I've seen daffodils and even tulips already pushing up out of the ground," Sabine said. "Will these low temperatures damage them, do you think?"

"They never mind the cold," Pru replied and then said the tarts were delicious and asked if she could have the recipe. Christopher offered a story of the Scout meeting on Saturday—the troop had taken on the project of repainting the church hall with a bit too much enthusiasm, and now the floor needed revarnishing. John said nothing.

When Sabine stood to collect the dishes, Pru popped up, too. "Let me help." She met with no resistance and so followed their hostess down the corridor to the kitchen, giving Christopher a backward glance as she left the dining room.

There was a door to the kitchen, and Pru made sure to close it. She needed to ask a question, but how was this subject to be broached?

"Thanks for the hand," Sabine said, not looking at Pru, but nodding at the counter. "Just set them there. I've chicken with lentils for our mains – and braised leeks. I hope that suits. I enjoy cooking, but it's rare that I can try out anything new."

Pru took the intended direction—away from anything too personal. "I never learned to cook, not until recently, when I began taking lessons. I've got a wonderful instructor. She was quite patient when my béarnaise sauce turned to scrambled eggs."

"Oh, sauces can be tricky—it's why I was hovering over the hollandaise. This is a lovely wine you and Christopher brought." She set it on the counter and kept her back to Pru.

No, this wouldn't do, edging our way round the gorilla in the room.

"Sabine."

"He didn't tell you, did he?" Sabine asked, whipping round. "He said nothing to Christopher about me? About being married?"

"No, he didn't. But why not?"

Sabine sighed and handed Pru a basket of crusty rolls. "We'd best get the next course out."

Not long into the chicken and lentils, and after a futile attempt at discussing politics—that's how bad it had got—Pru despaired of coming up with a neutral topic, and she was filled with annoyance that she was not giving Sabine's dinner the attention it deserved.

"Christopher," John said, "did Molly ever get you to volunteer at her mother-and-baby charity fête? She was always trying to rope in the junior officers."

"No, I don't recall I ever did that."

"Sabine," Pru said, "does Orchard House have fruit trees?"

"We've a couple of old apple trees at the bottom of the garden," Sabine replied. "But before you can get there, you must first beat your way through the wisteria to get out the kitchen door."

"You'll have to see the gardens at Greenoak," Christopher said.

"Molly started that charity in York," Upstone said, plowing on as if no one else had spoken. "It's still going strong."

Pru's eyes darted to Sabine, who had a pleasant expression but two red spots on her cheeks.

"Wisteria can so easily get away from you," Pru said. "I'd be happy to take a look at it for you." She shoveled another mouthful of food in and fumed about John's apparent lack of ability to speak about—or to—his wife. The living one.

Upstone waved a fork at Christopher, who moved out of its

way. "I can't count the number of times Sergeant Pearse and I ended up in the kitchen in the middle of the night with Molly doing a fry-up for us. Do you remember that assault case where the man was beaten with a model of a caravel from the Spanish Armada—"

"Of course, it's frustrating," Pru cut in, "not being able to dig in the garden right now. Usually, winter—as long as it isn't too wet—is a wonderful time to plant."

Upstone aimed his fork at Pru. "You phoned the victim the morning she died, didn't you?"

"John!"

That rebuke came from Christopher. Pru stopped chewing as Upstone threw his former protégé a look, and Christopher corrected himself. "Sir. Don't you think—"

"Yes, yes, all right," Upstone replied, recovering a bit of his good humor. Perhaps he believed he'd won a victory now that the spotlight had properly turned to murder. "Will you be able to come into the station tomorrow and give us a statement?"

"Yes, of course," Pru said. "I'll be there first thing in the morning."

Christopher gathered plates after they'd finished the chicken, and Pru—usually never the troublemaker—felt an unaccountable urge to suggest that he help Sabine in the kitchen, so that she could have a go at John. But, overcome with common sense, she instead followed their hostess again to the kitchen and returned with an apricot tart. After that, Sabine suggested coffee in the front room, and shooed Pru off with the men.

"Do you do much fishing these days?" Upstone asked Christopher as the three of them stood in the sitting room. "I remember Molly baking perch that you'd caught in the Foss."

"I take the Scouts out on the Test," Christopher replied. He nodded to the painting above the mantel. "Is that the Lake District?"

Sabine came in behind them with the coffee tray. "It is," she said.

Christopher took the tray from her and set it down. "A fine place for fishing," he said, "although, there's a visit a few years ago that stands out for me the most, when my son and I spent a couple of days near Cockermouth." He slipped his arm round Pru's waist. "It was a near disaster."

Pru, warmed at the memory, smiled and continued the story. "There was a rail strike. Christopher and Graham were stuck in the middle of nowhere, and I was about to flee the country—that is, move back to Dallas. You returned in the nick of time," she said to her husband and then turned to Sabine. "Where did you and John meet?"

"There." Sabine nodded to the painting. "I was living in Keswick for a year and had a show at a local gallery. This was last winter. Sometimes an artist sees her work in an entirely different light when it's hung. So, during the opening, I stood back to look at this one. Then, I heard a man behind me say, 'Cat Bells. It's as if—"

" '—I could walk right into that painting and climb the fell.' "

When John spoke those words, his face softened, but he dropped his eyes, avoiding his wife's gaze.

"It was my first sale of the show," Sabine added quietly.

The tender memory brought tears to Pru's eyes. "So, you're the artist. The painting is beautiful."

"Do you remember, Christopher," John said, "the time I took Molly up for a ramble in the Dales, and we got lost for almost an entire day because she ..."

They made it through coffee, and at last readied to take their leave. It had been an excruciating evening, the meal notwithstanding.

"Please do come back and see the garden in the daylight," Sabine said to Pru as coats were retrieved and "good nights" exchanged.

"I will," Pru replied as she and Christopher stepped outside.

The door shut. Pru dropped the smile and stomped off to the car, spinning round halfway there and hissing at Christopher, "It was as if she were invisible. How can he do that?"

Christopher herded her into the car as Pru seethed, yanking on the seat belt and shoving it into the lock. "Did he speak to her—even once? Did he ever acknowledge his wife was in the room?"

"Not a word to me about being married." Christopher reversed out of the drive abruptly, but then continued at a reasonable speed. "What is he playing at—all this talk about his dead wife? If he felt he were disrespecting Molly's memory, why even start something with Sabine? When did they marry? What are they doing in Hampshire?"

Pru crossed her arms and stared out into the darkness. "I intend to find out."

Christopher cut his eyes at her. "You don't want to get on his bad side." After a moment of silence, he added, "Pru?"

"You don't have to worry about me," she replied. "Sabine invited me. For a garden consultation."

The sky had returned to gray the next morning—still freezing, still no snow. A dull day, and it matched Pru's mood as she hunkered over a bowl of porridge at breakfast. Christopher had left early, giving her plenty of time to dwell on her morning activity: to go to the Winchester police station and give a statement. But what was she to say about the death of a woman she had met only once and who had either killed herself or … what? What did John Upstone suspect had really happened? But thoughts of Upstone led Pru directly to his shabby treatment of Sabine the evening before, and once her mind settled on that, her spirits sank deeper.

Evelyn loaded the oven with an enormous sheet of root vegetables—carrots, parsnips, and swedes mixed with rosemary and garlic—and then poured herself a cup of tea, and joined Pru at the table.

"Does your friend Acantha know about this turn of events? Did Christopher's superintendent tell her that it might not be suicide?"

Pru had thought it better not to mention the John-and-Sabine issue to Evelyn until she'd learned more, and so, had given only a brief account of the dinner party—what a delightful happenstance to find that Christopher's old boss was nearby, how lovely that he'd remarried, and look, I have a recipe for a crab-and-avocado tart.

"Superintendent Upstone didn't say any more than Acantha told us on Friday, except something about a 'concoction.' I wonder do they think she'd taken poison—or that someone had given it to her. Christopher was going to be briefed this morning, so we'll know more later." She sighed. "I'd better be on my way."

"You'll invite them for dinner, won't you?" Evelyn asked. "Superintendent Upstone and his wife? Wouldn't we all like to meet this man that Christopher admires so?"

Pru wasn't entirely sure the John Upstone that Christopher had known still existed.

CHAPTER 7

"I'm sorry, ma'am, but you aren't allowed any weapons inside the police station."

"What?"

The desk sergeant's comment grabbed Pru's attention. She'd been glancing round the lobby, but now turned back to the matter at hand—the search of her large canvas bag. It lay open on the table, exposing not only her purse, three extra hair clips, a notebook, four pencils and two pens, her phone, a handful of receipts, but also—at the bottom—a pair of hand pruners.

"My secateurs—so that's where they've been," Pru said. "I've been looking for this pair for ages." One of the words the sergeant had spoken drifted back into her consciousness. *Weapon.* She blushed to the roots of her hair. "I'm sorry, I didn't think to … I'm a gardener, you see. I remember now a couple of weeks ago I'd taken them with me up to the church because Bernadette—Reverend Freemantle—asked if I could cut the ivy away from the One Lost Lamb window. You know how ivy can be, and then I forgot to take them out again and … "

She stopped babbling. You'd think that being married to a

detective inspector would put her at ease in a police station, but that wasn't always the case.

The desk sergeant seemed unimpressed with her explanation. "You'll have to leave them here," he said, giving Pru a form to fill out and handing over a chit. He slipped the so-called weapon into a drawer and locked it, after which he gave the handle a test pull, just in case the pruners had a mind to escape of their own accord and snip the brown leaves off that quite sorry-looking spider plant hanging in the corner.

"Take a seat, please, and Detective Superintendent Upstone will be out to collect you."

Pru sat, glancing round at the Winchester police station. It felt vast, but she knew it was only because it wasn't Christopher's normal patch—the cubbyholelike station in Romsey seemed a bit more like home to her.

The door to the street opened, and Acantha walked in, looking smart in her mulberry suit and purple coat. She spotted Pru and made a beeline for her, ignoring the desk sergeant's greeting of "Yes, ma'am, what can I help you with?"

"Did they call you in because of Claudia?" she asked Pru, her stage whisper loud enough for anyone to hear. "What's this about? I spoke to them on Friday, but someone rang and told me to come in to the station today."

"Excuse me, ma'am," the desk sergeant called.

Nodding to the counter, Pru said, "Why don't you speak to him first, and then come and sit down."

When the desk sergeant performed his search on Acantha's leather satchel, he found a plastic bag of dried plant material. She identified the plant as clary sage, but still, he made a careful examination of the crumbling specimen before allowing her to sign in. She then gave him a short lecture on the benefits of the herb, which, when steeped in water, made an eyewash, and had been used as a remedy for more than a thousand years.

"Of course, it's better fresh," she said to Pru, sitting down at last, keeping her hands busy re-sorting her handbag, unbuttoning her coat, and smoothing her bun. "But as it's winter, I had to make do. I'm giving a talk to a garden club this evening, and I work better with a prop."

"Acantha, the police have more questions about Claudia's death."

"I don't know what else they could—"

Pru cut her off, wanting to get this over with. "My husband is a police officer—a detective inspector. He's been asked to work on the enquiry."

She and Christopher had talked it over. Pru had wanted the information out there so the others wouldn't learn about it another way and worry that she was a snitch.

Acantha paused. "Enquiry?" she echoed. "Police don't investigate suicides, do they?"

"No, I don't believe they do."

"Your husband—was he the one I talked with on Friday at Claudia's house?"

Pru shook her head, perhaps a bit too vehemently. "That was probably Detective Superintendent Upstone. I'm married to Christopher Pearse, and I wanted you to know so you didn't think I was trying to hide something. Perhaps he's the one you'll talk with today. Or maybe you're here only to sign your statement. It could be that simple."

"Not so simple for me," Acantha said. "You see, I need to get back into Claudia's house."

"Why?"

But Acantha had no time to answer, as Upstone emerged from a door behind the counter.

"Ms. Parke, if you'll follow me. Ms. Morris—someone will be along for you."

~

"You'll understand, I'm sure, it's better that I interview you instead of your husband." Upstone sat across the table from her with a file folder open and a pocket notebook nearby.

"Yes, of course," Pru replied to the detective superintendent, a man who appeared confident and assured in his role and his surroundings—so unlike the John Upstone from the previous evening.

The interview began, and it soon became clear he had more interest in Acantha, Rollo, and Finley than in her own encounter with Claudia. But Pru had no more information about the other members of the society than she did of the victim. If Claudia were truly a victim.

Pru waited for a lull in the questioning, and as Upstone flipped a couple of pages in his notebook and then wrote something in the file, she finally asked, "Why do you think she was murdered?"

He ran a finger over his David Niven mustache. "Pearse should have the autopsy results by now, and we'll know for certain. Let's just say, I didn't like the look of things at the scene."

A police officer's instinct—she'd seen it with Christopher, and when asked, his answers were just as vague, as if they couldn't really say *why* something was off, only that it was.

"I'm sorry I can't be of more help telling you about the society," Pru said, "but, you see, I met them only last week after I attended the lecture. Even so, I don't see how any one of them could be suspected of murder. Why would they do it? They had just received a huge donation from Claudia."

"A million pounds, was it?" Upstone leaned forward. "A great deal of money. Paperwork done and dusted? No hard feelings about it?"

Pru had no trouble following his line of thought, because on the drive home the previous evening, after exhausting the topic of John and Sabine, she and Christopher had gone over a few salient points, including the PHDHN.

"You're referring to the Protect Hazel Dormouse Habitat Now group. Because Claudia had reneged on her promise to give them the money. Do you think Terry Reed would kill her out of anger—if the dormice couldn't have her million, then no one could? Or do you think someone in the medieval garden society didn't want her to have the chance to change her mind again?"

The superintendent shrugged, as if now that he'd planted that seed, he could back off. "It's a line of enquiry. Two, actually." He closed his notebook.

"Is that it?" Pru asked. "I'm not sure I've been much help to you."

"Perhaps it isn't what you know now, but what you can find out for us. After all, as a new member of this society—and possibly new board member—you're perfectly positioned to see the enquiry in a different light from the police."

"Are you saying you need a mole?"

"I'm not asking you to join MI5. Your relationship to the enquiry doesn't need to be a secret. What I'm looking for is a connection to this group—someone who can explain to us the medieval aspect. The gardens, the plants, and what they were used for."

"Was she poisoned?" Pru asked.

"Let's leave it at that for now, shall we?" Upstone said, standing and smoothing his suit jacket.

Pru rose and moved to the door, taking the end of official business as permission to introduce another topic. "Thank you for dinner last evening—it was lovely to meet Sabine."

Upstone's eyes flashed, and Pru waited. *Go ahead, growl at me.* But instead, he blushed, and mumbled, "Yes, well," turning back into the bumbling husband from the evening before. She felt a pang of guilt for trying to poke the bear, only to have the bear whimper instead of roar. Although, it was quite a tiny pang.

He held the lobby door open for her and then returned to the inner sanctum of the station. The desk sergeant gave her barely a glance as most of his attention was being taken with an older woman complaining about an attempted bag snatching.

No Acantha in sight, but Rollo had arrived. He sat forward in his seat, elbows on his thighs and hands clasped. His face had a greenish tint to it, as if he'd spent the morning trying and failing to keep his breakfast down.

When he saw Pru, he popped up and said, "You, too? What's this about—have you any idea? The police rang me over the weekend. It was very awkward, I must say. I mean, it's dreadful about Claudia, but what questions would they have for me? If they wanted to ask anyone anything, it should be Finley—he's the one. Why me?"

With that, Rollo ran out of steam and dropped back into his chair. Pru sat beside him.

"Police are investigating Claudia's death, because they suspect it might not have been suicide."

"*What?*" Rollo gasped, clasping his chest and recoiling, with his eyes wide and his pupils reduced to tiny dots of black in a sea of green. It was, Pru thought, a bit over the top.

"I don't know anything else," she replied. "Although, I do want to tell you that the investigating detective inspector is my husband." Pru counted herself lucky that she would have to give this explanation only one more time.

Rollo's overwrought manner melted away. "Is he? Well, then, you can vouch for us, can't you? Because, what would we know about … " He frowned. "But, Pru, Acantha said Claudia had hanged herself. How would someone—"

At that moment, Finley walked into the lobby wearing his Cossack hat and gray coat. He went straight to the counter and, the desk sergeant having handed over the woman who had nearly been robbed to a police constable, blinked at this new arrival.

"Sir?" he asked.

Finley explained his business, signed in, and then turned. Spotting Pru and Rollo, he dragged off his hat, made his way to them, and sat down on the other side of Pru.

"Well," he said, toying with the edge of his hat, "bloody awful thing."

"Hello, Finley," Pru said. "You're here about Claudia's death. I want to explain something."

After giving him the details of her relationship, Finley's only comment was, "Is that right?"

Pru stood to leave, but it occurred to her she didn't know how to end the encounter. Would they want rid of her—out of the Winchester Medieval Garden Society because of her connection to the police? Would they think she was abandoning the effort to build the garden?

"I don't know what Claudia's death will mean for the society," she said. Rollo's head jerked up, and Finley flinched. "But it's a worthy project—the garden—and I hope I can … if you still want me to be involved in any way, just … well, let's stay in touch."

Both men mumbled a few unintelligible words, and then Finley's phone rang. He looked at the screen, stood, and walked a few steps away as he answered, saying, "Zoe?"

Rollo leapt up and followed Finley. "Zoe?" he repeated.

Pru took this as her cue to leave.

She'd reached the car when she remembered her hand pruners locked away behind the counter in the station, and turned on the spot to retrieve them. The desk sergeant was on the phone and so she waited, soon becoming aware of furious whispering behind her and off to the left. She looked out the corner of her eye. Rollo and Finley were nose to nose and, although she could not see the latter's face, the former was blazing.

"Sorted!" she heard him spit out. "You said it was sorted!"

Finley replied heatedly, but Pru caught only a few words. "Never promised" and something about a cart and a horse. What came out loud and clear was Finley's last statement: "At least we have Westcott Plumbing to fall back on."

The door behind the counter opened, and Acantha emerged, followed by Christopher. The men froze as his gaze swept the lobby. When he saw Pru, he smiled.

"Oh, Pru," Acantha said in a rush, "I'm so glad you're still here. You see now, Inspector Pearse—it would be fine with Pru there, wouldn't it? I'd be safe."

"That isn't the issue, Ms. Morris," Christopher said. "There are officers at the house. It's a crime scene."

"But my books," Acantha insisted. "I need to collect my books that Claudia had borrowed."

"Yes, fine. I can meet you there later, and we'll take a look together. Say, an hour and a half?"

Acantha looked at her watch, and Pru jumped in. "Would you like to go for a coffee in the meantime? I could certainly use one."

"Oh, yes." Acantha exhaled, and her face relaxed. "That would be lovely."

Christopher put his hand on Pru's arm. "I'll let you know if I'm held up." And then he turned his attention to Rollo and Finley, who looked like two schoolboys waiting for the headmaster.

Pru had spotted a café at the bottom of the hill from the police station, and that's where the two women headed, settling at a small table in the back. Pru had a cappuccino and a yeasty roll with a sugar glaze, and Acantha, a slice of ginger cake and a small Americano for which she had requested five shots of espresso.

"I hope I'm not causing any trouble by wanting my books back," Acantha said, rearranging her plate and coffee cup. "I didn't mind lending them to Claudia, but they are quite good, and I need them for an article I'm writing. Not just my copy of *The Apothecary Rose*, but particularly *The Leechbook Explained* and *Medieval Herbs to Try at Home.* I hope nothing's happened to them. What if police are emptying the contents of the house? How would I ever get them returned to me?"

Acantha took a breath. Pru wondered what she would be like after she'd had her coffee. Also, something she'd said had caught Pru's attention, but the conversation moved on before she had time to figure out what it was.

"It's so good of your husband—sorry, the detective inspector —to let me in, and I do appreciate you going along with me."

"Inside Claudia's house?" Pru asked. "Do you really need me there, because I don't think that's what Christopher meant when—"

"Oh, please, can't you? Just the thought of walking up to the door again makes me feel ill. All I can see is Ellis's face behind the glass. He looked dreadful. What if he's there? Why, Pru? I don't understand. What possible reason could the police have for suspecting it was"—she lowered her voice—"murder?"

A valid question. Why suspect that a woman, hanging from the landing fifteen feet above the ground floor, had been murdered?

Acantha didn't seem to expect an answer, and good thing, because as yet, Pru knew nothing. But Christopher had referred to Claudia Temple's house as a crime scene. He must've seen the autopsy results.

"How could anyone do that? Physically, I mean, in the actual moment. Use your hands to"—Acantha stared down into her coffee as one hand crept up to her own throat—"tie the scarf, her own scarf, round her neck, and fling her over ... " She broke off and covered her mouth. "Oh God."

They drank their coffee and ate in silence, Pru pulling apart her roll and Acantha picking at her cake. Much to Pru's surprise, the caffeine seemed to calm the woman, and they talked of other things for a while, but eventually, Acantha spoke of her hope to be included on the editorial board of—what she said—was an illustrious journal on medieval studies. "It raises one's profile, you know, to be associated with such a prestigious publication."

"Mmm," Pru said, reducing the paper napkin to shreds as she rubbed her sticky fingers with it. "Well, I suppose we'd best be off."

Acantha stood and buttoned her coat. "I wasn't talking of myself alone, you know. Think of Rollo's work."

Yes, both Rollo and Acantha were facing the same challenges —being taken seriously without the requisite degrees.

Rewrapped in her many layers, Pru led the way back to the police car park.

"The Temple house isn't really on Sleepers Hill," Acantha explained, as if Pru had taken exception to the description of where Claudia lived. "But near enough to throw out that name as their address—it sounds better. Claudia said it's what Ellis preferred."

As Sleepers Hill—or thereabouts—was on Pru's way home, they drove in tandem to a street of comfortably lived-in, brick semi-detached homes with white trim, black-painted gutters, and stained-glass side panels on either side of the front doors. But at a bend in the road, sat an exception to the rule. It was a large white stucco affair, and shot out of the ground like an enormous monolith—all straight lines and odd angles and with a great deal of glass.

Two blue-and-yellow-checkered police cars were parked at the curb, along with Christopher's BMW. So this was the home of Claudia and Ellis Temple. Pru stopped and lowered her window, calling to Acantha, who had already parked. "I could wait out here."

"No, please won't you come in, too?" Acantha asked, thrusting her hand through Pru's window to grab her arm. "I feel as if I'm robbing a grave or something."

It took little persuasion, because, although the thought of murder repelled her, curiosity had begun to reel Pru in, and, at the moment, it had the firmer hand. She accompanied Acantha to the door, where they stated their case to the uniformed police constable, who asked them to wait while she let Detective Inspector Pearse know they'd arrived.

They stood on the front step with the door open, shivering slightly. Pru peered into a window on the left and through the glare could see what might be a study with a large desk, one shelf of books, and not a stray paper in sight.

She looked through the door into the vast entry and beyond to the back of the house, into what looked like a combination kitchen and living room. On the left, there was a staircase that must lead to the first-floor landing where two strips of blue-and-white police tape had been tied to the railing, stretched down to the ground floor, and taped to the tile like an advertising banner. Again, Pru visualized Claudia's body, swinging from her own long red scarf. She swallowed hard and blinked the image away. Next to her, Acantha clutched her bag to her chest and kept her eyes on her toes.

The PC returned to the door, and in a moment, Christopher came down the stairs followed by a young woman wearing a smartly tailored trouser suit. It was Detective Sergeant Sophie Grey, who lifted her head in greeting to Pru.

Sophie had been in uniform as a police sergeant the year before, working with Christopher out of the tiny Romsey station. It had slipped Pru's mind that when Sophie had passed her exam and become a detective sergeant, she had got on at the Winchester station. Although not tall, she was a tough cookie, as Pru's dad might've said—and she'd need to be if she was now working under Detective Superintendent John Upstone.

Detective Sergeant Grey continued to the back of the house, and Christopher, with a quick look at Pru, turned to Acantha.

"Ms. Morris, you told me that, previous to this past Friday when Ms. Temple's body was found, the last time you were in this house was the Friday before."

Acantha nodded without looking up. "Yes."

"You never came to the house any other day?"

Acantha raised her head. "No—Friday was our day."

"And your tutelage was confined to study—reading books, discussing herbs used in medieval time. Did you ever give Ms. Temple any unusual herbs or make up one of these old herbal medicines to accompany your sessions?"

Acantha glanced down at her bag. "I may have brought dried samples, but they were ordinary plants. I told you this already. I swear I never gave Claudia anything that would harm her. Won't you tell me why you're asking me again?"

"Let's go into the kitchen," Christopher said, in that police habit of never answering a question. "You said you worked at the dining table, is that right? I want you to look round and tell me if anything seems different."

Pru tagged along as he led Acantha past the stairs and the blue-and-white streamers coming from the first-floor landing to the rear of the house, where the kitchen and living room formed one large room and the ceiling went up two stories. The entire back wall was glass and looked out onto the garden. This naturally drew Pru's attention. It consisted of a deep oval of grass edged with a hodgepodge of shrubbery, some with bare twigs waiting out the winter, and others, evergreen. At the farthest point, popping out of the middle of lower plantings, was an evergreen shrub about six feet high that drew Pru's attention. Its spiny-leaved stems were held at right angles to its vertical stems. Pru recognized it immediately—an Asian mahonia. A top-notch plant for winter, and a great contrast to low, mounding shrubs. But this mahonia sat askew, looking like the Leaning Tower of Pisa. Frost heave? It was cold enough.

It was cold inside the house, too—or seemed so. The decor was spare in that expensive sort of way—clean, square lines of tables and chairs, a kitchen in which the fridge was disguised as a cupboard and the stove top looked as black and smooth as the counters. Only a swan-neck faucet signaled the presence of a sink. In what must be the living-room area, a low-backed leather sofa and chairs in neutral shades kept a discreet profile, as if trying not to be noticed. Pru had met Claudia only once, but she could not imagine such a colorful personality thriving in this place.

In the middle of the vast space, a square black pillar rose from the floor to the ceiling far above. On one side was a wingback chair—upholstered in a cheerful chintz—and a low table teeming with loose sheets of paper, pens and pencils, and an untidy stack of books. A PC wearing gloves looked up from collecting the papers and stowing them in a plastic bag.

"There," Acantha said. "Those are my books. May I take them?"

"Hang on, let me make sure they've been logged," Christopher said.

And, Pru thought, fingerprinted.

When he stepped away, Acantha shivered. "It's hard to believe Claudia lived in this house, isn't it?" she asked. "Hard to believe anyone does."

Pru nodded to the messy table and smiled. "At least she had one spot of her own."

Christopher returned and asked Acantha to give the entire room another look. "Is anything different?"

Acantha shrugged. "No, not that I can see. Why? What did you expect me to say?"

"Thank you. The constable at the door will note the book titles. You can come into the station to sign your statement tomorrow."

Before he went back through to the study, Christopher put his hand on Pru's back. She felt the warmth through her sweater, interpreted the gesture, and smiled. His way of saying "See you later at home." She would've preferred to stick around and ask a few questions of her own, but there would be time enough for that over dinner.

The women remained where they were—Pru waiting for Acantha's lead to depart. Instead of moving, the woman sighed.

" 'I want to be like you,' she said to me. 'I want to know everything about medieval plants and give lectures and write articles.' " Acantha's eyes flashed. "Well, she couldn't be like me, could she? I've worked years to get where I am, and fought against people with university degrees who think I don't know what I'm talking about. What gave Claudia the idea she could swan in and become the belle of the ball in an instant?" Tears rolled down Acantha's cheeks, and she whisked them away with the back of her hand. "She loved making tea from black peppermint."

"No, sir"—the voice of the PC at the door carried to the back of the house—"you may not come in without permission from Inspector Pearse."

Pru turned to see a man, thin with a long face and thick brown hair, towering over the PC at the door, his overcoat unbuttoned and his tie crooked.

He looked up, saw Acantha, and scowled. Then his gaze shifted to Pru, and he narrowed his eyes.

"You there!" he shouted, pointing a finger as if picking her out of a lineup. "Are you another one of them? *Are* you?" he demanded, and Pru, stunned, had no answer. He attempted to push past the PC, but she stood her ground, and so he gave up the fight, but not the argument. "I'm the one who found Claudia like that, and now you let that lot in and yet bar me from my own house?"

Christopher burst out of the study followed by another PC, and the three of them—one detective and two uniforms—surrounded the man.

"Ellis," Acantha whispered to Pru.

"Mr. Temple, I'm Detective Inspector Pearse." Christopher dutifully held out his warrant card for inspection, but Ellis barely glanced at it, instead craning his head past his guard and keeping his attention on Pru.

She found her nerve, took a deep breath, and approached.

"Hello, Mr. Temple, I'm Pru Parke." Close up, he looked terrible. His eyes were bloodshot, he needed a shave, and she caught a whiff of whisky. Her heart hurt for him. "I'm sorry for your loss. I met Claudia only once, but I could tell she was a lovely woman. I've come along today to help Acantha collect a few books she'd lent Claudia. That's the only reason we're here—and we're going now."

As she spoke, he stood watching her, a frown on his face. "You're new. Then perhaps they haven't brainwashed you yet—convincing you that all this medieval business is worthwhile. Can you tell me how this happened? How they did it to her? If you know, you must tell me."

"Mr. Temple," Christopher cut in.

Acantha said, "Ellis, it's dreadful, but—"

He took a step toward her and shook a finger in her face. "I know what you did. I saw what you made her drink."

"Enough," Christopher demanded, and they all fell quiet. "Mr. Temple, go into the study and wait for me."

Ellis didn't budge. "I've lost my wife," he choked out and then drew a ragged breath. "I've lost my son—or as good as, because he accuses me of driving her to this. So if I want to ask every one of those people to stand up in court and testify to their part in her death, then I will."

At Christopher's nod, the PCs stepped forward. Ellis sniffed, and stalked off into the next room.

"Thank you, Inspector," Acantha said, hugging the books to her chest. "I'll be on my way now. Pru, ring me, will you?"

Acantha departed, but Pru remained. She sighed deeply, glancing at the study doorway.

"Finding her must've been terrible for him," she said to Christopher. "But, even with all that blame, it doesn't sound as if he knows you suspect it's murder."

"He knows. He's come here from the police station. John had him taken in to explain the case has become a murder enquiry and to give us a chance to get started here. It's the shock makes him react this way."

"And so you're certain it isn't suicide. How do you know?"

Christopher studied her, as if assessing how much she could take. They both knew that, at times, Pru's imagination could be entirely too vivid for her own tastes. But she would rather know than not.

"Claudia was dead before she was hanged."

CHAPTER 8

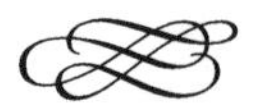

Pru stood on the pavement with her back to the Temple house. She plunged her hands into her pockets, and took a deep breath. Now that Ellis Temple knew his wife's death was murder and not suicide, perhaps someone was making him a sugary cup of tea while police continued to search for clues as to why and how someone had killed Claudia and then strung her up. This evening, Pru would ask Christopher what else police knew, but for now, she longed to clear her mind of the whole matter. She exhaled in a huff and watched a cloud of steamy breath disappear.

"Terrible business, that—isn't it?" said a scratchy voice nearby.

Pru glanced round and saw a woman on the pavement in front of the Victorian semidetached next door. She sat on a low, one-legged stool with a rounded base—Pru had seem them advertised to gardeners—her hands encased in mittens as big as boxing gloves as she rocked from side to side.

She dressed well for the cold, wearing what looked like several layers of sweaters over a housecoat. Her legs were covered in thick, rainbow-colored tights, and her feet were tucked into fleece-lined carpet slippers. She'd pulled one—possibly two—knit hats down to her eyebrows, leaving her apple-red cheeks her most prominent feature.

"Hello," Pru said, walking over. "Yes, it is sad. Did you know Claudia?"

"Didn't know either of them well, although her better than him. She was always bright and cheerful, waving and stopping to chat and the like. He's a bit dour, if you ask me. Are you with the police?"

"No." Well, yes. Sort of. "I'm involved with the medieval garden group that Claudia was a part of."

"Always interested in something, she was. They've come to talk with me, you know—the police. Doing their doorstep thing, asking if I'd seen anything unusual last Thursday night. Well, I'm not a good sleeper and I am awake during the night, but I had nothing to offer. Pity." The woman smiled, and her face, constricted by the layers of wool on her head, folded up into furrows. She stuck out a mittened hand. "How d'ya do? I'm Tabby Collier, but you call me Tabby."

"Pru Parke, pleased to meet you. Well, Tabby, looks like you have a lovely border. Is that corylopsis there, the winter buttercup?"

"Ah, you're a gardener," the woman said, grunting as she stood and tucked the plastic stool under her arm. "Then you understand the longing to plunge a spade into the ground. Frustrating, isn't it?"

"It is. But I doubt if the soil is frozen more than a few inches," Pru speculated, "so best to leave the roots undisturbed to wait it out. At least I hope that's the case—we kept our agapanthus in the ground."

"Oh dear," Tabby said. "Good luck with that."

They watched as a uniform came out from Claudia's house, heading for one of the police cars.

"Never did any gardening of their own," Tabby said. "Had

one of those services that came and cut the grass and hoovered any leaf out of place. Although they haven't been round lately, of course."

"How long have the Temples lived here?" Pru asked.

"Ten, eleven years, I'd say. But in all that time, no one in our street knew much about them."

"Do you know their son?"

Tabby frowned. "Son? I've never seen a sign of a child. It's like I told the officers, when neighbors keep themselves to themselves, you don't want to pry, do you? Mr. Temple, now, was off to work regularly, and I did sometimes think she didn't quite know what to do with herself. But then she'd have spells of activity and meetings and such and be ever so lively."

"Do you know what he does—his job?" Pru asked.

"No, only that he dresses well for it and he drives a fancy car. That's it over there." Pru looked across the road to a sporty red Jaguar. Tabby clicked her tongue and shook her head. "Such a loss. And you know what they say—things come in threes. I'd say he'd better brace himself."

Her fingers white with cold, Pru jabbed the heater settings in her car, waiting what seemed like forever for the air to heat up. To hurry things along, she stuck a numb hand inside her many layers of sweaters and cried out when it touched bare skin. Her cheeks prickled as they warmed. She had nothing else to do in Winchester, and so decided to go straight home and finish thawing in the kitchen at Greenoak with a hot bowl of anything going.

A quick look at the map on her phone to find the best way out to the Romsey road showed her there was, after all, something else she could do in Winchester. Fulflood, John and

Sabine's neighborhood, was quite close. Should she phone ahead? No, perhaps not this once, because if all else failed, she did have her pruners and there was that wisteria.

Pru almost lost her courage standing at the door, her finger hovering over the bell. Sabine could be out or at a crucial stage in a painting or cleaning the oven or—

The door flew open, and Sabine's smile swept away all worry.

"I looked out the window from upstairs and thought that was you. How lovely—please do come in."

"I happened to be close by," Pru explained. "I hope I'm not disturbing you."

"Not a bit of it." Sabine closed the door, pulled off a paint-stained smock, and stuffed it in the umbrella stand. "I so rarely get visitors—apart from the man to fill the oil tank or the missionaries. I was just about to make myself a sandwich. I couldn't interest you in one, could I?"

At the mere mention of food, Pru's stomach growled, reminding her of the time of day. "I'd love one."

In the kitchen, they exchanged a smattering of light conversation as Sabine gathered ingredients. "I've ham and cheese. Or ham. Or cheese."

"Ham and cheese."

"Tea or coffee?"

"Tea, please – shall I put the kettle on?" Pru asked, going to the sink to wash her hands.

A few minutes later they sat on high stools next to each other at the counter. Pru could see out the back to the garden through a tangled mass of whippy stems.

"I have my pruners with me. I thought I might sort out your wisteria."

"That would be wonderful—I'm afraid I don't know where to cut. Will pruning help it bloom?"

"Oh yes, a good hard prune will do wonders for the show you'll get in May." They continued to chat about the garden, and finally, halfway through her sandwich, Pru got up the nerve to ask, "So, when did you and John marry?"

Sabine looked at her out the corner of her eye. "September. Here in Winchester at the registry office."

"Are you local?" Pru asked, knowing that John Upstone wasn't.

Sabine shook her head. "We decided to start someplace fresh for both of us. John had been in York for—well, you know how long. I'd spent most of the past fifteen years or so wandering. A year or two at a time everywhere from the Shetlands to the Isle of Wight."

"Painting all the while?"

"Yes. And what about you?"

Pru took the abrupt change of focus in stride, knowing there was more to Sabine's answer and hoping they could return to it. For the time being, she told her own story of moving from Dallas, where she had lived all her life, to England.

"And how has it been with you and Christopher," Sabine asked, "coming into each other's already full lives?"

"It's been the best thing in the world," Pru said. "With all the accompanying struggles you could imagine. He can be overprotective, but that makes sense, because he's a policeman, and so, feels the need to save everyone. And I can be a bit stubborn." She shrugged. "Well, perhaps more than a bit. Occasionally our strongest personality traits crash into each other, but we work it out. And best of all, practically overnight, my family multiplied —including a stepson, Graham."

Sabine pushed the breadcrumbs around on her plate. Pru watched for a minute before she worked up the courage to ask, "I know John and Molly didn't have children. What about your side of the family?"

The breadcrumbs lost their fascination. Sabine brushed her

hands off and asked, "Would you like a glass of wine? And then I'll show you my studio."

"I'd love to see it."

"Red or white?"

"Red, please."

Sabine filled their glasses and said, "Cheers."

They took sips, and then Pru followed her up the stairs and up another set and through a door into a vast space that smelled of paint and was full of color. Frames—from gold gilt to austere oak—were stacked against walls, along with blank canvases pulled tightly across stretcher bars. Charcoal sketches littered the walls and were thumbtacked to the corners of partly finished works on easels.

"Wow." Pru, breathless, could barely take it all in. Finally, her eyes rested on one particular canvas. She saw a stone castle sitting atop what she knew to be an extinct volcano, and exclaimed "Edinburgh!" On closer examination, she spotted the shops along the Royal Mile that led to the castle's esplanade. "Christopher and I were married in Edinburgh—at the Botanics."

"It's one of my favorite cities," Sabine said.

"Your work is … it's difficult to put into words. It's finished and yet leaves so much to my imagination."

" 'A rough beauty.' " Sabine blushed. "The art critic in the *Birmingham Mail* wrote that. It's my favorite review of all time."

"Have you always been an artist?"

Sabine sat on a low stool and nodded toward a window seat for Pru.

"Most of my life I painted what other people wanted, and made good money from it. I was a dab hand at ginning up a piece of art from any old snapshot sent to me. Happy newlyweds, houses, grandparents, babies, dogs. During the school holidays, my son and I would go on rambles, and I'd free myself to paint what I wanted. Tom would say, 'But Mum, why don't you sell these?' I asked him who'd pay money for them, and he said he would. I told him he could have them for free, and so, he made a collection of all the dashed-off holiday art and papered his room with them." She smiled, but did not look happy. "He was twenty-six when he died. Afghanistan—he was army."

"Sabine, how dreadful."

"Yes," she agreed firmly, but without tears. "A sniper." She pointed to a small painting tacked up on the wall near them. It had worn edges and deep creases where it had been folded. It was a spring scene with a forest floor carpeted in bluebells and a young boy walking away, rucksack on his back and walking stick in his hand. "They found that on him, tucked inside his uniform. I'd given it to him before he left."

The painting melted into a blur of greens and blues as Pru's eyes filled with tears that spilled over and splashed into her wine.

"How did you ever manage to recover?"

"I'm not sure a full recovery is ever possible," Sabine said and smiled again, but this time, it was genuine. "But I'll tell you one thing I did. I stopped painting what other people wanted. From then on, I painted for myself—and for Tom. I went back to all the places we'd been on holiday, and I painted and painted and painted until I could breathe again."

Pru wiped her cheeks and searched her sleeves in vain for a tissue. Sabine came to her rescue with a piece of muslin, smeared with paint and smelling strongly of turpentine.

"Thanks." Pru blew her nose on the cleanest corner. "But you've done all right, haven't you? You have shows and sell your work."

"Yes, I'm fine. Tom had been right all along."

They were quiet for a moment. The sun was sinking, and one last ray of light found its way through tree branches and into the west window and hit the easels, throwing long, thin shadows on the floor that looked like giant insects.

"Sabine"—Pru cleared her throat—"you and John."

"Yes, well." Sabine looked into her empty glass. "For that we'll need another drink. Or would you prefer coffee?"

Pru followed her downstairs, where they fortified themselves with coffee before moving to the sitting room. Sabine lit the fire and switched on the lamps as she said, "John and I met at my show in Keswick. You heard that part."

"And it sounded as if he was fairly taken with you from the start," Pru replied, unsure of the truth of her statement.

Sabine grinned. "The feeling was mutual. We had dinner together that first night and never stopped talking about … everything. We took the walk up to Cat Bells the next day and on the way down ran into a squall and ended up soaked and shivering in front of the fire at the Dog and Gun." She looked into her own fireplace now. "We seemed to fit perfectly into each other's empty spaces. Does that make sense?"

"Yes," Pru said, "it does."

"He told me about Molly—of course he did—and how much she meant to him. I understood that. But we were happy, and we committed ourselves to each other. I admit it was quick, but was it too quick? I don't know. I do know we were both looking forward to the future. He said, Wouldn't a change be the best way to begin? and so we chose someplace new for both of us. He managed a transfer and came down here to find us a place to live. I thought we'd get a flat, but John found this house. He said when he saw the room upstairs, he knew it would be perfect for my studio. He was right."

Pru found it difficult to reconcile the John Upstone that Sabine described with the embarrassed, uneasy man from dinner the night before.

"But then," Pru said, "something happened."

"Yes, and whatever it was, it happened suddenly and only a few weeks ago. He's closed himself off. I've asked what's wrong, but he won't talk about it. He does, however, talk about Molly, as you well heard. I could be an accessory in this house for all his attention. It's as if he's trying to goad me into disliking him, to save me from ..." Her face drained of color, and she took a quick breath before going on. "I think he's ill. I'm afraid he's dying."

CHAPTER 9

It was just after six and dark when Pru left Orchard House—it had been dark for a good while. Even so, she would arrive before Christopher and get their dinner in the oven. And then they would have the evening before them.

But when she pulled into the drive at Greenoak, the light in the kitchen was on and the BMW already in residence. She hurried in to meet Christopher in the kitchen, his phone in hand.

"Sorry," she said, shedding her coat and boots. "You weren't sending out a search party, were you? I didn't realize the time—but still, I'm surprised you're home first. I stopped to see Sabine." He raised his eyebrows, but she had her excuse ready. "The wisteria is in desperate shape, and I wanted to get a start on it. We had lunch and then got to talking."

"How was that?"

"Oh." Pru didn't know how to begin that subject, and so said, "I'll explain all that later. But, how did the rest of your day go—your interviews with the others and Claudia's husband? Why were you asking Acantha to look round the house? Did you think she'd notice something missing?"

"I found chicken goulash in the freezer," Christopher said, "and have just put it in the oven. The library fire is going." He took her hand. "Come on."

They sat in front of the fire with glasses of wine, and it occurred to Pru that Christopher might be home early on a regular basis, at least for the run of this enquiry, because they would have notes to compare.

"Well, Inspector, what's your report?"

"The medical examiner said there were no signs of a struggle, as such," Christopher said.

"'As such'?"

"A chair had been overturned, making it look as if Claudia stood on it and then kicked it away. That could appear to be a suicide. But then, how did she get the contusion on the back of her head? Was it the result of a fall or a blow? To create the impression this was suicide, the killer would want to make it look as if she had taken something first and then hanged herself. If that's the case, he or she might've given Claudia an overdose."

"An overdose of what?"

"To be determined, but there was an open jar on the table. The liquid inside is being analyzed, so we'll be able to compare it with what was in her system."

Pru knew that toxicology reports did not appear within the hour as they so conveniently did on television detective programs. It could be days or even weeks before they would know.

"Is this what you were asking Acantha about? Is it what John meant when he asked me about a 'concoction'? Have you seen it —is it an herbal mix?"

"It's a murky color—greenish brown—and it had a sharp odor combined with the smell of overcooked vegetables."

"It was there when Ellis found her?" Pru asked. "Wait now. I just realized something. He found Claudia on Friday morning. Where had he been?"

"Oxford," Christopher said, staring into the flames. "On business."

"What business?"

"Ellis Temple deals in luxury cars—Temple Motors has a small showroom off the Petersfield Road. He was in Oxford for a meeting with a business consortium, a sort of sales and marketing support group. Eight of them with various businesses gather at a hotel for a seminar every six months. Begins Wednesday and finishes Friday morning."

"So, he's off the list?"

"No one is off the list as of yet. As far as Temple's story is concerned, I need to talk with each of the other attendees. And the hotel."

"Do you know what time she died?"

"Not long after midnight."

"And he didn't find her until morning." Pru shivered. "If it's some herbal brew—well, I realize that would point to Acantha first, because she was teaching Claudia about medieval herbs and their uses. But she couldn't've done that—drug Claudia and hang her." She felt Christopher's eyes on her. Yes, she did have a tendency to think the best of people, but she wasn't making excuses now. "Physically, I mean. How would she ever have managed?"

"Claudia might not have collapsed until she'd gone up to the first-floor landing. Or the murderer could've had help."

"A conspiracy? What, did she talk Rollo into ..." Her mind moved briskly along a path making unwanted progress. She drew her feet up onto the sofa. "Rollo and Finley were arguing in the lobby of the station today."

Christopher nodded. "I can imagine. Finley Martin told me it was Wednesday late morning when he delivered the papers that Claudia needed to sign for the donation. Then he took her out for the day, and left her house back at her house about seven that evening. On Thursday, he gave her a lift to your meeting at the site of the garden, dropped her at home, then went back to collect the papers on Thursday evening. But she was unable to put her hands on them."

"What?" Pru said. "She'd lost them? Or was she stalling, about to change her mind again?"

"Finley Martin said she swore she'd signed them and put them somewhere. He said he went back to his office and printed out the lot again to have ready for her to sign the next day."

"The next day, she was dead. Could she have put them in the post? Could she have gone out and delivered them herself and Terry Reed had been watching and followed her? No," Pru said, disagreeing with herself. "She was killed at home."

"Not in a fit of anger—this required planning," Christopher said. "I wonder what is Reed's knowledge of herbal mixtures?"

Pru shrugged. "You didn't find herbs or anything that looked like leftover ingredients in the house?"

"Nothing," Christopher said.

"Rollo, Finley—Acantha, too—talked as if the million pounds was a done deal. I think they have even spent some of it. If they believed the papers signed, and didn't want Claudia to change her mind again ..."

"I'll have a word with Claudia's solicitor, Zoe Bagshaw. She has an office on Southgate in Winchester."

Zoe, Pru thought. She's the one who rang Finley. "So, you and John think Claudia's death has something to do with the money and the medieval garden, because there was some herby liquid on the kitchen table?"

"There's something else odd. The pockets of her cardigan were stuffed with dried plants—rosemary and lavender, I think —and something else. Small pieces that looked like resin. Quite fragrant. We don't know if she put them there or if the killer did, but I want to know their significance. When you go in to sign your statement tomorrow, will you take a look? I've told the officers in charge of evidence, so there would be no problem."

"Yes, I will. There's nothing harmful about rosemary and lavender. They could be samples that Acantha had given her. I'll ask her, because she's invited me over, you see. And after all," Pru added, ready to deflect any protest Christopher might mount about staying safe, "that is my assignment from Detective Superintendent Upstone. To chat up the board members."

Acantha must be low on the suspect list, Pru thought, because Christopher only nodded.

"What about their son?" Pru asked. "Tabby said she'd never seen any sign of a child."

"Tabby?"

"Tabby Collier. She's the next-door neighbor. She was out in her front garden, and I stopped to talk."

"She just happened to be outdoors in freezing weather, did she?" Christopher asked. "The son—Daniel Temple—lives in Inverness. John was having difficulty reaching him."

"Hadn't his father done that—told him about Claudia?"

"Apparently, yes, but we need a full understanding of the family background, and so either John or I will interview him."

Police building their case. "Acantha said Claudia talked about him all the time. Danny. But she got the idea he left home early. How old is he?"

"Temple said he was about twenty-five."

"About?" Pru asked. "Doesn't he know how old his son is?"

"Or possibly twenty-six."

Pru looked into her empty wineglass. "Twenty-six. That's how old Sabine's son was when he died."

Pru took Christopher's hand and told him Sabine's story. The death of a young man—the loss of a son. Although Pru didn't mention it aloud, she was reminded of Christopher's son, Graham, who was very much alive. They'd celebrated his twenty-seventh birthday in early

January, when he visited over Christmas. He was a wonderful young man, and although Pru could not claim any responsibility for his many fine qualities, she loved him dearly and could not help thinking at that moment what a fragile thing is life.

"His death is what led her to paint as she does now. Also"—Pru studied her sock feet, but watched Christopher out the corner of her eye—"Sabine and I talked about how John is acting."

A shadow crossed Christopher's face. "What did she say?"

Pru wished she had one more sip of wine for courage. "They came to Winchester in September and married. It was meant to give them both a fresh start. John chose that house just for Sabine, because the room at the top has fantastic light for her studio. They were happy. But he changed suddenly a few weeks ago, and he refuses to talk about it." Pru couldn't keep her chin from quivering—this conversation had far too much darkness in it. "She's afraid he's dying."

Christopher didn't look surprised. He didn't look happy, either. He and Pru proceeded to dissect John Upstone's every move and phrase since Christopher had reconnected with him—only the day before—hoping to find clues to his behavior. Without coming to any firm conclusion, they gave up and moved to the kitchen and their dinner. The meal was silent and contemplative, until the subject of the enquiry rose to the surface.

"Claudia had really taken to the study of medieval herbs and their uses?"

"She loved it," Pru said. "At least as far as I could tell. But perhaps she had loved dormice just as much. I wonder what happened there."

"I rang Terry Reed," Christopher said. "I'm driving over to Plymouth tomorrow to see him."

"After I sign my statement in the morning and take a look at the herbs from Claudia's pocket, I need to go back to Orchard House—I didn't get to the wisteria today."

Her husband made an unintelligible reply.

Pru, an unfulfilled matchmaker, had taken to assisting in the repair of what she saw as other people's worthy but broken relationships in the desire that everyone find that balance of contentment, happiness, and hard work that she and Christopher had. Her record was spotty, but that didn't stop her from taking on a new case.

"Will you talk with John?" she asked.

"What would he tell me he wouldn't tell his wife?"

"Can you find out another way—if he's ill?"

"I can't request my superior's medical records," Christopher said. "It isn't as if he's not doing his job. His energy level seems fine, his attention to the case is good, and analysis of what we've found so far is as sharp as I remember."

"When you came home yesterday, you said he looked old."

"You told me that was inevitable."

"And that he seemed uneasy about something," Pru reminded him.

"Yes, and now we know that was about Sabine—because he didn't have the courage to tell me he'd remarried."

Pru stabbed the last piece of chicken off her plate and said in a casual tone, "Of course, I could ask him about it myself."

"Am I being strong-armed?" Christopher asked, but with that ghost of a smile.

Pru intended to spend the first half of the morning at her computer, writing the article about medieval herb gardens, but she'd no more sat down in the library than she heard voices in the kitchen. Polly and Bernadette had arrived. Pru met them in the entry as they emerged from the kitchen.

"I've got an appointment with a client in Stockbridge," her sister-in-law said.

"And I've got the mothers-and-babies group arriving at the church hall in an hour," Bernadette said.

"Well, then," Pru said, "lovely of you to stop. Come again sometime."

"Silly," Polly said.

"Actually," Bernadette said, "we thought we'd better look in and see how you are."

"You and the enquiry," Polly said. "When did Claudia's suicide turn to murder?"

The swing door to the kitchen opened and Evelyn asked, "Coffee?"

Polly made a show of looking at her watch. "Oh, I daresay I've time for a coffee. You?" she asked the vicar.

The three of them went into the kitchen. Pru put the kettle on and reached for the cafetière and measured grounds, Polly got out cups and saucers, and Bernadette filled the milk jug. Evelyn stood at the sink washing stalks of chard, but the others settled at the table. Pru popped the lid on the biscuit tin and offered shortbread.

"Christopher has been asked to take over the enquiry," Pru said.

"In the paper it said that a Detective Superintendent Upstone was running the investigation," Bernadette said.

"Yes, but …" Pru looked at the expectant faces across the table from her. "Right, I'd better start there. On Monday," Pru said, "I met John Upstone."

They could well have spent the rest of the day on the story of Christopher's first boss and his surprising appearance in Winchester, replete with a wife he pretends isn't there, but there wasn't time, and so instead, Pru gave Polly and Bernadette a précis on John and Sabine. As she described Sabine's art, Polly grabbed her phone and searched.

"Sabine Noakes," she reported. "Several galleries sell her paintings. Look at this one of the Forest of Dean."

They gathered round Polly's phone.

"Amazing," Bernadette said.

"That's a picture, that is," Evelyn said, leaning over Pru's shoulder. "Even that tiny, I feel as if I were there."

There were no conclusions to draw from the Upstone story, although Pru did ask Bernadette if she thought it could be true that John was ill and pushing Sabine away to save her from hurt.

"Don't our minds work in funny ways," Bernadette said. "Thinking we could stop someone from caring just like that."

"I'm going to invite them to dinner on Friday evening," Pru said with a burst of inspiration. "Will you come, Bernadette? And you and Simon, Polly?"

"And what will you serve at this dinner party?" Evelyn asked.

"Scrambled eggs?" Pru offered, and Ev laughed.

"Right, now," Polly said with a quick check of the time, "what about Claudia Temple?"

Pru quickly introduced the players in the enquiry, starting with Rollo.

"Yes, I remember him," Polly said. "He's the short fellow—he introduced Acantha. And he's Westcott Plumbing? They're everywhere, they are. 'We treat your pipes as if they were our own'—isn't that their motto?"

It didn't take long for Pru to get them up to speed, because Pru was short on details, and even if she had known firm evidence against anyone, she couldn't've passed it on unless it was general knowledge.

Bernadette reached over and gave Pru's hand a squeeze. "And well done, you, for being asked to assist in the enquiry. Especially as it may put you in the position of helping John and Sabine over this rough patch of theirs."

"I'll do what I can," Pru said, "but as far as I can tell, John isn't one to brook interference in his personal life."

"On the other hand," Polly said, "he doesn't know how persistent you can be."

"Yes," Pru said. "Beware, John Upstone."

Polly popped up from her chair. "Must dash. Sounds as if it's early days yet. You have no word on what was in the jar on the table, and if she actually drank any of it? No sign of forced entry —isn't that something they look for? Fingerprints? Did she argue with anyone the day before?"

Those were questions Pru should be asking, because the answers would lead to actual clues, not just vague impressions.

As Polly and Bernadette buttoned up their coats, Pru reached for hers, too.

"Are you not getting back to work on your article?" Evelyn asked.

Pru tried to look regretful. "I have to go into Winchester to the police station—to sign my statement."

The wisteria on the back of John and Sabine's house grew from a fat, gnarled, and twisted trunk and reached as high the studio's windows on the second floor. Pru had seen wisteria that had climbed to the top of hundred-foot trees, so this particular vine was only mildly out of control. Still, the long, whippy stems that had grown the previous summer now made the plant looked like a monster centipede waving its arms about in the air. Were they arms or legs? Pru contemplated what centipede appendages were called and how many they actually had as she set to cutting the stems back to two pairs of buds.

She had arrived late morning as Sabine had been leaving for an appointment with a gallery in town. "Not to worry," Pru had told her. "I've my work cut out for me here. But before you go—will you and John come to dinner at Greenoak on Friday?"

Sabine had seemed delighted with the idea, but had accepted

the invitation provisionally, upon John's approval. Before she went on her way, she had laid a hand on Pru's arm and said, "I didn't know anyone when we moved here—neither of us did. I feel like my world is expanding at last."

Left alone to work, Pru entered that Zen-like state of pruning—snipping and thinking and snipping. She thought about the Friday dinner, and realized there might be something more difficult than persuading John to attend—preparing the meal. She would need a consultation with Evelyn.

After an hour, a knee-high pile of long, unruly stems had accumulated at Pru's feet—and she'd got only as far as clearing the back door. Her toes were numb and her fingers well on their way to being so. She would give herself another fifteen minutes before seeking out the warmth of her car's heater. As she reached high to catch a stem above the kitchen window, a form loomed up from inside. She squealed, dropped her pruners, and jumped back into the stems, which wrapped round her ankles like snakes. As she stumbled and kicked to get free, John flew out the door and caught her arm.

"Are you all right?" he asked.

"Fine." Breathless, she put a hand on her chest and panted. "Just surprised."

"I didn't know you were here," he explained with a slightly injured tone.

"I had mentioned to Sabine I would prune the wisteria," Pru said. "I dropped by unannounced, and she was on her way out to an appointment, but she said for me to go ahead." The situation came into focus—John Upstone had come home for lunch only because he believed the coast to be clear. "You knew, didn't you—that she'd be out?"

Upstone ignored the question, and instead studied the wisteria from ground to rooftop. "You'll need a ladder for that."

"I won't need one. I'll find someone local to come and finish it for you."

"Are you afraid of ladders?"

"No," Pru replied, "ladders don't scare me. It's heights I can't handle."

John laughed.

Pru smiled in return. "And I don't mind admitting it. Christopher knew quite soon after we'd met that I have this problem. I think that's important in a relationship—sharing."

All humor evaporated from Upstone's face. "Well, then—shall I leave you to it?"

"Actually, I'm finished for today. I'll be back to look over those old apple trees. For now, I need to sign my statement, and Christopher asked if I would look at what you found in Claudia's pockets."

"Good," Upstone said, his voice firm now that he was back on his own turf of a murder enquiry.

"And that liquid that you think she drank." Pru dropped her pruners into her bag and added, "By the way—you and Sabine are invited to dinner at Greenoak on Friday. Just a small gathering—my brother and his wife. Our vicar. Sabine loves the idea, and Christopher and I are looking forward to it."

Before John could object, Pru hurried off.

At the station, the desk sergeant greeted her as an old friend and made a little joke when she handed over the pruners to be locked away. "You haven't been at the roses in the cathedral garden, now have you?"

"I wouldn't think of it," Pru said. "I once killed off a Mr. Lincoln by pruning too early—learned my lesson."

When she stated her purpose for being there, the desk sergeant made a call and then passed her along to a PC, who led her into the depths of the station. He left her at a counter in an open office and returned in a few minutes with the evidence bags and the jar of unknown mixture.

Even though it came straight out of the station's evidence fridge, the murky liquid smelled bad—the odor of decay, along with the twang of wine. She could identify nothing in it. Next, she examined what had been found in Claudia's cardigan pocket —a few stems of rosemary and lavender. The sharp, piney odor of the rosemary was strong and fairly fresh. The lavender had only a few leaves—in winter the plants looked like little more than a bundle of gray sticks.

A plastic bag held the small, rocklike substance Christopher had mentioned. Pru opened the bag and breathed in—it had a strong aroma that reminded her of licorice and earth at the same time. Acantha would need to see this and the contents of the jar in person, but she could at least give her a first glimpse. Were photos allowed? Pru glanced round the office. Everyone looked busy, and no one was paying attention to her. She pulled out her phone.

Acantha lived not far from the train station on the busy Stockbridge Road in a second-floor, two-bedroom flat. She answered the door with a pencil stuck through the shiny black bun atop her head, a thick bundle of loose papers under one arm, and an open book in her hand.

"Thanks for seeing me at such short notice," Pru said.

"Not a bit of it," Acantha said. "I'm glad you rang. You're my excuse to take a break. Come through now, and I'll put the kettle on." She deposited books and papers on a desk already heaped with more of the same, and went to the kitchen while Pru hung her coat on a peg on the back of the door and stood still, taking in the sitting room. An enormous green sofa and two matching side chairs vied for floor space with a myriad of occasional tables. Underneath the furniture, several round rugs covered the hardwood floor, overlapping like a Venn diagram. Books were stacked haphazardly on the coffee table—at the top of one pile lay *Betony, Bistort, and Borage: The Authentic Medievalist*—and protruding pencils, used envelopes, and drinks coasters used as bookmarks. All the many lights in the room, from floor lamps to sconces, were switched on, illuminating overstuffed bookcases and framed botanical prints.

Pru crept up to one to get a closer look and found these were not prints, but actual herbarium specimens. Pressed under glass were plant parts—leaves, stems, flowers—carefully arranged for proper identification along with a handwritten label affixed at the bottom.

Always up for a plant ID quiz, Pru refused to read a label until she'd had a good guess. The first one, dill, was easy, because of its umbrellalike inflorescence that divided into delicate filaments—although it could've been fennel or one of the other plants in the same family. The next, betony, she knew in a second, given away by its magenta spikes of tiny tubular flowers. She got stuck on the one after that. It had pointed oval leaves and faded yellow flowers with a dark throat. She had to read the label—henbane. Determined to increase her score, she moved on to the next plant, and smiled at its large leaves and the three different flower clusters—one each of white, pink, and purple.

Acantha stuck her head out of the kitchen. "Are you all right with caraway seeds?"

"Comfrey," Pru said, pleased with herself.

"No, dear, I said 'caraway.' "

"Caraway?" Pru echoed. "Yes, fine—sorry. I was admiring your herbarium."

"Ah, comfrey." Acantha nodded to the specimen. "Also known as boneset."

Pru stepped over to the mantel next, which was populated by a host of photographs.

"And this is your family?"

Acantha smiled. "In all their glory. See at the far end—the old snapshots? My father was in the Windrush generation. Do you know it? His family came from Jamaica after the Second World War. He was the youngest of five. Now, would you mind tea in the kitchen? We'd have more space."

Marginally. A stack of journals—*Medieval Times Today*—had to be shifted off the table and onto the counter to make room for the cups and saucers, teapot, and cake plate.

"I remember you told me that you don't have a university degree," Pru said, "but you certainly know a lot about herbs and medieval times. Has it always been a passion?"

"I started young, that's for certain," Acantha said. "My dad had a small but well-chosen culinary herb garden in window boxes outside the kitchen of our flat. He set me assignments to learn what each one was, where it came from, and what dishes it could be used in—probably to get me out from underfoot."

"He was a cook?"

"He was a mechanic for London Transport. But at home, he was a master chef."

"Was your mother Jamaican, too?" Pru asked.

"No, French. She was a chemist and worked at the sugar factory in Peterborough. She met Dad on a girls weekend in the Big Smoke." As Pru tried to work out the geography of this relationship, Acantha continued. "After I was born, my three brothers came along, and so she quit the factory. But my parents both instilled in me the idea that I could make myself into whatever I wanted to be, even if it never paid the rent. So, I made my living as a bookkeeper, but at heart, I'm a medievalist, and that's how I am determined to be remembered."

As they ate their way through the plate of seedcake, Acantha told stories of medieval times—the people and how they lived. She got to the end of a tale about monks and their propensity for turnips, and Pru broke out in peals of laughter, ending in a snort.

"Right," Acantha said, clearing the tea things away. "Now, what do you have to show me?"

Back to the business of murder. Pru brought up the photos she'd taken at the police station. When it came to the shot of the rocky bits, Acantha leaned over and enlarged the picture.

"Myrrh," she said.

"Are you certain?" Pru asked.

"Rosemary, lavender, myrrh," Acantha counted them off on her fingers. "These are some of the herbs of death. It was quite common in medieval time—anything strong-smelling would be tucked round the body or inside the clothes to cover the odor. It might've been several days before burial, you see, and the body would lie in state in the home."

"Shouldn't you see this sample in person and smell it to be sure?"

"No need, I'll show you." She stood and reached over to a wall shelf lined with a jumbled collection of small jars and tins that Pru had taken for a spice rack. And it was, so to speak.

Acantha selected a jar with a faded label that read "Tiptree Orange Marmalade," gave it a shake, and held it up to the light. It appeared empty except for a few brownish bits that rattled round the bottom.

"I thought I had more than that," she said quietly, and then her eyes met Pru's. "I pass the jar round at talks, you see, and I never get back as much as goes out. Smell." She unscrewed the jar, and Pru took a sniff.

"Yes, that's what it is. Myrrh. Did you talk about this with Claudia—how people were buried in medieval times?"

"I ... no ... that is ..." Acantha clasped the jar to her chest. "I suppose it's possible. After all, we talked a great deal. Claudia bounced from one subject to another—this herb, that use—

always with a million questions. I answered and answered, but so little of it sank in. She couldn't settle on anything."

Pru thought that summed up Claudia all round—she couldn't settle on anything. "How about this?" In the photo, the jar of murky liquid looked nondescript. "There were no bits in it, but it smelled of vegetation."

Acantha stared at the picture with a small frown. "I don't know. Why? Where did this come from?"

"Police found the jar on the kitchen table, and they're testing it to see what it is and if she drank any."

Acantha shrank away from Pru's phone. "Well, perhaps it's a vitamin drink or an energy boost or whatever it is that people take nowadays. How would I know? I don't see how you can point fingers and try to lay blame on a person for teaching—at least, trying to teach—about old herbal customs."

"I'm not pointing a finger," Pru said, laying her phone, screen-side down, on the table. "But the police now know that someone killed her, and so there has to be an enquiry. It would be helpful to them if you could go in and take a look at what they found. Perhaps you can explain to them how Claudia came to be interested in medieval herbs." Pru would like to hear that one.

Acantha chewed on her upper lip for a moment, as if trying to keep words from spilling out. When a *ping* drifted in from the sitting room, she leapt up and retrieved her phone, rushing back into the kitchen to say, "Oh my—we need to leave!"

"We?" Pru asked.

"I rang Rollo to say you'd be stopping by, and he thought now would be as good a time as any. We shouldn't be late."

"Late for what?"

"We need to be at the solicitor's office in ten minutes," Acantha said. "Good thing it's only on Southgate. No, leave the dishes, I'll take care of them later."

Acantha threw on her coat and dashed out the door. Pru

followed, and, waiting on the landing as the door was locked, she asked, "Whose solicitor?"

"Claudia's. Her name is Zoe Bagshaw. She needs to meet with the board. To explain about the donation, I suppose."

"But Acantha," Pru said, following on the woman's heels down two flights of stairs, "I'm not on the board."

Acantha stopped abruptly at the front door of the building. "You won't desert us now, will you, Pru?"

CHAPTER 10

She followed Acantha's blue Polo on the short drive to Southgate. Pru thought this road eventually became St. Cross Street, where the Hospital and site of what was to be the medieval herb garden lay. Here, a row of neatly kept Georgian revival houses lined one side of the street. They had no front gardens to speak of—black wrought-iron railings guided visitors to the front door, where many displayed tasteful brass plaques.

Acantha pulled into a car park across the road marked Church Parking Only that was occupied by one other vehicle, a cornflower-blue sports car. Pru followed suit, but when she got out of her car, she pointed to the restriction. Acantha nodded to the honesty box with its own sign: "Thank you for your donation £2 for 1 hour."

After dropping coins into the box, the women crossed the road to a house with a black-and-white-checkerboard stone entry. A white portico held up gleaming columns atop ziggurat plinths. Bagshaw & Churchill, Solicitors, the brass plaque read.

"Is her partner related to Winston Churchill?" Pru asked as they rang the bell.

"God, no," Acantha answered. "It was Martin & Bagshaw

before she and Finley divorced. Churchill is the name of her dog. Zoe lives above the office."

"Finley was married to—"

But Acantha had rung the bell and the door buzzed open, so Pru had no more time to clarify this new piece of information. They walked into a small but elegantly decorated entry—white woodwork against sage-green walls and marbled floors with gold flecks. The reception desk was empty. Acantha didn't stop, but walked behind it to a door that stood ajar. She gave a single knock and continued through to the inner office with Pru following. There, Finley stood talking with a woman whose white-blond hair was cut in a sleek bob and who was dressed in a well-tailored, rose-colored suit with a wide collar and deep V-neck. A lacy black camisole peeked out to almost cover her décolletage.

"Acantha, good," the woman said, approaching and holding her hand out to Pru. "Hello, Pru, I'm Zoe Bagshaw." She had a viselike grip. "Where's Rollo?"

"On his way, I imagine. I'm just nipping into the loo," Acantha said, and disappeared.

"Hello, happy to meet you," Pru said. "Hello, Finley." She turned back to the Zoe. "I hope Finley has explained I'm not actually on the board, and so I understand if you'd rather I leave while you discuss any business matters."

Zoe tilted her head and gave Pru a sad smile. "Do you know practically the last thing Claudia said to me? She said, 'Zoe, you'll never guess—we've found the most wonderful addition to the society. Pru Parke. She's a gardener and knows ever so much about everything, and truly we couldn't find anyone more suitable. Write her name down this minute.' That's what she said."

Acantha had reentered the room to hear this. "Were you the last one to see her alive, Zoe?" she asked.

"No, I wasn't," the solicitor said. "I saw her Thursday morning." Under heavy-lidded eyes, she threw her ex a look.

Finley coughed. "After our outing to the site, I went back to see her Thursday, early in the evening."

"Ooh, Finley," Zoe cooed, "while the husband's away … "

"It was nothing like that," he snapped, his bald head blushing. "You know that isn't how I operate."

"Don't I just?" was Zoe's reply.

The doorbell rang. Zoe glanced at the open laptop on her desk and said, "Here he is." She pressed a key, and after a distant buzz, Rollo strolled in. He frowned at Finley and nodded to Acantha and Pru.

"Right," Zoe said, "we're all here. Take a seat. Drinks, anyone?"

They sat round a small table near an oriel window—the men fortified with whisky, Acantha clutching a glass of sherry, and Pru resolute with fizzy water. She had the idea she'd better stay on top of things.

Zoe cleared her throat and began. "Claudia distinctly asked that her will not be made public until all named parties are present. And so, until we can locate Danny, there will be no announcement. I will, however, say—as you already know—the papers for the donation were not signed. At this point, I'm not sure what, if anything, can be done about that."

Rollo jabbed the table. "Finley said he'd seen her sign."

"I never said those words," Finley countered. "I said she told me I could pick up the signed papers Thursday evening."

"So you should've!" Rollo said in a loud voice.

"And I would've done," Finley said, louder, "but she'd misplaced them. You should never have spent the money before we had it. But of course, you couldn't help getting ahead of yourself, Rollo, could you? We all know what you think you can get out of this—your shiny new career as a landscape gardener."

"And you?" Rollo leaned across the table. "What did you

want, Finley? It wasn't enough to swan around with Ellis's wife—you needed more than that to put him in his place."

"You had no compassion for her life," Finley said.

"It was all part of the Finley plan to rub elbows with the rich and famous," Rollo declared to the table.

"Enough!" Zoe snapped. "Is this what you've sunk to, this bickering?"

"What you're telling us," Acantha said, a calm voice in a rough sea, "is that we won't get the money for the garden."

"Does Danny inherit?" Rollo asked. "Or will Ellis take it all?"

Zoe sighed and sat back. "I thought if I had you all here at the same time and looked each one of you in the eye, I could make myself clear, but perhaps I was wrong. But whether you will listen to the truth or not, it stands—you'll have to wait for Danny."

"She could've left us a legacy," Finley said. "That could be in her will."

"Yes, a gift"—Rollo nodded—"although perhaps not for the full amount. Is that it, Zoe?"

"Nothing"—the solicitor drew out the word—"about Claudia's estate will be leaked until Danny is present."

"Where is he?" Pru asked.

The board members turned their attention to her in surprise before shifting their focus to Zoe.

"Yes," Finley said, "where is he?"

The solicitor crossed her legs, clasped her hands in her lap, and offered a smile. "He's on his way."

On his way where, Pru wondered—to the office or to Winchester in general? He lived in Inverness. Scotland wasn't the ends of the earth.

"We should talk to Danny," Rollo suggested.

"You'll do nothing of the kind," Zoe snapped. "Let him alone. What does he care for gardens or dormice or ... He's a young man who has lost his mother. Leave him to grieve."

Acantha's phone rang, and she stepped out into the reception area to answer while Zoe told the others, "I'll let you know when I hear. It can't be too long, I'm sure. Not that he won't have other things on his mind, remember. Police haven't released Claudia's body yet, but when they do, there'll be arrangements to be made."

"Police asked you where you were Thursday evening, didn't they?" Rollo addressed his question to Finley, but gave Pru a significant look. "What did you tell them?"

"I told them I saw Claudia—do you think I tried to hide it? And when she told me she'd misplaced the papers, I left. First, I stopped by my office to print them out again and then home. I was propped up in bed with a book by ten."

"With a witness, I suppose?" Rollo asked with a smirk.

"And what about you. Do you think Ken is your alibi?" Finley retorted, turning to Pru and rolling his eyes. "It's the easiest thing in the world for your spouse to claim you were at home, but it's the first thing a prosecutor will go after."

"Just because he's my husband doesn't make it a lie."

"Give it a rest, you two," Zoe said. "Pru isn't Queen's Counsel —you don't have to prove anything to her."

"Yes, but even so—"

Rollo got no further before Acantha stuck her head into the office and reached an arm out for her coat.

"Sorry. I need to pick up my granddaughter from her minder. Let me know about ... you know."

After she left, the men seemed to think it was time to call it quits, too. While he pulled on his coat, Finley said, "Pru, this sad turn of events in no way alters our offer to you—we would welcome you as a board member. Perhaps we could meet and go over a few details?"

"Yes, that would be fine."

"Pru," Rollo interrupted, "I'd love to get feedback from you on my garden designs. I feel as if we're on the same wavelength, as it were, when it comes to imbuing the landscape with the appropriate sense of age and authenticity while keeping an eye on Health and Safety regulations. Say, you and your husband could come to dinner one evening. How about that?"

"Lovely," Pru began, wondering if Rollo remembered that her husband and the DI on the case were one and the same. Or perhaps, that was the point. "I'll need to—"

"And how would that look, Rollo," Finley scoffed, "inviting the police to dinner?"

The two men continued squabbling as they left. Pru, not meaning to be the last one out, reached for her coat and bag.

"Wait." It was Zoe's tone more than the word that stopped Pru. "Please. Could you stay just a minute more? I wanted to say—"

What she wanted to say was put on hold as her phone rang. Zoe grabbed it, held up a finger to Pru, and answered. As she moved to her desk, she chatted with someone about magistrate's court, and leaned over to type into her laptop. Pru moved nearer the window, and so went unnoticed when a man stormed in the door.

He was thin with spiky gray hair and a face worn from what must've been a hard life. He wore no sweater or coat, only black sneakers, black denims, and a skintight black T-shirt that had a colorful logo of some kind on it.

"Zoe, babe," he launched in with a raspy voice, "have you heard from him yet? Because he isn't answering any of my texts—"

"*Arlo!*" Zoe's voice sliced through the air. She gave a sharp nod in Pru's direction, and the man stopped short. Zoe ended her phone call and straightened. "This is Pru Parke, the newest board member for the medieval society. Pru, Arlo Hartfield."

"Hello, pleased to meet you," Pru said. "Well, I'd best be off."

"Hang on," Arlo said. "You're the gardener, aren't you?"

"I'm *a* gardener."

"I hope you're not one of these that only goes in for neatly trimmed hedges and bedding out," he said. "There's more to the landscape than begonias. You must understand the threat our countryside is under—we're losing it at an alarming rate. You must realize how important it is to restore native habitat. You wouldn't condone the sort of behavior that would wipe out an entire species?"

"Yes. I mean, no, certainly not."

"Think of the bumblebees," he continued, his voice growing deeper with fervor. "Think of the role a plant like field cow-wheat can do to keep down grasses while wildflowers are establishing."

Pru glanced at Arlo's T-shirt again and realized the artwork was a spiky pink-and-yellow flower. Ah, the field cow-wheat people—the group before the dormice.

"Not now, Arlo," Zoe said. "Pru, you probably recognize Arlo from his band The Guard—he was lead singer. They were an enormous presence in the British music scene a few years ago, always being compared with The Police."

"Oh, The Guard," Pru said. No, that name didn't ring a bell. She remembered The Police, of course, but that had been more than a few years ago. "You're absolutely right, Arlo, it's vital that native habitat be retained and restored wherever possible. Wasn't Claudia interested in something like this? Did you know her?"

Arlo cut his eyes at Zoe, who stepped in.

"Claudia's interests were far reaching, no one can deny that. Well"—Zoe grabbed Pru's coat and bag and handed them over—"I know you need to be on your way, so we won't keep you."

The front doorbell rang, and Zoe spun her laptop round to look at the screen. Pru could see it from where she stood—the security camera showed a close-up of a police badge and warrant card. A detective inspector, as a matter of fact. Pru couldn't read the name on his card, but she didn't need to. She could see his wedding ring.

"Well," Zoe said under her breath, "I'd better get this over with," and buzzed him in.

Arlo faded into the woodwork, Zoe opened her office door, and Christopher walked in from the reception area. He didn't blink an eye when he saw Pru.

"Ms. Bagshaw," he said, "I'm Detective Inspector Pearse. I rang earlier to tell you I'd be stopping by. I hope I'm not interrupting anything."

"Yes, well," Pru said, "I should be on my way." She nodded at Christopher. "Inspector."

"Arlo, you'll need to be going as well," Zoe said.

"No, I want to—"

Pru didn't wait for the end of this conversation, but slipped out and crossed the road to her car—and found Christopher's parked next to it. No wonder he hadn't looked surprised. She got in and started up the engine, waiting for the heater to put out a bit of warmth and watching the door of Bagshaw & Churchill. Not a minute later, Arlo burst out. He stuck his hands in his armpits and stalked off down the pavement.

CHAPTER 11

"Did John ask you to go the solicitor's?" Christopher asked.

He and Pru sat at their kitchen table with slices of Evelyn's apple cake and mugs of tea.

"No," Pru said, "I was at Acantha's showing her photos of what was found in Claudia's pockets. While I was there, she got a call, and off we went for a board meeting at Bagshaw & Churchill. Medieval garden society, you see, so still part of my remit. Are you home early so that you can question me?"

"According to John, you're part of the team now, so we can consider this a debriefing."

"'Part of the team,'" Pru said. "Do I get my own warrant card?"

"Don't push it."

"Just think," she said, casting a sly glance at him out the corner of her eye. "Instead of an undergardener, I'm an undercover gardener."

He tried for a stern look, but she could see it was half-hearted.

"All right," she said," I'm not even undercover. Everyone knows about my connection to the police. And so, I can't imagine they would let anything untoward slip. What did you find out from Terry Reed about dormice?"

"Claudia showed up at one of their meetings about eighteen months ago and immediately became involved, talking about a donation. They had nothing in writing, and nothing in particular drove her off. After about a year, she seemed to lose interest."

"You've heard of the field cow-wheat people?"

"The group Claudia promised money to before the dormice? Reed mentioned them."

"Well, do you know who that fellow was at Zoe's office—the one in the black T-shirt?"

"That was Claudia's first husband."

Pru sputtered into her tea. "What? No one mentioned that to me. Zoe introduced him as the lead singer in a band called The Guard. Do you know them?"

"The Guard," Christopher repeated, as if searching his memory banks.

There's a ringing endorsement, Pru thought. She would ask Polly and Bernadette about the band.

"In addition to being Claudia's ex," Pru said, "Arlo Hartfield is an advocate for the field cow-wheat. I need to look into why it's such an important plant. I'll do that first thing tomorrow." Wait, was there something else she was supposed to do in the morning?

They cleared the tea things, and Christopher went off to the library to light the fire. Pru looked into the fridge to find that Evelyn had left them a lentil-and-sausage stew for dinner. Bless her.

Pru hauled the pot of stew out of the fridge and onto the counter, removed the lid, and gave it a stir before putting it on the stove for a slow reheat. Her phone rang, and she leaned over to check the screen—it was Rollo.

"I had so hoped to ask both you and your husband to

dinner," he began as soon as Pru answered. "Ken is a fabulous cook—wait till you taste his duck à l'orange—but we'll need to save that for another time. Perhaps you and I, Pru, could have coffee tomorrow? I'd love for you to stop in. I feel as if we haven't had the chance to talk shop, as it were—the garden."

Pru accepted, and Rollo gave her his address. Christopher came back into the kitchen and she told him about the invitation to coffee.

"Rollo's renderings are quite good," she said. "But, I wonder if the garden can be built without Claudia's money. Did Zoe tell you she won't read the will until Danny arrives?"

"The son. He sent word he was on his way, but there's been no sign of him yet," Christopher said.

Pru tapped her phone against her chin and thought about her visit to Bagshaw & Churchill.

"Here's a funny thing," she said. "No, here are two funny things. When Acantha and I arrived at Zoe's office, we pressed a button and were let in. The same with you. Zoe's got the camera feed on her computer, so she can see who is waiting and unlock the door. But when Arlo arrived, he just ... appeared."

"So he must know the key code," Christopher said. "That speaks to a certain intimacy."

"He called her 'babe'—although he seems the type to call any woman that."

"What's your other funny thing?" Christopher asked.

"Arlo—Claudia's ex-husband—was a bit frantic. The first thing he said was 'have you heard from him' and something about 'he isn't answering my texts.' Who was this 'he'? Is it someone to do with the enquiry? If so, who hasn't been heard from?" Christopher watched her silently. She added, "And, why didn't Ellis know how old his own son is?"

"Why, Ms. Parke," Christopher said, "are you suggesting it's possible that Danny is not Ellis Temple's biological son, but Arlo Hartfield's?"

"I might be," Pru said. "What do you say?"

"I say, well done."

"Thank you, Inspector."

Was the father of Claudia's son, Danny Ellis Temple or '80s rocker Arlo Hartfield? Pru wasn't sure that Christopher hadn't already wondered the same thing, even though he did give her credit for the idea and said he would check on it. Would it matter to the enquiry? It might, if his father was interested in Danny's inheritance—would he receive Claudia's one million pounds she had promised to the herb garden? And the dormice. And the field cow-wheat—represented by Hartfield, and wasn't that convenient? Or would it go to Ellis Temple? Did he need it? He appeared well heeled, to say the least. Look at that shiny red Jag he drove.

These thoughts occupied Pru's mind on the drive to Rollo's the next morning. She pulled up to a brick-and-stucco semidetached Victorian on St. Cross Road, not far from the site of the medieval garden. Potential garden. She spent another few seconds in the warmth of her car before getting out and dashing up to the door past a front garden the size of a postage stamp that was decorated by cones of clipped box in a checkerboard pattern.

Rollo greeted her and led her through a modern interior design that was nonetheless warmer than the Temple house. In the back, sun filled a large space that combined kitchen and breakfast room. On the table, he'd laid out his drawings. The three-dimensional model of the garden sat on the deep sill of the oriel window.

"Cappuccino?" he asked.

"Yes, lovely."

"Ken is at work, but he's left us with these." Rollo nodded to a plate of shortbread with a dusting of chocolate and almonds.

While the espresso machine hissed, Pru peered into the model garden. The walls had been painted as if they were brick, and paper cutouts colored brown and green represented trees and shrubs while spray-painted cotton balls stood in for the herbaceous plants.

Rollo noticed her attention and said, "I've portrayed the landscape as it will be—perhaps a bit unkempt for some tastes, and certainly not the bold swathes of color that are popular today." Rollo handed Pru her coffee. "Say 'historic garden' to some people, and they envision a Gertrude Jekyll border. We need to educate them otherwise. This is medieval history, not a pastel painting. Not that there's anything wrong with that."

"It's fascinating how the attention to function and beauty changed from society to society down the ages," Pru said.

For a moment, Rollo stood still, cappuccino in hand and with an expression akin to a five-year-old on Christmas morning.

"It is, as you say, truly fascinating." He set the coffee down and clasped his hands. "In fact, I've written what I see as a series of articles about just that. Well, I shouldn't say written … they do need a bit of work. I've done it for my own satisfaction, of course, because who would … and my plant knowledge isn't quite up to snuff, so I would really need someone with a sharp eye to … " He came to attention. "Now, more to the matter at hand."

Pru settled at the counter and Rollo picked up a plan-view drawing. "You couldn't ask for a better backdrop than the Hospital of St. Cross and, in turn, the walled garden will lend an atmosphere of time and place. You might have noticed that in the elevations, I've included the figure of a monk. Doesn't he look right at home?"

By the time she'd finished her cappuccino, Rollo was

explaining the type of mortar used in medieval times. Pru resisted scraping the foam from the inside of the cup and perked up when it sounded as if he might be reaching his concluding statements.

"Signage notwithstanding, the visitor will be able to—" His mobile rang and, after a glance at the screen, he said, "Sorry, I should take this. I told them to ring only in an emergency."

He walked off into the sitting room, to answer and Pru half listened to the one-sided conversation about two workers out sick and the refurb of a Victorian Grade II-listed maisonette in danger of not meeting its date of completion. This was followed by something about testing for lead in the water, and the mains not shut off by the council and so there had been a flood at the site. Pru studied the drawings and the model, ate another shortbread, and fifteen minutes later, Rollo returned, his face red as he slapped his mobile repeatedly into the palm of his hand.

"There, that should hold them," he said, exhaling in a huff and then offering a chagrined smile. "I never saw myself running a plumbing company, I can tell you that, but neither of my brothers was interested in carrying on the family business. It had been our dad's life, and so I stepped in. I don't mind, really. I suppose I saw it as a way to make up for other things."

"Sounds as if you do more than the usual plumbing repairs," Pru said.

"Yes, we've recently expanded to restoration work with listed properties, but that has required more outlay before the income, which means that in no way could I … Finley and the others seem to look at Westcott Plumbing as a fallback, you see. They think the company could cover anything Claudia's money couldn't. That isn't the way a business works—there are obligations. No, we were relying on Claudia's donation. No one thought she would change her mind."

Change her mind—again.

"How did Claudia become interested in medieval herbs?" Pru asked.

"How does anyone ...?" Rollo frowned. "Yes, I see what you mean. About two years ago, Acantha and I met at a lecture at the Hospital of St. Cross and found we had this mutual interest. It didn't take long before we'd formed the society and attracted a fair number of people to our cause. At the time, Ken said before we went further, we should contact a solicitor and make certain we were legal. He'd met Finley through work, and suggested we ask him to help us with all the paperwork to become a registered charity. One day, I suppose about a year ago, Finley was at Zoe's office—oh, did you know they had been married?"

"Yes, Acantha told me."

"Right, so, Finley was at Zoe's office, and Claudia arrived for a meeting with her solicitor, and heard from Finley what we were about. She thought it sounded fascinating, and ... well, Bob's your uncle."

And goodbye, dormice. "Do you know Claudia's husband?"

"Ellis? No. We barely knew Claudia, she'd been with us such a short time."

"Her death must be difficult for him. And for her son."

Rollo had the good grace to look chastised. "Yes—puts the whole thing in perspective, doesn't it? The loss of a partner and a parent by such means. Is there any news on that front?"

She fell back on the usual. "I believe police are following several lines of enquiry."

"To think it happened while the rest of us were going about our normal lives—spending a quiet evening at home. At least, I know I was. Another cappuccino?" Rollo asked, taking her empty cup and starting the process before she could answer.

"Did you know about the dormice people?" Pru asked.

Rollo shrugged one shoulder. "Barely. Zoe explained it to us —it just wasn't a proper fit for Claudia."

"Have you met Terry Reed?"

"Is that his name?" Rollo frowned. "Yes, he's the one. He emailed about what he thought they were owed."

"And had you heard of the field cow-wheat?"

Rollo kept his eyes on the coffee dripping into the cup. "We all thought the world of Claudia, and she had every right to do with her money whatever she bloody well liked. But the truth of the matter is, she promised it to the garden, and Finley, for one, was totally taken in. He told us she had signed. But, of course, Finley had his own reasons for believing that."

Pru thought Rollo wanted to leave her with Finley's name uppermost in mind when it came to Claudia, because he then returned the conversation to the subject of historic landscapes and their worth in today's world. When he offered a third cappuccino, Pru declined, thanked him, and left.

At the curb another car pulled up behind hers—a tiny BMW that made no noise. Must be electric. A man popped out, his ruddy cheeks picking up the same color in the tartan of his overcoat.

"Are you Pru?" he asked. "I'm Ken."

"Yes. Hello, Ken," she said. "Sorry to have missed you this morning."

"I'd hoped to get away, but was cornered by my manager for a team meeting," he said.

"You left us well supplied—the shortbread was delicious."

"Look," he said, glancing up at his front door, "the circumstances are dreadful, but I'm awfully glad you've appeared on the scene. Rollo feels as if he's got someone else in his corner now—someone who knows about gardening and can appreciate his design ideas."

"He's quite good," Pru said. "I don't know how he finds the time to work on designs and run a business, too."

Ken gave a single nod. "He works night and day—literally. He'll be up at one, two o'clock in the morning and go off to the company offices to use the drafting board and work on garden designs, just to keep his hand in. That's where he was the night Claudia died—I'm sure he told you that."

No, Pru thought as she drove back to Greenoak, Rollo hadn't told her he'd been at his plumbing company's offices at the time Claudia died. In fact, he'd made it quite clear that he'd been at home, safely tucked up in bed. Pru considered this contradiction. Ken had offered the information freely. If Rollo needed an alibi, wouldn't he and his husband have given the same excuse? Her mind on the enquiry, Pru drove slowly along the Straight Mile, especially at the bends where the ice on the roadway wouldn't melt until the temperatures made it above freezing and stayed there.

Alibis. What had Rollo told Christopher? Had the others been accounted for during the window the medical examiner gave for Claudia's death? It had been the middle of the night—how do you track movements for a time when most people were in bed? She needed to get her thoughts organized when it came to Claudia Temple's murder, the Winchester Medieval Garden Society, its board members—plus dormice, an exhusband, a missing son, and one million pounds. People, motives, and alibis. A flow chart or a timetable would give her a clearer view.

She needed a murder room. That's what the police set up for an investigation. Christopher would have just such a thing at the station, but she wouldn't be allowed access to that any old time she pleased—imagine the look on John Upstone's face if she tried. With her own murder room, she could keep things straight.

At Greenoak, Pru went straight to the potting shed. Did she have the space here? The large wooden seed cabinet took up a great deal of room. Another wall was filled with spades, hoes, and rakes hanging from pegs and the third had shelves lined with wellies, bins of fertilizer, tins of linseed oil, and the like. The far end of the shed was mostly glass—that's where she and Simon started their seeds. No room in the potting shed. Pru opened the door to leave, but then closed it again. On the back hung last year's calendar, the December photo a frost-covered parterre garden in York.

Her phone rang and she answered while she took the calendar off the door.

"Pru Parke?" a raspy voice said. "Arlo Hartfield. We met at Zoe's office yesterday, do you remember?"

"Yes, hello Mr. Hartfield."

"None of that—it's just Arlo. Look, I was in a right state at Zoe's, and I don't think I left you with a good impression. I'd like to talk with you, if that's all right. Sort of, explain things."

"Yes, of course," Pru replied. Because, she told herself, it was probably about the field cow-wheat, and that was certainly her remit on the enquiry.

"Brill. Say, tomorrow morning? Do you know the Royal Oak in Winchester?"

"The pub near the cathedral?"

"If you can make it before opening, that'll be grand."

In the mudroom, Pru shed her coat as she asked Evelyn, "Do you remember a band called The Guard?"

The cook paused stirring a pot. "Oh, yes, I saw them on *Top of the Pops*. Wasn't that a long time ago?"

Evelyn stayed busy at the hob, while Pru gathered blank paper, various colored pens, and three pads of sticky notes in neon shades, and set to work at the kitchen table—by far, the coziest place in the house. Meanwhile, Evelyn peeled carrots for roasting, set potatoes on to boil, rolled out pastry, and rummaged in the pantry. This went on for the better part of an hour, both working comfortably and quietly, until Evelyn lifted the lid on a simmering pot and said, "Potato leek soup—are you ready for a bowl?" She turned and took in the expanse of the old farm table, now covered with sheets of paper and sticky notes like a patchwork quilt.

"What's this in aid of?" the cook asked.

"I'm making my own murder room," Pru explained, shifting a sticky note from one sheet of paper to another.

"On my table?"

"No, not on your table. It's meant for the back of the door in the potting shed. I'll take everything out there when I've finished my initial ... organizing." She shuffled the papers into an untidy heap. "Later."

"Good thing, too, because after that bowl of soup, we'll need the table as we spend the afternoon sorting out your dinner for tomorrow."

"All afternoon?" Pru asked, incredulous. "There won't be a sauce, will there?" She meant it as a question, but it came out as a plea.

"This." Evelyn pulled a folded paper from the pocket of her apron and handed it over. "Chicken marengo. Made for Napoleon, no less."

Pru's eyes grew large as she saw the number of ingredients—and the number of steps. "It looks ... involved."

"That's why we're starting on it this afternoon. It's a dish that's best prepared the day before. Tomorrow, all you'll need to do is pop it back in the oven."

Evelyn, always careful to make any recipe sound easy so as not to frighten Pru, had missed the mark once or twice. That delicate, eggy, roasted vegetable dish far too close to being a soufflé, for example, which she had overcooked until it dried to the consistency of shoe leather.

"What about the pudding?" Pru asked. "I'm not ready for meringues again."

That elicited a snigger from Evelyn, and Pru couldn't help joining in. Her first attempt at baking meringues had resulted in a stiff but gooey mess that had to be gnawed off the spoon and then seemed to form a permanent bond on the teeth.

"Apple crumble," Evelyn said. "Although, there could be a toffee sauce to go along with it."

Pru sighed. "Better get stuck in."

At the end of the afternoon, Peachey arrived to a clean kitchen. No one could ever guess that an entire dinner for seven lay at the ready. He and Evelyn loaded the pensioners' meals into his van and were off. Pru spread out her murder-room paraphernalia on the table again, but then retired to the library, lit the fire, and fell asleep on the sofa.

She awoke to a kiss from Christopher. He sat down on the edge of the sofa and watched as she gathered her thoughts.

"It isn't late, is it?" she asked, blinking.

"No, just half six."

"Evelyn and I cooked this afternoon for tomorrow evening. A do-ahead recipe someone invented for Napoleon."

"I suppose he was as short for time as anyone," Christopher said, and Pru giggled.

They went to the kitchen, to be met with a tableful of murder-room papers and sticky notes.

"I thought I'd organize my thoughts," she explained, examining her layout. "But I'm short a fair amount of detail. Anything on fingerprints?"

Christopher looked over her work. "Nothing out of the ordinary—Claudia. Ellis. The woman who cleans weekly. Acantha Morris."

"Of course—because she was Claudia's teacher. She was there every Friday morning." Pru took a pen and scribbled something on a sticky note.

Christopher tapped on another. "What's this? 'Rollo wasn't home.' "

"Did he tell you he was?" Pru asked. "Because that's what he told me this morning, but then, when I was at my car, Ken, his husband, arrived home, and we talked for a minute. Ken said that Rollo spends time in the middle of the night at the plumbing company's offices so he can use the drafting board for garden designs, and that's where he was the night Claudia died."

"Well done, Ms. Parke," Christopher said. "Rollo Westcott did indeed tell me he was at home."

"Although," Pru said, chuffed at acquiring this investigative brownie point but thinking that she needed to admit there was a problem, "if Rollo needed an alibi, wouldn't he and Ken have agreed to say the same thing?"

"It's often one little error that leads to an unraveling," Christopher said.

"And so, Rollo really is a suspect? Yes, I know," she said before he could remind her, "everyone's a suspect. So, what about the others—do they each have their own alibi for the middle of that night?"

"Safely tucked up in bed," Christopher said. "Apart from Terry Reed, who was in Devon carrying out nocturnal dormouse observations."

"Don't dormice hibernate?"

"They do. He's studying predatory damage to hibernating nests."

"Sounds a bit dodgy, don't you think?" Pru asked.

"He has seven other witnesses."

"Seven? You wouldn't think it would take that many people to watch dormice hibernating. So, are these the only suspects?" Pru waved her arm over the table. "The herb garden people. Terry Reed—except, he seems to be alibied out. Arlo Hartfield for field cow-wheat as well as being her ex-husband. And Ellis, her current husband." She pulled over a clean sheet of paper.

"Wait now, Zoe Bagshaw. She's the solicitor, but you never know, do you? Especially if she's involved with Arlo."

"What did you call the contents of the victim's pockets?" Christopher asked.

"Herbs of death." Pru set down the felt marker. "That's what Acantha said they were. Perhaps they studied the subject. For all the tutoring Acantha did, it didn't seem much of it stuck with Claudia, yet, whoever killed her tried to make it look as if she knew enough to have prepared herself."

"And the contents of the jar?"

"Acantha wasn't sure. When will you have the analysis?"

"With a bit of luck, tomorrow," Christopher said. "If not, it might be Monday."

Pru riffled through her papers. "I've managed to find photos online of everyone, to accompany each person's possible motives. Although, all the motives boil down to one thing—money."

Christopher pointed at one of the photos. "That's a bit dated."

"Yes," Pru replied. "Arlo Hartfield from his glory days with The Guard." Arlo's disheveled blond hair had had a bit of curl to it then—now it was short and gray, although still unkempt. But nothing had changed his aquiline nose.

"I also printed out a color photo of the field cow-wheat." She handed Christopher a close-up of a cluster of flowers. "They're actually quite small, but it's a pretty little thing. And I have a dormouse here somewhere."

"What else came of your coffee with Rollo Westcott?" Christopher asked.

"Rollo. He would rather design gardens than run a plumbing business. And he's worried about money." She looked up from her papers. "He was quite sure that Finley said she'd signed the money over. Also, Rollo said that the others think he could pay for the whole garden, but he can't. He and Finley don't always agree." Pru rested her chin in her hand. "I should talk with Finley. How is Ellis Temple holding up?"

Christopher laid a hand over hers. "You do remember that you are to be a resource concerning the herb garden, don't you—and not an investigating officer on the entire enquiry?"

She wondered when that would come—the "you are not the police" warning.

"It does have to do with the garden, because Claudia's husband sounded as if he thought her death was all their fault. Wait now, there's this." She wrote on another sticky note. "Do you know how Claudia came to be interested in medieval gardens?"

"Do you?"

Oh good, Pru thought, she'd come up with something new. She explained how Claudia had by chance met Finley at Zoe's office.

Christopher gave her a nod. "It's like following a trail of breadcrumbs, isn't it?" he asked.

"It is." But there was a gap in the trail. "Arlo must've tried to talk her into supporting the field cow-wheat efforts, but who got her interested in the little hazel dormouse?"

"Terry Reed said he didn't know," Christopher said. "He told me she showed up at one of their meetings. I'll have another talk with him, but tomorrow, I'm driving up to Oxford to speak with the members of Ellis Temple's business consortium."

"You won't forget our dinner party."

"It's an easy drive up and down the A34 to Oxford and back. I won't forget—although John tried to."

"He what?"

"I mentioned it today, and he did his best to act surprised," Christopher said.

Pru picked up her phone. "I'll ring Sabine this minute and say how much we're looking forward to it. John Upstone," she muttered, "crafty old—Hello, Sabine."

~

The next morning, Pru rose early and went out to the garden to cut a few sprays of foliage for the church flowers. It was slim pickings other than conifers, because most evergreens had protected themselves from the cold by curling their leaves under—it was a good strategy to hunker down and wait out the weather. To the foliage, she added a flat of crocus and a few pots of early little narcissus that she and Simon had planted weeks earlier.

Pru motored over to St. Mary's and found Polly and Bernadette in the kitchen of the church hall sitting with coffee in front of a two-bar heater.

"I can't stay," Pru said when asked. "I'm off to Winchester to see Arlo Hartfield. He's—"

"Arlo Hartfield?" Bernadette echoed.

"He's the field cow-wheat guy. Claudia was going to give them her money, but then she switched to the hazel dormouse before the medieval garden."

"Arlo Hartfield?" Polly repeated.

"He was married to Claudia," Pru added.

"He never!" Polly's eyes grew wide behind her red-framed glasses. "Not the actual Arlo Hartfield? The Guard?"

"Yes, The Guard," Pru said. "That's him. Did you know the band?"

Polly and the vicar exchanged eye rolls.

"Were they not popular in the States?" Bernadette asked.

"Not that I recall," Pru said. "He's asked me to meet him at the Royal Oak in Winchester."

"All right for some," Polly said. "Do you remember, Bernadette, that he bought a pub in Winchester? He made a big announcement that he was finished with the band and the industry."

"Retired from music," Bernadette said. "That must've been at least ten years ago. Or fifteen."

" 'I said goodbye to love and hello to eternity alone,' " Polly said and sighed.

Bernadette began humming a tune, and Polly joined in. Pru left them to it.

The door of the Royal Oak creaked when Pru pushed it open. The entry was dark—a signal that the pub wasn't open for business yet—but she walked through into a long room with a bar in the middle. The Royal Oak, with its low ceiling and even lower beams, had possibly been a coaching inn a few centuries ago. At the bar, bottles rattled as workers restocked for the new day. Beyond that at the far end of the room was a small stage, and on the stage was Arlo Hartfield, in his tight black jeans and his tight black T-shirt that was emblazoned with an image of field cow-wheat. He had a guitar in hand and an amp at his feet. He turned a knob on the speaker, plucked at a string, and a *twang* blasted the air.

"Sorry," he called out, and then saw Pru. "Oh, yeah, here you are."

"Good morning," Pru said as she made her way to the back.

Arlo unplugged his guitar and climbed down from the stage. "'Morning, Pru. Frankie!"

"Yo!" the call came from behind the bar.

"Coffees over here." Arlo turned to Pru. "Unless you'd like something stronger?"

"Coffee," Pru said.

Arlo gestured to a table, and they sat. He kept hold of the guitar.

"Do you perform here at your pub?"

"What—this?" Arlo asked with nonchalance. "No, this is

something entirely new." He glanced round them at the empty seats and leaned forward. "You're practically the first to know. I'm getting the band back together."

"Are you?" Pru asked.

Arlo looked down at the table. "Well, not all of them, of course. Not Gerry. Poor lad—gone too soon." The coffee arrived, and Pru wrapped her hands round a mug, as Arlo continued. "I haven't been able to locate a replacement drummer—not a real quality one. Not yet. You don't play, do you? Meanwhile, I spend a bit of time up here before the punters arrive to work on a new song or two. There are still things to iron out for the concert—venue and such. Costs are through the roof these days."

A reunion of The Guard would be big news for some, but it wasn't the reason Pru was there. At least, she hoped it wasn't.

"Arlo, you wanted to talk with me."

"Oh, yeah, so see, I don't know what sort of tosh those others have been filling your head with, but I thought I'd better set you straight." He clicked his tongue. "Greed is a terrible thing." He plucked a guitar string. Unplugged, the sound was dull and muted. "Greed is a gremlin in your gut." He strummed a couple of chords and nodded. "Yeah, writing that one really took it out of me."

Really—the man quotes his own song lyrics?

"So, you and Claudia were married," Pru said, and Arlo cut his eyes at her. Did he not know that she would know? "Did you see much of her?"

"What?" Arlo asked sharply. "Oh, yeah, no, not really. You know how it is. Hadn't laid eyes on her in yonks. Sad." He beat lightly on the guitar strings as if keeping time. "Awhile back, we had a really good conversation, and she decided to donate the money her dad left her to a good cause. You know, something worthwhile."

"The field cow-wheat?" Pru asked. *Or the reunion of The Guard?*

"Doesn't matter now, does it?" Arlo asked. "What I want you to know, Pru, is that after Claudia's ... you know, death ... those others are thinking of only one thing, and that's her money. I'm sure even Temple wouldn't say no to an extra million. They all think they have a claim to it, but where should the money rightly go? Well, at least we can trust Zoe to keep hold of the reins, can't we?"

Why was Arlo Hartfield talking with Pru about Claudia's money? Why had he wanted to talk with her at all? She hadn't known Claudia and she knew nothing about her finances or her personal life. Had Rollo or one of the others told him she had the ear of the police?

At the opposite end of the building, the pub door creaked open, and Arlo glanced at his watch.

"Opening time. I'm afraid you'll have to excuse me. But you think about what I said, Pru. Another coffee?"

Pru declined and stood to pull on her coat. She had nothing to show for her time, except to note that Arlo had done his best to point the finger of blame at others—not necessarily for Claudia's death, but for their greed.

He walked her halfway across the pub, ducking at each low beam, chatting about The Guard's reunion, and inviting her backstage after the concert—whenever and wherever it might be. Perhaps Pru would take him up on it and ask groupies Polly and Bernadette along.

"You'll let me know, won't you?" Arlo asked Pru. She didn't answer, because she wasn't sure what he was talking about. "You'll let me know if you have any questions for me, because"—he laid a hand on his chest—"my heart's an open book, written in the permanent ink of love."

Arlo veered off to the bar, and Pru continued to the unlit entry and held up when her phone rang.

"Pru, John Upstone here."

This had better be an official phone call, Pru thought, because there was no way she would let him wiggle off the hook for dinner.

"Yes, Detective Superintendent Upstone. What can I do for you?"

"These herbalists—have you spoken with every one of them?"

Finley, she thought. "I've talked with almost every board member of the medieval garden society. Still on it."

"Isn't someone coming in to take a look at that liquid?"

"Do you have the results from the analysis?" Pru countered.

"No," John said, making it sound like a grumble. "We're still waiting for that."

"Ms. Morris will take a look as soon as she can. I'll go with her."

"Have you asked them their whereabouts the night of the murder? I'd like to compare what they've told you with what they've given us. When can you come into the station?"

"Well I can't come into the station this afternoon, because I'll be putting the finishing touches on this evening's dinner with you and Sabine"—a sliver of a pause—"so, how about tomorrow, even though it is Saturday?"

"Yes, fine." He ended the call.

Did a single reminder of his personal life send John Upstone running scared? Pru followed their short conversation with a call to Christopher.

"How is your day out to Oxford?"

"Without anything of interest thus far. I'll stop at the hotel last and then start back. How was your talk with Arlo Hartfield?" he asked.

"Vague—Arlo's fairly vague about everything. What of Danny? Have you heard anything? Here he's just lost his mother. He's probably devastated. Maybe he doesn't want to walk into the middle of the enquiry. Maybe he just needs to sit down and talk with one person."

Pru pushed open the door of the pub and was hit with a blast of frigid air and bright sun. She turned her face away, and as she did so, she caught sight of someone standing behind her in the dim entry. The person backed away and disappeared into the darkness.

In her Mini, Pru started the engine, put the call on speaker, and rubbed her hands together, waiting for the heater to get going.

"Arlo talked about Claudia's money," she continued with Christopher. "But he said he hadn't seen her in a while. Not much of a report, is it?"

"It's slow going most of the time," Christopher said. "Are you off home now?"

"I have one more stop. To see Tabby."

"The neighbor?"

"The very one. I know someone from the police has already talked with her, but my visit is about her garden. I'm giving her some flower seeds and it's the middle of the day, so Ellis Temple won't be home, will he? He'll be off selling a Bentley or a Rolls."

Pru looked in the rearview mirror. A tall, thin man came out of the pub—she thought he was the one who had been standing in the entry as she left. He looked round the small car park and then went to a silver Honda, started the engine, and sat.

"Have you spoken with John today?" Christopher asked.

"He just rang to check up on me. He won't bring up the enquiry at dinner this evening, will he?"

The red Jag was parked in front of the white monolith of a house. Perhaps Ellis Temple was taking time off from the business after his wife's death. Pru preferred not to run into him, because she didn't know what she could say. Would he remember shouting at her? She drove past the Temple house, and continued past Tabby's, too, before she pulled her Mini over.

The street was quiet and Tabby was not in her garden, but she came to the door only a moment after Pru rang the bell. The knit hat was gone, and she'd taken off a layer or two, but her cheeks were still apple red.

"Hello, Tabby, do you remember me? I'm Pru Parke. We met a few days ago when you were out in the front garden."

"On Monday," Tabby said, "when the police were here about poor Mrs. Temple. Of course, I remember. Come in now out of the cold."

"I've brought you some cosmos seed we collected last summer," Pru said, stepping inside and producing a brown envelope from her coat pocket as if it were her admission ticket.

"Why, isn't that lovely," Tabby said, holding the packet at arm's length to read the handwritten label. "Here now, take off your wraps, and we'll have a cuppa."

Pru shrugged out of her coat, untied her scarf, and hung them on a peg, then followed Tabby, who padded back to the kitchen in her carpet slippers.

"Summer before last, we planted five different varieties," Pru said, "and this past summer, they had crossed on their own. We had quite a display—shades of pink, some white, others bicolored, a few with frilly petals. So, I can't tell you quite what you'll get."

"It'll be a happy surprise, I'm sure. Just thinking about their lovely summer faces warms me," Tabby said, stuffing the envelope in the pocket of her cardigan and filling the kettle. "Sit now, and tell me about your garden."

Over tea and ginger nuts, they exchanged tales of working the soil. Eventually, at a pause, Pru asked, "I suppose the police have gone from next door. Is Mr. Temple all right, do you think?"

"Wouldn't know, would I? I took over a jar of soup, but had to leave it on the front step as no one answered—even though that red car of his was sitting out front like it is today. Chicken and veg. Probably froze before he took it in."

"Perhaps he's working from home," Pru said. She gazed out the kitchen window to the Temple house. "It's an unusual style, isn't it? I mean, for this street."

"Calls attention to itself, it does," Tabby said, "here on a street of Victorian semi-detacheds. The one that was there was hit by a bomb during the war. Before my time, but this house I'm in was my mum's house and she remembered the land next door sat empty for near twenty years before someone built what's there now. It's an odd-looking place, to be sure, and doesn't seem homely, if you know what I mean. The rest of us on the street are long-termers, but that house never seems to hold on to anyone for long. The Temples have been in for five ... six years now."

"And you don't know much about them?"

"Like I said, I didn't even know they had a little dog."

"A dog?"

"The one they lost," Tabby said. "Or was it a cat?"

"I don't know."

"Well, it's too bad, either way. And then this happens with Mrs. Temple. They do say things come in threes."

"Do you know Acantha Morris? A Black woman with her hair up in a bun. She used to come here to teach Claudia about herbs."

"Oh, I do. She introduced herself one day in the autumn, and we got to talking about bay laurel. Yes, very nice woman."

"She came every Friday morning," Pru said.

"Not just then—other times, too," Tabby said.

Was that right? Hadn't Acantha said she'd been to Claudia's house only on Fridays?

"Not that there weren't others stopping by," Tabby said, dunking a biscuit in her tea. "There could be quiet spells, but then there would be months and months of people going in and out. Since last summer, I've seen Ms. Morris, and also a fellow in a little blue car stops occasionally during the day." *Finley?* "And, another man—thin, short gray hair. It seemed as if I should know who he was."

Pru knew who he was—Arlo Hartfield, who said he hadn't seen Claudia in "yonks."

"Did you tell the police this?"

"No, all they wanted to know was who had been there had been anything visitors the day or the evening before," Tabby said. "There was only the man in the little blue car. Do you want me to have a think about visitors who came during those busy times lately?"

"Would you? If you can remember, that is. You could make a list. Police would be ever so grateful."

"You aren't police, though." Her tone made this part statement, part question.

"No," Pru said. "But I am married to the detective inspector on the enquiry—his name is Christopher Pearse. He's not the detective you spoke with that first day. I'm sure if Christopher comes round again, he'll introduce himself."

Pru had donned all her layers and set out, making it to the end of Tabby's front walk when she heard a sharp "You there."

She turned to see Ellis Temple stalking out of his house wearing a suit but no coat. He motioned Pru over. She walked partway, and he met her on the pavement.

"I remember you," he said. "You're one of them, aren't you?

This is harassment, and I won't put up with it. You can take that back to your society of herbalists or whatever you are. I'm not going to forget what you did to my wife."

He couldn't still think Claudia's death a suicide? Surely Christopher had disabused him of that idea.

"Mr. Ellis, I'm sorry for your loss. But I haven't stopped by to see you—I was calling on your neighbor, Tabby."

Temple jerked his head slightly toward next door. "That one?"

"Ms. Collier," Pru said. "That's her name. But you remember me because I was here that first day—I came with Acantha Morris."

"Oh yes, I certainly know who she is. She was always leaving jars of things for Claudia on the doorstep—plants or liquids containing God knows what. Do police know about that?"

"I'm not privy to the police enquiry," Pru said, telling herself that wasn't a total lie.

Ellis passed a hand over his forehead. "I'm sorry, yes. It's only that ... you have no idea what it was like, coming home that morning and finding her. It's done such odd things to my thinking. The questions keep swirling round in my brain, and I can't concentrate. Where is Daniel? What sort of secrets is that Bagshaw woman keeping? It's as if I'm on the outside of my life and I can't get back in again."

"The police are doing everything they can to find out what happened to Claudia." Should she mention Christopher?

"God, it's freezing out here," Ellis said, as if he'd only that moment become aware of the cold. "Well, again, I'm terribly sorry."

He spun round and walked back in the house. Pru glanced over to Tabby's window and saw movement behind the stained-glass panel at the front door. She smiled, then headed down the pavement toward her car. Just beyond her Mini, a silver Honda had parked. As she neared, a man got out. He was tall and thin, and he made straight for her so quickly she took a step back. He stopped short a few feet away.

"Who are you?" he demanded.

It was the man from the pub. Now, closer, she could see he was young—in his twenties—with curly brown hair, an aquiline nose, and a generous mouth. Pru thought that when he smiled, it would be wide and engaging. He wasn't smiling now.

"I'm Pru Parke," she said. "Are you Danny?"

CHAPTER 12

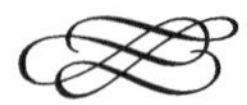

"Who are you?" he asked again, but the anger had left his voice and he sounded like a boy. "How do you know who I am? Did you know my mother?"

"I met her just once. I'm sorry for your loss—she was a lovely woman."

"Pru Parke," he said. "You're the gardener?"

"Yes, I am. How did you know?"

"Mum mentioned you when we talked last ... Thursday, last week." He looked away from her, blinking red-rimmed eyes, his face drawn.

Thursday, the day before Claudia died. Was murdered.

"Have you just arrived?" Pru asked.

Danny took a sharp breath. He stuck his hands in his pockets and looked round the street. "Yeah."

"You must be eager to get home, then, and see your—"

"Father?" Danny asked in a hard voice. "Is that what he told you, that he was my father?" His gaze shot past Pru to the Temple house.

"He's worried about you."

"He's worried about himself." Danny pivoted and headed back to his car.

"Where are you staying?" Pru asked, following on his heels.

He pulled a hand out of his pocket and stared down at his car key. "I'll find a place."

"Will you stay with Arlo?"

Danny looked up. "For meeting my mum only once, you know a lot."

"Well, I did notice you at the pub—why else would you be there? And you look like Arlo as well as your mother." Pru's fingers, deep in the pockets of her coat, had gone numb, as had her toes. "I'm on my way to lunch—will you join me?"

Pru thought the young man was tired and hungry or lonely and scared—or a messy combination—because he didn't question the invitation, only shrugged, and said, "Yeah, all right."

Pru led them to a café she'd noticed on the drive over. She asked Danny what he wanted and then sent him to a table. She ordered and paid, then brought over coffees to warm them while they waited for the food.

"Colder here than it is in Inverness," Danny said. "A real winter."

"You had a long journey," Pru said.

"I didn't do it all in one go—I stopped near Leeds and then left early this morning and came the rest of the way."

Pru wrapped her hands round her coffee mug. "Had your mum talked about plans for the medieval garden?"

"Oh yeah," he said, "she's been going on about it for a while. She said she was learning all the plants and how they were medicines and food, too."

"You said your mum told you about me. Do you remember her talking about the other people involved?"

"I remember some woman teaching her. That wasn't you. I remember she wanted to give them her money. The money Granddad left her. But hadn't she been trying to do that for years—to give it away to someone?" Danny crossed his arms as if to protect himself. "Do you know what happened?"

"The police will want to talk with you," Pru said. "They can explain."

"You're involved with the police," Danny said. It sounded like a challenge.

"Yes, in a way. Who told you about your mother?"

"Annamarie rang—a police detective had told her. Then he rang me. Detective Superintendent Upstone."

Pru didn't know who Annamarie was, but hoped John had been kind.

The food arrived—an enormous toasted sandwich for Danny, piled high with various meats and cheeses and with a mound of greens alongside—and a bowl of mushroom soup for Pru. She wondered if Danny would be interested in eating, but after a moment of staring at the plate, he tucked in.

After a while, Pru asked, "When did you leave home?"

"You mean here, Winchester? When I was fifteen. There was no 'home' by then. Ellis had started sniffing round a year or two before that, and Mum bought all his smarmy charm and they were married. And to top it all off, he adopted me."

"Well, that must mean that he—"

"Didn't mean anything, but it looked good, didn't it?" Danny stabbed at his salad. "I said yes only because he'd talked Mum into it. He was always wanting to play Happy Families."

"What's wrong with Ellis?"

"I don't like him." Danny shrugged as if to ward off Pru's next question. "It isn't that he did anything, it's only that the world had to be run his way."

Not for the first time, Pru counted herself lucky that she became a stepmother only after Graham had grown into adulthood. It couldn't've been easy for any of the Temples during Danny's teenage years.

"So, you left here and went to Inverness?"

"First, I went to stay with my granddad and Annamarie, his partner. She was a fair bit younger than he was. They lived in this big old house at the edge of Leeds. When Granddad got sick, Annamarie took care of him. He died the year after I got there. He left his money to Mum, and left the house to Annamarie, but she had nothing to live on, and so she turned the place into an old people's home—said if she could look after one, why not a dozen? I stayed and worked for her. I like old people—they tell good stories."

He took a mouthful of his sandwich, stopped, and looked at Pru. "Not like … I mean, these are seriously old people."

She laughed. "Thanks. So, how did you make it to Inverness?"

"A few years ago, Annamarie said I should try my wings, that I could always come back and work at the home if I needed to. So, I wandered a bit and ended up in Inverness, thinking I'd get work on a fishing boat. Turns out, I get seasick, so I got a job in a caf near the docks. We're open all night. Fishermen come in after days out on their boats, and the last thing they want to eat is fish and chips, so we mostly do fry-ups."

"When your mum married Ellis and you wanted to leave, why didn't you live with your … with Arlo?"

"When I was growing up, Arlo was so out of it he couldn't put two words together. I know he's better now, but back then I wanted away from all of them." His eyes darkened. "But, I should've come back before this. I shouldn't've left her like that. She was always so trusting."

Danny may have been racked with guilt and sorrow, but he didn't cry at the thought of all those lost years. Pru was another matter. She grabbed a paper napkin and daubed at her eyes. Danny looked away.

"Do you feel up to talking with the police today?" Pru asked, but then remembered that Christopher was in Oxford. "Or perhaps you'd rather wait until Monday for that. Did you mean to have a word with Arlo? I believe he's quite worried about you. And you know your mum's solicitor, Zoe Bagshaw, is waiting for you."

"Yeah, sure, I'll see them," Danny replied with not a shred of conviction in his voice.

Pru's phone lit up with a text from Evelyn—only then did she notice it was past three o'clock and remembered the dinner party that evening. She put her arm in her bag and dug round in the bottom for her cards.

She'd had them printed for general purposes at Polly's urging. "Calling cards are still a thing," her sister-in-law had explained and had presented Pru with a lovely little brass case to carry them in. But it had spent several weeks bouncing round in her bag, and now, when Pru located it, she found it had come open, and its contents were lost to the deep. Another scramble, and at last she came up with a card so battered she might well have picked it up off the street. She straightened its bent corners and handed it over to Danny.

"We live just the other side of Romsey," she said. "Look, I should tell you that my husband, Christopher Pearse, is the detective inspector on this enquiry." Danny's eyes flickered and Pru rushed on. "He's a good man, and he will find out what happened to your mum. You'll be talking with him, I know, but meanwhile, you stop by Greenoak any time, whether you need a place to stay or all you want is a cup of tea."

Pru watched Danny drive away. Where would he go? She'd have to hope for the best, because Evelyn's text had reminded her to stop at the bakery. Ev had also asked if there were to be a centerpiece for the table. Pru put her Mini in gear, but kept her foot on the brake when her phone rang.

"Pru, Rollo Westcott here. I'm terribly sorry to disturb you—end of the week and all—but it's just come to my attention that Ken ... well, rather spilled the beans on my whereabouts that Thursday night."

"Oh?" Pru kept the engine idling, waiting for the heater to kick in and for Rollo to continue.

"I do own the company, after all," Rollo said, "and there's no reason I shouldn't take advantage of the facilities at Westcott Plumbing. Otherwise, I'd be drawing on the kitchen table, you know? It's only that ... there's a design competition coming up sponsored by a garden magazine, and I thought well, why not put my name in for it. Couldn't hurt to try, could it?"

He sounded a bit out of breath, but Pru heard a ring of sincerity, reminding her of how she sounded when she'd told friends in Dallas she was moving to England. *Couldn't hurt to try, could it?*

"I'm sure you'll want to tell the police as well," Pru said.

"Absolutely," Rollo said. "It's only that it didn't seem important at the time."

"I appreciate you clearing that up for me," Pru said. "And good luck to you."

And now, she needed to get a move on. In Romsey, she stopped at the bakery, panicked at the almost-empty shelves before spotting a good-sized Italian loaf, and made it back at Greenoak just gone five thirty. After handing the bread over to Evelyn, she went straight back outside to cut greenery and trailing stems of ivy. Those she washed off in the mudroom, after which she made a trip to the potting shed, bringing in the last few precious containers of narcissus. She reviewed her dinner instructions with Evelyn, who had written everything out in detail. Peachey arrived to collect his wife and the pensioners' dinners, and Pru went to the dining room to start on the table arrangement. She got in such a tangle with the lengths of ivy that when Evelyn looked in to say goodbye and saw the state of things, she shooed Pru upstairs to change clothes. By the time Pru arrived back on the ground floor, panting slightly, Evelyn and Peachey had gone, the dining table looked fabulous, the large dishes of chicken marengo sat awaiting a splash of brandy and the oven, and there was a text from Christopher to say he was caught at the back of a queue after a road-traffic accident just before Newbury and might be cutting it close.

Pru poured herself a glass of wine.

~

"I'll pass on your compliments to Evelyn," Pru said as nearly everyone went for seconds at the table.

"You were the cook," Christopher said.

"And you've done a marvelous job," Bernadette added.

"Well, I helped," Pru said, inordinately pleased with the meal.

"You and Ev worked side by side," Polly said. "Fifty-fifty."

"Probably more like thirty-seventy," Pru said, remembering what seemed like hours of chopping and browning and sautéing and reducing the day before.

"How about this bit?" Simon asked, holding up a chicken-leg bone. "Was this Evelyn's seventy or your thirty?"

"Mine, definitely," Pru said.

"You did well," her brother replied.

The conversation went on and Pru listened with her chin in her hand and elbow on the table. She had been worried about so many things for this evening—the meal, of course, but also how the group would mix. Most especially, which John Upstone would show up.

But he had been the model dinner guest, for the most part. In the library with drinks, Pru had heard him mention Molly only once when talking with Christopher and Simon. Christopher had adeptly shifted the conversation in a different direction. Sabine seemed relaxed, although her eyes had darted to her husband once or twice. Pru imagined she could see a distance between them, but perhaps that was only because of what she knew.

During dinner, Pru had heard Bernadette say to John, "You and your wife were quite brave to make such a move to Winchester from York. It's good you have each other as you get to know the area." John had flashed Pru a suspicious look, but she had smiled and turned to her brother and asked what his favorite summer bulb was.

Pudding—apple crumble with cream rather than a toffee sauce, thank goodness— was served and eaten, and Christopher and Pru sent everyone back to the library and cleared the table. In the kitchen, she put the kettle on and turned to find herself in Christopher's arms.

"Well done, you," he said. "I'm sorry I was late."

He'd made it home a few minutes after their guests had arrived, and this was the first moment they'd had alone.

"No matter. But I have loads to tell you when everyone is gone. Did you find anything out?"

The swing door opened, and Simon stuck his head in.

"I've been sent to carry the coffee tray," her brother said. He and Christopher set about counting cups and saucers while Pru poured up two cafetières.

At the end of coffee and brandies, Pru felt herself drifting off into that pleasant place where she listened to the lively conversation round her but felt no compunction to join in. She sat on a love seat next to her brother, who was engaged in a discussion about rugby with John. Polly and Sabine chatted about something and laughed. Across the way, Bernadette and Christopher went over the upcoming Scout schedule.

The dinner party broke up when Polly, Simon, and

Bernadette rose to leave. When those three had gone, John asked Christopher about the set of Gibbons he had noticed on a library shelf, and Pru showed Sabine the way to the loo, then took the coffee tray back to the kitchen where only the lamp on the counter burned, giving off a low, comforting light. She set the tray down and turned to go back to the library, but heard a tap at the mudroom door. Looking through, she could see straight out the glass half and recognized the late-night visitor. Danny.

The cold air swept round her when she opened the door. "Come in," she said.

He hesitated, standing on the flagstone with his hands stuffed in his pockets and his breath puffing in the cold air.

"Looked as if you had company," he said. "I shouldn't've stopped."

"The guests are gone—almost gone." Only Detective Superintendent Upstone lingered. "Come along now and warm up in the kitchen."

He stepped over the threshold into the mudroom and stopped. He looked no better than he had at midday, and possibly worse—his face ashen, his eyes redder. Pru glanced out to the yard, but didn't see his car.

"Where did you park?"

"Down the lane. I drove through and saw the lights and the cars and thought …"

Pru gave him a light nudge toward the kitchen. "I hope you haven't eaten," she said, "because we have some lovely chicken left from dinner. I had a hand in it, and I'm not much of a cook, but this turned out all right. Take your coat off and sit down."

That was what he had needed—firm direction. He did as he was told, while Pru dished out the food. She had poured him a glass of wine when the swing door opened and Sabine appeared. All three of them looked startled. Danny paused, fork halfway to his mouth, and Sabine blushed.

"Sorry, I didn't realize ..."

"It's fine—come in," Pru said, although in a quiet voice. The swing door closed softly. "Danny, this is Sabine. Sabine, Danny."

Danny stood. "Hello."

"Oh, do carry on," Sabine said, looking unconcerned that Pru hadn't said who Danny was and why he was eating leftovers at nearly eleven thirty. "Pru, I only wanted to say that we're getting ready to leave and I thought—"

Pru rushed to her. "Time already? Well, of course. Danny"—he had remained standing and chewing—"please don't go anywhere. Sit down again, all right? I'll be only a few minutes."

The two women moved into the entry. Pru could hear Christopher's and John's voices from the library, getting closer.

"Look, Sabine," she said, just above a whisper, "it was a surprise, Danny showing up, and I'm not sure this is the best time to tell John he's here." At Sabine's raised eyebrows, Pru continued. "It's to do with the murder enquiry. Danny is Claudia's—the victim's—son, and he's only just arrived from Inverness."

Sabine's gaze cut to the closed swing door to the kitchen. "How awful for him. Does he have no one here?"

"He has a father and a stepfather, neither of whom he is inclined to see."

For a moment, Sabine looked as if she would head back into the kitchen, but the men came out of the library, and it was time to say goodbye.

"I'll give you a ring over the weekend," Pru said to Sabine, who nodded.

The front door closed, and Pru spun round and leaned her back against it.

"Okay," she said to Christopher, "here's what I haven't had the chance to tell you—in a nutshell. I met Danny today. And now, he's here in the kitchen."

She heard the crunch of tires on the gravel as John and

Sabine drove off. She watched Christopher, who watched her.

"He saw me at the Royal Oak," she said, "and he followed me to the Temples' house and wanted to know who I was and if I'd known his mother. He's ... sad and confused. At the moment, he doesn't want to see Ellis or Arlo. I don't believe he has anywhere else to go, and I told him he could stop here any time." She glanced toward the kitchen. "I'm a bit surprised he took me up on my offer."

"Does he know—"

"I told him who you were."

Christopher ran his hand up Pru's arm. "All right. Let's see how he's doing."

Danny sat at the kitchen table, doodling on the back of the dinner-party to-do list Evelyn had left Pru. He leapt up when he saw Christopher.

Pru turned more lights on and carried out the introductions. "This is Danny Temple."

"I'm not using Temple," Danny said.

"What surname is it, then?" Christopher asked.

"Dunno yet. Might be Hartfield. Might not."

"Well, whatever you decide, you'll need to get that changed by deed poll," Christopher said.

"Yes, sir."

He looked at Danny's empty plate. "I can recommend the apple crumble—would you like some?"

"Yes, sir. Thank you."

The two men sat at the table. While Danny ate the pudding, Christopher asked him about the drive from Inverness, about Scotland, about football. Pru smiled to herself as the young man relaxed—she could hear it in his voice.

When Danny had finished, he asked, "Do you know who killed my mum?"

"We've talked with many of the people who knew your mother," Christopher said, "and we're following up on several pieces of evidence." *Herbs of death,* Pru thought. *That green concoction in the jar. What else?* "We will find who did this. Did you talk with her regularly?"

"Once or twice a week."

"Had she said anything to you about donating money? Did you know she planned to give it away?"

"Yeah. She didn't want it. She knew I didn't want it. Granddad left me some, but I gave most of it to Annamarie. Mum always said that money should go to where it's needed, and if we didn't need it, there was someone or something that did. I know it sounds a bit barmy, but it was the way she was and what I heard my whole life. We were never skint."

Danny closed his mouth and took a sharp breath as he stifled a yawn.

"You must be exhausted," Pru said. "We have a room ready for you"—Evelyn made certain that there was always a guest room ready at Greenoak—"so why don't you get your bag and bring it in."

"I don't mean for you to put me up," he protested, but weakly. "I don't want to be a bother."

"You're not anything of the sort." But she feared he might walk out the door and not return, and so Pru turned to Christopher and said, "Danny parked down the lane. He could bring his car in here now."

"Why don't I walk out with you?" Christopher said.

Danny didn't object further, and in a few minutes they returned, the young man carrying one small bag. Pru led him upstairs, down the corridor on the other side of the stairs, and to a room with its own bath. He stood looking at it for a moment, and then turned to Pru.

"Thanks," he said, and she heard a break in his voice.

"See you in the morning," she said and closed his door.

~

Christopher had stayed behind to turn off lights and lock doors, and by the time he came upstairs, Pru had her bath water running and was adding a splash of jasmine oil, causing a cloud of fragrant steam to rise. She settled into the tub. He sat on a low chair against the wall, and she gave him the details of her day—Arlo, Ellis stopping her on the front walk, Danny waiting for her far enough away that his stepfather didn't see.

"Rollo rang to confess he'd been at the drawing board at Westcott Plumbing when Claudia was killed—just as Ken told me."

"Well, then, I'm sure the company's CCTV will verify that," Christopher said.

"Rollo is a busy man. He owns a business, he's drawing garden plans, and he's writing articles about the history of ..." Pru lost her train of thought.

"The history of plumbing?" Christopher offered.

Pru laughed. "No, not plumbing. Let's see, where were we? Tabby knew Acantha. She saw her several times at the house, and not only on Fridays. She'd seen Finley visit and Arlo, too, even though he told me he hadn't seen Claudia in yonks."

"Where is Finley Martin in all this?" Christopher said.

"There was something Rollo said to Finley when they were arguing—about how Finley treated Claudia. I wonder was there anything between them. But, aren't big donors always handled like rock stars? Now, what of your day?"

"I talked with the others in Ellis Temple's business group," Christopher said. "There are three men and two women. They've been meeting every six months for the past seven years in the same hotel—a fine country house—on the outskirts of Oxford. He's quite a hit with the staff there, apparently, because he always lets one or two of them take his Jag out for a spin."

"Do all the people in the consortium sell cars?"

"No, it's rather like a support group, exchanging ideas on sales and marketing. Although they all sell something—bespoke bath fixtures, British woven upholstery fabrics, artisan garden ornaments carved from Portland stone."

Pru perked up. "What sort of ornaments—gnomes?"

"She didn't go into detail. Art in the Hedges is the name of her business," Christopher said. "The others reported that Ellis was there the entire time from late Wednesday evening—they meet for drinks—all day and evening Thursday and up until Friday morning. Two said they saw him about six thirty Friday before they all left. They were all quite sorry to hear about Claudia."

"So, that's Ellis accounted for."

"Possibly," Christopher said. "The hotel has CCTV on the drive showing comings and goings—they're sending it to me, just to be sure."

"Do they have cameras inside?"

Christopher shook his head. "Doesn't suit their clientele."

"Posh place, is it?"

"Hmm."

"Ellis must do well in the luxury-car business. You won't make Sophie watch all those hours of cars going in and out?"

"I'll have a uniform get on it. Sophie's been pulled off this case and onto a GBH enquiry." Christopher stretched his legs out and rested his head against the wall. "We're running background checks on the members of the medieval garden society, Terry Reed, and Arlo Hartfield. Getting financials. The results have come back for the liquid in the jar at the crime scene, but I was running too late to stop for them. I'll see them tomorrow."

Pru pulled the plug and rose from the tub, water cascading off her. Christopher took her towel off the warming rack and held it open and ready.

"Now," he said, wrapping her up with both the towel and his arms, "are we finished with our day?"

Pru snuggled her damp hair against his chest.

"I'd say we are."

CHAPTER 13

The next morning, Pru woke to gray light and no Christopher beside her. She checked the time—half past nine. During the week, even though she had neither set hours nor an employer breathing down her neck, she always rose early, making Saturday morning perfect for a lie-in. She wondered if Danny had gone. Only one way to find out. She leapt out of bed, hurried into the bathroom, and, standing as near to the radiator as she dared, dressed.

Downstairs, Pru put her head in the library, saw no one, and went to the kitchen. It was empty and clean—all the dishes washed up from the night before. She detected a breakfasty aroma of toast and bacon. She put the kettle on and checked her phone, to find a text from Christopher to say they had gone into the station in Winchester. A cold wave of fear swept over Pru. Would Danny have to identify his mother's body to make it official? Then she thought, no, Ellis, her husband, had done that when he'd found her.

Pru sliced bread and opened the cutlery drawer. Here, next to the knives and forks and spoons, was where she'd stashed her murder-room papers and sticky notes. She took them out and set them on the counter, then reached for the jar of marmalade, which was sitting atop the list Evelyn had written up of Pru's tasks for the dinner party. She turned it over to find a pencil sketch of the kitchen.

It was a view from the opposite end, the artist's back to the stove and looking toward the Welsh dresser lined with plates and with the long antique farm table between. On the far wall, the swing door stood partway open, and the edge of a tray stacked with cups and saucers could be seen, as if someone was pushing in. Somehow, the pencil had caught the spirit of the room—the heart of Greenoak—homely and warm with sunlight streaming in from one side. An inviting place to anyone who needed a cup of tea and comfort.

This must be Danny's work—he had been doodling when she'd come back into the kitchen. No, not doodling—drawing. This was art. The kettle came to a boil. Pru left the drawing on the counter and had her breakfast.

She took her murder-room papers out to the potting shed and stuck them up on the back of the door, but she didn't linger, because the sky had cleared and was doing its best to push the temperature up a degree or two. That had been the pattern during this extreme cold—below freezing overnight and then, perhaps, a bit above during the day. Never enough to thaw the soil, though.

The sun lured her into the walled kitchen garden, where she forked another layer of straw onto the bed of carrots, beets, and parsnips, and then walked over and stood up against the brick wall with eyes closed, imagining monks at work in their monastery gardens all those centuries ago. They'd've kept their root crops in the ground for winter, too, and probably piled straw over the rows for extra mulch just as she did. Harvest what you need when you need it, digging deep below the frozen layer, but leaving alone permanent plantings. In times of extreme cold, the roots of trees and shrubs were best left alone.

Her phone rang, and she woke from her medieval reverie.

"Good morning," Christopher said.

"Good morning. I was just thinking how nice it is we don't have to live on a permanent diet of turnips and carp through the winter."

"Is that what Evelyn left for the weekend?"

"Fortunately, not," Pru said as she started back to the house. "Are you at the station?"

"I am. I've had a look at the report on the ingredients in the jar—it's quite a concoction. How much did Claudia know about herbs?" Christopher asked.

"I believe she was on a pretty basic level."

"But Acantha Morris knows a great deal more. I'd like her to take a look at the report, and I want you to be here when she does."

"You don't suspect her of poisoning Claudia?" Pru asked. "Acantha is a teacher. Herbalists don't go round killing people as a rule. Even if she knew how to get hold of all the ingredients, she ..." Pru stopped in the mudroom.

"Pru?"

"Yesterday, Ellis said that Acantha would sometimes drop off herb samples for Claudia to study—leave them on the doorstep. But certainly this sort of thing wouldn't have been one of her lessons. Couldn't it be that someone else is trying to fit the medieval garden society up for murder?"

"Before we can know that, we need to understand what we have. Do you want to ring Acantha Morris, or shall I?"

"I'll ring her this minute, and I'll come in with her. Now, where has Danny got to?"

"He's gone to talk with Arlo and said he would see Temple after, but I'm not convinced he'll follow through there."

"We can't make him talk with his stepfather, can we? What good would it do?" In the kitchen, Pru took Danny's drawing, and put it in her bag. "You didn't need to wash last night's dishes before you left."

"I didn't," Christopher replied. "I walked in this morning to find Danny at the sink. He said it was no bother, that he was both cook and dishwasher at the café in Inverness."

"It was good you didn't go into details last night about Claudia's death—Danny looked exhausted. But did he ask for more this morning?"

"He did, and I told him as much as we know. Not about suspects, but about how she died."

Pru swallowed. "Well, you can tell me, too, can't you?"

"Pru—"

"I want to know," she said firmly. "How could she be forced to drink whatever that was and then hanged?"

For a moment, she didn't think Christopher would tell her, but then he began, describing the likely scene in a rather sketchy fashion, how Claudia may have collapsed downstairs and been carried up. Or, perhaps she had collapsed upstairs on the landing.

"It's likely the murderer hadn't intended for her to die so soon, but had hoped to … position the body so that it looked as if Claudia first drank the liquid and then hanged herself."

"Poison—that's what was in the jar?"

"It poisoned her. Once on the landing, the killer used the long red scarf, securing it to the railing and then tying it round Claudia's neck—before lowering her over the side. Bruising doesn't occur after death, and that's what caught John's attention."

Pru put a hand over her eyes in a vain attempt to unsee the image in her brain. "You mean, she was thrown over the banister like a … sack of rubbish?" Pru asked.

"No, not thrown," he said. "If she had been, it's likely it would've broken her neck."

Pru sank into a chair and put her head between her knees.

"Pru?"

Still upside down and her voice thick, she replied, "Yes, I'm fine."

~

Pru rang Acantha, about meeting at the police station, but the woman had all four of her grandchildren until after lunch—happy squeals in the background attested to the fact—and so they arranged to meet that afternoon. Pru didn't give a reason, and Acantha didn't ask.

That left her loads of time for other stops. There was something Pru wanted to see, and it was at Tabby's. The idea had come to her that morning standing in the kitchen garden at Greenoak. She couldn't remember what it was, only that it was something. Perhaps being on the scene would jog her memory.

"I'm like a bad penny," Pru said when Tabby opened the door.

"Not a bit of it," the woman said. "Company is always welcome. And here comes the post behind you."

Pru turned to see the carrier at the end of the front walk, sorting through his bag. "How are you, Tabby?" he called.

"Right as rain, Sameer," Tabby said. "And you?"

"Not too bad as long as I keep moving. Here you are," Sameer said, coming up the walk and handing over a stack of what looked like mostly advertisements.

"Cheers," she called as he walked off. Tabby stepped back to let Pru in. "Come through now, I'll put the kettle on."

The door closed. Tabby set her post on top of what might have been a week's worth of mail and headed for the kitchen. As Pru followed, half the pile gave way and slid to the floor. She stooped to gather it up and noticed what looked like a newsletter—pages folded in half and stuck together. The return address read: PHDHN.

Pru carried it into the kitchen. "Are you a member of the hazel dormouse group?"

"Oh yes," Tabby said, "I send them twenty-five pounds every year and write letters to the council and my MP. I'm also a member of Beaver Dam Betterment, Save Shingle Beaches, and the one about the Scottish wildcat. They're all worthy causes."

"Do you know Terry Reed?"

Tabby looked up from filling the kettle. "Isn't he the fellow in charge of dormice?"

"Did you know that Claudia had become involved in the group?"

"I didn't, but I'm not surprised," Tabby said, reaching for the biscuit tin. "She learned about dormice from me. You see, one of my newsletters was misdelivered—not Sameer's fault, it was stuck to the back of a Lakeland catalog meant for next door." She nodded toward the Temple house. "Mrs. Temple brought it over, and we got to chatting. She asked ever so many questions about the hazel dormouse and its endangered habitat. Said she had a mind to join herself. She was like that—very enthusiastic about things."

And so it was by chance that Protect Hazel Dormouse Habitat Now had become near and dear to Claudia's heart.

"Did you know she wanted to give them money?" Pru asked. "More than the twenty-five pounds for membership—a great deal of money."

"Did she? Wouldn't they have loved that? Although, there are so many worthy causes, I don't know how you would decide which one needs it the most."

Pru poured milk in her tea, reached for a Garibaldi from the plate of biscuits, and looked out the window, over the brick wall, and into the back garden of the Temple house.

"Lovely of you to stop today," Tabby said. "Saturdays are good for visiting, aren't they? It's the day I talk to my daughter in New Zealand. Just a good chin wag for no particular reason."

Pru was reminded she had no particular reason for this visit —or, at least, not one she could name.

Then one did occur to her. She plunged an arm into her bag, feeling round at the bottom. She'd collected the stray cards and put them back in their case, and now handed over the cleanest of the lot.

"I wanted you to have my mobile number in case you remembered anything else about Claudia and any visitors she might've had and you want to tell me."

"Tell you instead of the police?" Tabby asked with sly smile.

"Well ..." Pru blushed.

Tabby tapped her finger on the side of her nose. "Will do. Isn't he a smart man, that detective inspector husband of yours —sending you out undercover, so to speak?"

Pru found she had plenty of time for lunch before meeting Acantha at the station and so went into the city center to the Royal Oak, glancing round in case Arlo—or Danny—was about. She saw neither, and carried her half pint of bitter to a small table in the same back room, away from the piped-in rock music. She didn't recognize the band. Could it be The Guard? A server followed with her lunch order, and Pru dug into the bowl of rather stodgy beef stew. A few spoonfuls in, her phone rang.

"Pru? Finley Martin here. I hope I'm not disturbing you on your day off. Gardeners do get days off, don't they?" He laughed lightly.

She hadn't encountered this chatty version of Finley up to now, and decided to match his tone.

"How are you, Finley? No, gardeners never get a day off—I

was out spreading straw only this morning. What about solicitors? Always answering a law question, I suppose."

"Yes, yes," he replied as if his attention had moved along to something else. "I wanted to have a word with you, if you don't mind, about Claudia."

It was as she had suspected—she'd become the clearinghouse for the enquiry. Pru understood how John Upstone could scare someone off, but why were these medievalists afraid of Christopher? True, he could be firm with his questioning, but not aggressive. Unless he needed to be.

He did, however have that penetrating gaze—Pru had encountered it the first time they'd met, when she was living in London and Christopher was with the Met. She had found a body in a client's potting shed, and Detective Chief Inspector Pearse had gone to the house in Chelsea to question her. Those intense brown eyes. She had felt as if he could see right through her. That could be why Rollo and Finley wanted to approach her first—especially if they had something to hide. They thought she was soft. But she wouldn't be soft, she told herself. Not with any of them.

Pru put her spoon down, leaving the bowl of stew unfinished. "Of course, Finley. Although I don't know how much help I can give you."

"You see, it's that I've made my movements clear to your … Detective Inspector Pearse, but I do believe others might try to undermine the truth." And by others, he meant Rollo. Anyone else? "Here are the facts."

Pru hoped he didn't expect her to keep notes.

"During the week in question, I was with Claudia on Wednesday—most of the day, as it turned out. She wanted to visit a plant nursery she'd heard about that specializes in herbs. It's north of Bristol and not even open in winter, but I was able to secure a time for her to view the place. I invited Acantha along, but she turned me down, saying something about the commercialization of knowledge." He clicked his tongue.

"I know that nursery," Pru said.

"Well, there was very little to see at this time of year, but Claudia toured the place, raved about the gardens although they looked empty to me, and seemed happy about the expedition."

"And that was the point—to keep Claudia happy?"

"Charity giving is its own field of interest, Pru," the solicitor said. "I was happy to be Claudia's driver if it meant she was more comfortable with her donation."

"But, she never signed the papers?"

"I was certain she had—and this is what I don't understand. I left her with the papers earlier in the week. On Thursday, when I drove her home after our meeting at the site, I went in with her to collect them, but she couldn't find them and said she needed to have a good shufti. That house is devoid of anything out of place, apart from Claudia's little desk, but nevertheless, I left her to the hunt and said I would return that evening."

Pru would check Finley's comings and goings with Tabby's account.

"And you did return?"

"Yes, but she was, I must say, a bit at sixes and sevens. She swore she'd signed the papers, but now couldn't put her hands on them. I calmed her down and said I would print out a fresh set and get them to her as soon as I could."

"Friday?"

"No, I had other things on my schedule. I had planned to do it Monday, but then over the weekend I heard from Acantha, and … well, that was that."

One of the pub servers came by collecting dishes, and Pru relinquished the congealed bowl of stew but kept hold of the roll and butter.

"It's a pity the papers went missing," she said.

"Well, now that Danny has inherited," Finley said, "we may

have another chance. Unless he has a particular passion of his own, and would like to see the money go there. Either way, I am ready to assist."

"Do you think Arlo would expect part of Danny's inheritance?" It was a wild idea, but one that kept bouncing round Pru's head. "To give to the field cow-wheat cause?"

"I've no doubt he'd like Claudia's money—for himself," Finley said. "He has an idea that if The Guard's comeback album is tied to a cause, it'll take off. So, he's chosen to champion this little flower no one's ever heard of, and he tried to persuade Claudia to back him. Arlo Hartfield's only true cause is Arlo Hartfield. That's something you won't get Zoe to admit."

Pru finished her roll and butter, downed the last swallow of her half pint, and still had time to swing by Orchard House to see Sabine.

John Upstone answered the door wearing a cardigan and worn canvas trousers. He greeted her politely, but with a certain wariness.

"I hope I'm not disturbing you," Pru said, putting on a smile and wondering why the detective superintendent wasn't at the station, even if it was Saturday. "I was nearby and stopped to see Sabine."

"She's gone up to London for the day," John said, thawing a bit.

"Oh, I see." No wonder he felt safe to stay home, Pru thought. But here was an opportunity to get to know John better. Should she take advantage of it? Pru wished she had Bernadette at her side—the vicar could crack even the toughest nut. "Well, if it's no trouble, I'll just nip round back to take a look at those old apple trees you've got."

"Yes, all right," John said. "But you don't have to go round, come through." He took Pru through the house and directly to the back door, which he opened. "Here you are." Then, he followed her out.

The ancient trees sat at the very bottom of the back garden. There must've been more before the houses were built on this road—why else would theirs be called Orchard House? —but here, only these two wizened specimens remained. Their bare limbs were twisted and adorned with clumps of yellow-green lichen. High up in the tree tops sat balls of mistletoe.

"Apple trees live a long time," Pru said, patting the gnarled trunk. "A bit of careful pruning would do them good." She reached up, picked off one of the dried leaves, and examined it as she continued. "It was a big step for you and Sabine to move to a new place. I understand how difficult that can be—not knowing anyone, because it's what I did—moved to London from Texas without knowing a soul. At least you have each other."

John didn't reply but neither did he growl, and so Pru decided to move forward carefully and stay positive.

"Sabine told me how you found this house and knew it was perfect because she could use the top floor as her studio." She looked up to those windows, and when she looked back, it was in time to see John's jaw tighten.

"Are you here about the apples?" he asked. "Because I'm not looking for anything else. Just because Pearse and I have known each other for twenty-five years doesn't give you the right to meddle."

Pru felt her face go hot. "I'm not meddling, I'm concerned. Sabine and I have talked only a few times, but I know she's confused."

"This is nothing to do with you. "

Quite true, and Pru knew she should keep her thoughts to herself. She was practiced at avoiding confrontation, but this was different—Sabine was hurt and something was wrong with John. This once, she would not let it go.

"Are you telling me to stay away from your wife? Are you ordering me?"

"What I've asked of you concerns the murder enquiry, nothing more." John's eyes were hard. "I don't need your nose in my private affairs."

"And I don't need you dictating who I can and cannot be friends with. If you choose to ignore your wife, then she certainly needs someone to talk with."

John lifted his chin and looked down his nose at her. "You'd best be careful. I doubt you want your actions reflecting on Pearse's status in the department."

Pru stepped back. "Are you threatening Christopher through me? Are you so afraid to say what's wrong that—"

"I think you'd better forget the apple trees and be on your way."

"If you think you've made a mistake by marrying Sabine, shouldn't you—"

"Get out!"

CHAPTER 14

Pru sat in her car, shaking. She opened her fist to find the dried leaf crumbled to nothing and brushed the bits off and onto her lap. She regretted what had happened—letting her stubborn streak get the better of her and taking advantage of a man who was … what? Ill? He seemed in fine fettle. Pru, on the other hand, needed to calm down. She took slow, deep breaths of cold air until her stomach stopped churning.

When she'd got herself under control, she drove to the station, but once there, found it difficult to release the steering wheel. She pulled her hands off and wiggled her fingers to bring the feeling back, then took the alligator clip out of her hair, combed it through, and reclipped.

The desk sergeant had just locked away Pru's secateurs when Acantha walked in, sporting a smear of green paint on her jaw.

When Pru pointed it out, Acantha touched her face. "Oh, we were painting."

"With your grandchildren?" Pru asked as Acantha located a compact in her bag. "How old are they?"

Taking a tissue from her pocket, Acantha said. "Six, four, nearly three, and nine months. They love to paint, but you can imagine the chaos, the little dears. I always make sure to keep the messiest activity for when I'm at their house, not my flat."

Acantha licked the tissue and got to work on the green paint, and Pru took the chance to tick a question off her ever-lengthening list.

"You and Rollo know a lot about herbs and garden history, but is Finley as knowledgeable about medieval times?"

"Ha! He knows even less than …" Acantha sighed. "Finley has made it a point to be interested in various aspects of the garden —those bricks, for example—but for the most part, his role was to be Claudia's escort. Her keeper, you might say. Although he could sometimes be a bit too obsequious for my tastes, but perhaps that's what's needed when it comes to asking for money. For charitable purposes, of course."

"So his interest in Claudia was for the money, not for … anything else?"

Acantha dropped the compact back into her bag and stuffed the tissue into her sleeve. "Other than to make himself look good?" she asked.

At that moment, Christopher came out to meet them. Her exchange with John came crashing back like a wave, almost knocking her over. She attempted to ignore it and smiled at Christopher, but she'd made a poor job of it, apparently, because he didn't smile back. His eyes narrowed, and, although she looked away, she could feel his gaze on her—those penetrating brown eyes.

"I hope you don't mind, Inspector," Acantha said, "but I don't have a great deal of time."

Christopher took his eyes off Pru and said, "This shouldn't take long." He escorted them back to an interview room, and the three of them sat at a table—the two women on one side, the detective inspector on the other. A PC arrived with the jar containing the murky liquid and a file folder.

Christopher took a single sheet of paper from the folder and pushed it across the table to them. "Ms. Morris, this is a list of ingredients found in the mixture at the scene. I'd like you—both of you—to read through and tell me about them."

Acantha searched in her bag, came up with glasses, and perched them on the end of her nose. She ran her finger down the list and then took hand away abruptly. She removed her glasses, folded them, and held them in her lap. "It's ... these plants are used as ingredients in dwale."

"And what is dwale?" Christopher asked.

Acantha hesitated, and Pru thought she could see the woman caught between fear and her desire to instruct. "Dwale was used as an anesthetic in medieval times—something to put a patient to sleep during surgery. Or for childbirth."

Pru looked at the first item on the list and wrinkled her nose. "Bile?"

"Bile was used as an emulsifier in some mixtures," Acantha said, and, as if kick-started, she read the list aloud. "Hemlock, lactuca—"

"Lettuce?" Pru asked.

"Mmm," Acantha replied. "Inert, of course. But this"—she tapped on the paper—"this isn't right."

Pru looked where she indicated. "Hydrocodone?"

"It's an opioid," Christopher said.

"Opium is the correct ingredient," Acantha said.

"Perhaps the prescription drug was easier to get hold of than pure opium."

"Opium comes from *Papaver somniferum*," Pru said, happy to offer the little she knew. "Breadseed poppy—it's a garden flower, and the seeds aren't dangerous."

"No," Acantha said, "it's the pod that contains the narcotic. And lastly, here's henbane—*Hyoscyamus niger*."

Pru had seen that name recently. It had been one of the herbarium specimens in Acantha's flat. "Henbane. It's poisonous—and hemlock, too, of course."

"And, apart from the modern drug," Christopher said, "this is the recipe for dwale?"

"There was no one recipe set in stone," Acantha said. "Many contained belladonna and perhaps bryony."

"Bryony," Pru echoed. "The hedgerow vine?"

"Yes. Recipes from the continent might've called for mandrake, but that isn't native to Britain and was difficult to obtain. Bryony roots look a bit similar, and so it was often a substitute. But it's a strong purgative and needed to be used wisely."

Red wine was last ingredient on the list. Pru thought it would've taken a great deal of wine to make her drink this stuff. Why did Claudia?

"This is a poisonous mixture," Christopher said. "Have you ever made it?"

"No!" Acantha said in a sharp tone, but then she frowned. "Just because I've studied it doesn't mean … and dwale wasn't meant to kill anyone. Although, obviously, too much of … This must've been mixed incorrectly—the wrong amounts used and administered."

Christopher pushed the jar to the middle of the table. "In this dwale there's enough of any one of those poisonous plants to cause death."

"I'm a teacher, Mr. Pearse, not a murderer," Acantha said, her chest heaving.

"Did you teach Ms. Temple how to make dwale?"

"Claudia couldn't keep the ingredients for bouquet garni straight," Acantha said, "why would I ever try to instruct her on how to make something that had the potential to cause death?"

"Bouquet garni?" Pru asked.

Acantha shook her head, and that errant tress of hair came loose. "It's not important. It's only that I use it as an example to students of how ancient herbs are still with us today."

"Did you introduce dwale in any way into your lessons with

Ms. Temple?" Christopher asked. "Because the word was found in her notes from your classes."

Acantha's gaze darted round the room from her lap to the door to the jar on the table, then up to Christopher. "We talked of so many things having to do with medieval times," she said. "It could be difficult to keep Claudia on a single topic. I suppose there's a chance the word came up. But I wasn't running a hands-on workshop with her, and we never made anything more than black-peppermint tea."

"I imagine some of these ingredients are not easy to find," Christopher said.

Acantha stared at the report and didn't answer, and so Pru said, "Hemlock grows wild. So does henbane. Anyone could find them."

"You wouldn't need to bother. You can get everything online," Acantha added. "It's quite easy to be a medievalist these days."

"Ms. Morris, you've said you visited the house on Friday mornings for lessons."

Acantha kept her eyes on the report. "Friday mornings, yes."

"You've said you had not been there other days or times," Christopher said.

"I never … did I say that? I meant for lessons. There may have been a time or two I dropped something off for Claudia to study."

"What did you leave for her?"

"Herbs!" Acantha cried, gripping her hands as they shook. "Harmless things—mint, sage, betony. Are you accusing me of cooking up dwale—incorrectly—and forcing her drink it? To what end? Why would I want Claudia dead? She was a benefactor of the … would've been a benefactor who …"

But Pru saw that Acantha laid great store in her reputation. She held a not insignificant role in the establishment of the medieval herb garden at the Hospital of St. Cross and that place would gain her a great deal of respect. So Acantha, too, was afraid Claudia would change her mind about the money. But if that had been the motive for the murder, the killer had got his or her timing wrong.

"I am not accusing you of anything," Christopher said, "but you do understand how important it is that you hold nothing back?"

Acantha pulled out the tissue stained with green paint from her sleeve. "Yes," she said, "of course. I'm sorry I wasn't more ... clear about these things."

Christopher nodded. "Thank you both for coming in." With that dismissal, he walked them back to the lobby, and when they arrived there, he put his hand on Pru's back. She knew the signal and waited. Christopher turned to the desk sergeant, as Acantha turned to Pru and grabbed her arm.

"I didn't do this to her," Acantha whispered. "And I don't believe Claudia would ever consider making dwale herself. She knew her own limitations, I'll say that for her."

Pru didn't want to think Acantha was guilty of poisoning Claudia, but someone was.

"Did any of the other members of the society know as much about herbs as you do?" Pru asked, although she couldn't actually name any "other members" of the society, apart from Rollo and Finley. Certainly neither of them seemed likely to know what henbane was and where to find it.

"No." Acantha let go of Pru's arm, sniffed, and buttoned her coat. "We have a growing membership who is interested in the creation of the garden, but not to the extent we four are, and we each have our own areas of interest. Rollo knows the history of design. Finley knows charity law. You have the necessary combination of garden history and plant care. The knowledge of herbs and their uses in medieval times—that was mine. I suppose that makes me the prime suspect," she said glumly.

"Certainly not," Pru said. "At least, not necessarily. As long as you tell them every little thing you can remember about Claudia."

Acantha's furrowed brow lifted. "Yes, well, then." She turned her collar up. "Best be off. I've the grandbaby the rest of the day."

"Your daughter has her hands full with four little ones," Pru said. "Is she . . ."

"Married?" Acantha finished. "Yes, but it's a busy household. My daughter is an emergency-room nurse and works odd shifts. My son-in-law's schedule is as bad or worse. So, I do what I can. Sometimes I stay overnight helping her with the children."

"What does your son-in-law do?"

"Laundry." Acantha laughed. "Not his own, of course. He owns a laundry business for hotel linens."

"Well," Pru said, "you go on. I'm going to stay for a moment."

Acantha's eyes darted to Christopher, his back still to them. "Of course."

She left and Pru lingered in the police station lobby perusing a poster about a midwinter fair at the cathedral. When Christopher finished at the desk, he went to her.

"Do you have time for a coffee?" he asked.

They walked down to a café at the corner and sat in the window, Pru with a latte large enough to swim in and Christopher with a cup containing several shots of espresso. He stirred in milk and didn't speak.

"Is Acantha a suspect?" she asked.

"Why would she kill Claudia Temple?" he countered.

"Because Claudia tried her patience?" When Christopher didn't reply, Pru added, "Acantha is self-taught and she knows a great deal and she's quite proud of that. Wanting other experts to consider her their peer in the field is important to her. But would she go this far? It doesn't seem like a strong enough motive."

"The strength of a motive lies with the perpetrator," Christopher said. "What looks like a flimsy reason to us may mean the world to the killer."

"In that case, the others were counting on the donation just as much as Acantha—including Finley. He rang me earlier."

Pru told him what Finley had said.

Christopher nodded. "It's as he told me."

"It's Acantha's impression that Finley wants to move in better circles—in the world of charity giving."

"He did sound a bit too altruistic when I questioned him."

They drank in silence for a moment. Pru wondered when they would get to the topic at hand—her run-in with John. She knew Christopher suspected something.

"There's no record of Claudia ordering those herbs online," he said. "Not on her credit cards or coming from their joint bank account. We'll keep looking and start at the other end—checking with the companies in the country that sell the stuff and looking into recent orders."

"I can see someone tracking down the herbs," Pru said, "but what about the hydrocodone?"

"Claudia had a prescription for painkillers—Ellis Temple said she'd had back trouble last year, but said she had taken only a few at the time. He can't remember how many. The bottle was still in their cabinet, opened, four tablets gone and no prints apart from hers."

A vital aspect of the case occurred to her—one so obvious Pru couldn't believe she hadn't thought of it before that moment. "But if someone did this to her, how did that person get in? Were there signs of a break-in?"

"Fair question. The back door was unlocked."

"She let the person in—so it was someone she knew?"

"Was it? Temple said she often didn't set the alarm system and occasionally left doors unlocked during the day. He said her mind didn't work to practicalities."

That certainly fit with the picture of Claudia that everyone painted.

"No signs of a struggle," Pru said.

"And no sign that she was forced to drink that liquid."

It had been no common break-in. Someone who knew her had been after Claudia and set it up to look as if she'd killed herself. But the murderer failed in that.

"And now"—Christopher reached across the table and took Pru's hand—"what has upset you?"

"Oh, that," Pru said. The black cloud that was John Upstone moved back to fill her mind. "It seems I've annoyed your boss, and so he's threatened retribution." She winced—it sounded worse than she had hoped.

"John?"

"I stopped to see Sabine. She was gone, but John was there. I said I was concerned about her—about them—and I was told in no uncertain terms to keep my nose out of their marriage." Christopher waited, and so she went through the entire exchange, ending with, "But I believe Sabine needs a friend now."

"He threatened you? You're to keep your nose out or—what?" Christopher asked.

"Something about my actions reflecting on you."

Christopher slammed his spoon down on the table. "Empty threats. What is he playing at? I'll have a word with him."

Pru grabbed his hand. "No, don't! I'll ... I'll tone it down. I promise." She saw that ghost of a smile. "No, really I will. I won't bring up the subject with him again. But I won't desert Sabine."

"Best to set realistic goals, isn't it?"

Pru laughed. "Now, have you heard from Danny?"

"I told him we'd be at the Blackbird this evening and hoped to see him there."

~

Pru went home and watched two episodes of *Cadfael* before Christopher arrived and they walked to the Robber Blackbird—a frigid journey in the dark with a flashlight beam bobbing along in front of them down the familiar lane. They were quiet, but the trek helped clear Pru's head. She made a plan for the next day, Sunday. She needed to talk with Sabine—confess her part in the set-to she'd had with John and find out what he'd told his wife about it. But Pru would play it safe this time. She wouldn't show up at the house unannounced, but instead give Sabine a ring first. If John were at home, she would arrange to meet her elsewhere.

There you are, John Upstone—you ordered me to keep my nose out of your affairs and you've forced me into subterfuge. Happy now?

Christopher took Pru's hand as they turned down a farm track—the shortcut to the pub—and stepped carefully round and over the deepest ruts that were like miniature frozen ponds. Her thoughts shifted to the enquiry and what she saw as her responsibilities: finding out what the medieval garden society had to do with Claudia's death.

It had to start with them, because Terry Reed, hazel dormouse supporter, had spent the night Thursday to Friday morning in a Devon woodland when Claudia had been murdered, and he had seven eyewitnesses to prove it. Everyone else, as far as Pru recalled, had been tucked up in bed. No, wait—Rollo was at Westcott Plumbing working on a garden design. And Arlo Hartfield? Was it proper conduct for Claudia's solicitor, Zoe Bagshaw, to be involved with the ex-husband of the deceased?

Pru had solved nothing by the time she and Christopher

reached the pub. As they passed under the creaking sign—an illustration of a blackbird with a bag of loot slung over his shoulder—she gave up her worries for the evening. Indoors, the place was heaving. It was just past seven, that crossover time when early drinkers had yet to leave for home while others had started to arrive for their evening meal. Pru scanned the room, wondering if they would find Danny holed away in some corner looking at his phone. If they found him in the pub at all.

He was there, all right—sitting at the end of the bar with a pint in front of him and listening to an old farmer from up the lane. By the look of the wild gesticulations of the farmer, he was in the middle of a story. Behind the bar, Ursula Whycher, no spring chicken herself, patted down her tangerine-tinted hair and added a comment to the conversation, and they all three broke into laughter. Pru smiled at how relaxed Danny seemed. And how much he looked like his mother.

When she and Christopher approached, Ursula said, "There you are, ducks. What can I get you?"

Simon and Polly came in soon after, and, drinks in hand, the five of them decamped to a table in a raised area at the back and away from the crowd.

"Isn't Bernadette coming?" Pru asked.

"She said she'd try to pop in," Polly replied, "but she's polishing her sermon. Saturday evening, you know."

They were at the end of their meals when the vicar appeared, half pint in hand.

"There now," she said, "I've put that sermon to bed. Do you remember, Pru, the afternoon I saw you swatting the sweet-pea seedlings and you told me it helped them form stronger stems? I've used that analogy, because isn't it the way? Adversity turned to strength." They shifted down on the long bench, and she scooted in next to Polly and across from Danny. She looked at the young man and smiled. "Hello, are you Danny?"

Pru made the introductions, and the vicar followed with "I

hear you're at Greenoak."

"Yeah," Danny said. "I mean, I need to—"

"You're welcome to stay with us as long as you like," Pru said. She couldn't see Danny sleeping upstairs in the white monolith that was the Temple house. "You're absolutely no bother, and we want you to make yourself at home. Understood?"

Danny nodded and thanked her. During the next half hour, Bernadette teased bits of information out of him in her inimitable way, and soon the young man was pulling out his phone to show them snapshots of his grandad's partner, Annamarie; the café in Inverness; and Libby, his girlfriend.

"She's lovely," Bernadette said. "And look, here's the two of you together."

Danny grinned at the photo and set his phone on the table.

Pru ventured into a new topic. "Christopher said you went to see Arlo today. How did that go?"

"All right, I suppose," Danny said. "He said he was sorry about Mum. Sorry we hadn't seen each other more. Sorry he missed Granddad's funeral. Mostly, he talked about the band." Danny's face darkened. "He's getting them back together—huge reunion concert. Maybe a tour. He asked me didn't I want to get in on it, that I could have any job I wanted—stage manager, roadie, his personal assistant. He said it would cost a lot upfront."

Some father-son reunion that must have been, Pru thought. Arlo wanted the money. Forget the field cow-wheat—Danny would inherit, and Arlo needed backing for his band. Had he asked Claudia and she'd said no?

"Are you interested in working with the band?" Bernadette asked.

"I'm not," Danny said and slammed his empty pint glass on the table. "Bloody stupid—" He looked up at the vicar and reddened.

Pru jumped in. "So, I hear he needs a drummer."

Danny laughed. "Yeah, he offered to give me lessons."

"Did you see Ellis today?" she asked.

"No. I will do—tomorrow," Danny said, looking as if he were anticipating a tooth pull without anesthetic.

"Would you like me to go along?" Pru asked.

A light flashed in his eyes like the reflection of a beacon of hope, but then he shook his head.

"No thanks. It's only that ..."

"It's difficult for him, too, I'm sure," Bernadette said.

Danny didn't respond.

Sunday, Pru rose in time for church.

She leaned over and gave Christopher a kiss. "You stay in bed. You deserve a lie-in."

But he got up, too. Downstairs, there were signs Danny had been about—a spent tea bag, a plate with crumbs in the sink. Pru and Christopher had tea and toast of their own in a hurry, and started out for St. Mary's. How comforting it was that the young man had made himself at home, she thought. It made her wish Graham would come back for a longer visit. She rather enjoyed being a stepmother at this stage of a young person's life —Graham certainly was trouble free. Of course, he and Christopher had always had a good relationship. Would Ellis and Danny get along better now that the stepson was well into his twenties?

It was a fine church service, although Pru couldn't keep here eyes off the arrangement in one of the windows when she spotted the daphne drooping over the side of the vase. Past its time, or the water level had gone down. She'd cut fresh stems later in the week for next Sunday.

They returned to Greenoak to find Danny sitting in the sun on the stone terrace with his sketchbook and pencil, looking out at the Hampshire countryside to the south where the land fell gently away.

"Hello," Pru said, glancing at his work. "You're quite a good artist."

"Art? Oh, I don't know. It's just something I do. At home—in Inverness—people ask me to draw boats or dogs or people. I've done a fair number of the caf—Otts, the owner, sticks them up on the wall, and people can take one if they want."

"Have you had lessons?" Christopher asked.

"No, I just look at something, and then I seem to know where the lines go."

"You drew a lovely sketch of our kitchen the other night," Pru said. "Look, we know an artist, and I was wondering if you would mind if I showed it to her."

Danny shrugged. "Sure, that's all right."

"Ready for lunch?" Pru asked. "There's soup."

Instead of soup, Danny offered to cook. Pru protested—weakly—but the young man insisted, and they soon sat down to a proper fry-up for their Sunday brunch. "I miss the cooking," he said, "and I don't want to lose my touch with the fried bread, now do I? Too bad there's no black pudding."

Eggs, bacon, sausage, mushrooms, grilled tomato, a pile of toast—plus the fried bread—served them well enough. At the end of it all, Pru thought she might need a nap, but instead rose and collected the dishes.

"You're relieved of washing-up duty today," she said, "because I'm sure you want to be on your way. But, we'll see you this evening, and you won't need to cook. There's something in the freezer for us—a casserole or something. I didn't fix it, Evelyn Peachey did. You'll meet her tomorrow."

Danny grinned. "She fixed it? Was it broken, this casserole?"

"That's the Texas influence at Greenoak," Christopher explained.

"You cooked the meal on Friday, didn't you?" Danny asked.

"It was good."

Pru blushed. "Thank you. Are you off now?" She didn't want to push, but he might as well get it over with.

"Yeah." Danny rose from the kitchen table and readied himself to see Ellis, pulling on his coat as if it were a suit of armor. "Arlo reminded me tomorrow's the reading of Mum's will." He looked at his shoes, his brows knitted. "A lot of people want her money, don't they?"

"Has anyone been bothering you about that?" Pru asked.

"Arlo told me. 'Be prepared,' he said. 'They'll be like vultures.' "

There's the pot calling the kettle black.

"I suppose there'll be quite a few people at the reading." She aimed the comment at Christopher. Danny needed an ally—someone to go with him for support when the will was read. He didn't seem to think much of Ellis, and Arlo was one of those with his hand out. Who would be on Danny's side?

Christopher nodded—only a slight movement. "Would you like me to be there?" he asked Danny. "It isn't unusual in an enquiry for the police to be represented when the will is read. It's public information."

Danny played with a button on his coat for a moment, and then said, "Well, I suppose I would, if you don't mind, sir."

After Danny left, Christopher stretched out on the sofa in the library, and Pru went out to the potting shed. When she opened the door, a pink cloud swept out like a candy-floss whirlwind.

The sticky notes. They had come unstuck from the witness-suspect pages on the back of the door. The cold, Pru decided. They would need reorganizing and then sticking back up with … what would adhere in below-freezing temperatures? She gathered them up and left the bits of paper in a heap on top of the seed cabinet as her phone rang.

"Pru? It's Sabine. Have you seen John?"

CHAPTER 15

Have you seen John? How could four words hold such a sense of overwhelming fear and foreboding?

"Today?" Pru asked. "No, not today, but I saw him yesterday afternoon. Why?"

"You talked with him?"

"Yes," Pru said. *Talked—if you could call it that.* "I stopped by and you were gone and I wanted to look at the apple trees and … didn't he tell you?"

"He wasn't here when I got back from London," Sabine said, her voice flat. "He didn't come home last night, and I haven't heard a word today. He left no note, and he isn't answering his phone."

Pru left the potting shed, pulling the door closed behind her, and hurried back inside.

"I hope I didn't … it's just that, John and I got into a brief argument. I'm sorry, I should've kept my mouth shut, it's only sometimes a person outside a problem can see more clearly"—at least, it was always that way with Bernadette, although Pru wouldn't fancy even the vicar's chances with John Upstone

—"and I only wanted to offer support. Because, you've no one else to talk with here."

"No, of course it wasn't you, it's only that I'm not quite sure what to do."

Outrage fought with fear as Pru rushed into the library. "Look, let me ask Christopher."

At the sound of his name, Christopher's head popped up over the back of the sofa.

"Oh, would you?" Sabine asked.

"And Sabine, do you want to come here to Greenoak?"

"I don't think I should leave," Sabine said. "This is silly, I know—he could be off doing I don't know what. It's only that, even lately when he's been so distant, he at least tells me where he is. Is this the end of it? Won't he let me close enough to say goodbye?"

"That's no way to think now," Pru said. "We're on our way."

"It's my fault," Pru said as Christopher drove them to Winchester and Orchard House.

"How can it be your fault?" Christopher replied, his voice calm and even, the way he talked in any crisis. "He's in turmoil over something—anything could've set him off. He's always been well able to handle conflict. Why, I've seen him confront a violent suspect and walk away all the better for it."

"But this is personal," Pru said. "I only wanted him to consider Sabine. Doesn't he see what this is doing to her?"

Christopher put his hand on her knee, then removed it to downshift as he took a bend on the Straight Mile. "I'll see what I can find out."

They fell into a silence that lasted the rest of the journey.

Sabine must've been keeping an eye out, because she opened the door the minute they pulled up.

"I'm so sorry, both of you," she said, as she ushered them into the sitting room. "I shouldn't've dragged you over here on a Sunday afternoon. Really, I'm sure there's no worry. John's probably working on the enquiry. Do you think, Christopher?"

Pru didn't believe that, and she doubted that Sabine or Christopher thought it possible.

"Let me ask round," Christopher said.

"Thank you," Sabine said, and managed a smile. "Coffee?"

At least it gave them something to do. The women left Christopher to his phone and went to the kitchen, where Pru apologized again.

"John was right, I shouldn't've interfered. It's none of my business," she said.

"Please do make it your business," Sabine said, switching the kettle on and swiping away a tear in one smooth move. "At least on my behalf. I rather like having someone to talk with."

"Good, then I certainly won't give up." Pru filled the milk jug and then leaned against the counter. "Isn't it odd," she said, "how some people think you get to a certain age and you can no longer make friends? I don't believe that's true." She set her bag down on a kitchen stool. "Now, look—I have something to show you."

She drew out Danny's sketch of the Greenoak kitchen, unfolded it, and laid it on the counter.

Sabine glanced at it and then picked it up to study it. "That's a fine illustration. There's something about it—a touch of character, a way of looking at life. Technique is good, if a bit rough. And look how the light pools on the counter from that single lamp. Whose work is it?"

"It's Danny's—remember, you met him in our kitchen."

"The young man whose mother … yes. Does he ever work in color—pencil or paints? Do you know where he studied?"

"As far as I know, he's self-taught."

"Is that right," Sabine murmured. "You should bring him

round—that is, I'd love to meet him if he wants."

Danny's sketch had taken Sabine away from her own troubles, but only for a moment. Pru could hear Christopher's raised voice in the sitting room—even over the kettle coming to a boil. The women exchanged looks, and Sabine paled.

"Biscuits?" she asked quickly.

"Yes," Pru answered. "That is, I'll just go and see." She hurried out of the kitchen, but crept up to the door of the sitting room. The kettle's noise faded, and Christopher's voice grew stronger.

"Where the hell are you?" he shouted into the phone.

Shouting of any kind from her husband was nearly unheard of. On this occasion it may have been prompted by worry for Sabine, but Pru suspected its root cause to be Christopher's discovery that his idol John Upstone had feet of clay.

"Well, then," he continued, "you bloody well get back here and explain yourself to your wife." Only a moment's pause, and then, "No, John, you don't pull rank on me—not with this."

Sabine came out of the kitchen with a tray, the cups and saucers rattling enough to make her presence known. Christopher said something else, but in a low voice, and Pru didn't catch the words. Then he stuffed the phone in his pocket.

"Well, then," Sabine said, her voice shaky with false cheer, "shall we sit?"

Coffee was poured and handed out and each of them added milk, stirred, and reached for a digestive biscuit. Thus supplied, Sabine set her cup on the table without taking a sip. She laughed, and a shudder went through her. "So, what do you say to people when your husband's done a bunk?"

"He'll be back," Christopher said. "He wouldn't say much to me, but I'm sure he'll be home this evening."

Relief eased the pained look on her face, but it was replaced with something else. Something steely. "Will he now?" she replied, but quietly, as if to herself.

"Won't you come out to Greenoak for dinner?" Pru asked.

"It'll be a simple affair, just sitting round the kitchen table. You could talk with Danny."

Sabine took her coffee and drank half of it down as if it were the caffeinated version of Dutch courage. She sat up straight and stuck out her chin. "Thank you—both of you—but no. I hope to talk with Danny another time. As it happens, I'm off away myself. A gallery in … Somerset rang and wants to see a few things."

"Where in Somerset?" Pru asked.

"Just some little place. I'll be back in a day or two."

"He wouldn't tell me where he was," Christopher said to Pru on their way home. "But I don't think he's gone far. He's rattled, I know that. 'It's a fearful thing,' he told me, 'when someone brings light into a dark place.'"

Pru hadn't thought John Upstone to be so poetic. Had he been talking about Sabine? Or had Pru's visit pushed him over the edge?

"Are you worried about him?" she asked.

Christopher was quiet for a moment. "No. He'll be all right."

It sounded like wishful thinking.

Pru's phone rang. "It's Acantha," she said, and then answered.

"Pru, I'm so terribly sorry to disturb you on a Sunday afternoon." There were squeals in the background, and, in a muffled tone, Acantha said, "Granny's on the phone, love, I won't be a minute. Don't put that in your mouth." The phone went dead, but before Pru could decide what to do, it rang again. "Sorry about that," Acantha continued.

"Hello," Pru said. "That's a lively bunch, isn't it?"

"Yes, the little dears. I won't keep you, Pru, it's only, I'd love to have another chat with you—herbs, the garden, you know.

How about tomorrow? I'll be home all day, because I've got a deadline. And the children."

The word *deadline* startled Pru, as if someone had given her a light slap. Then, she heard a crash and a shriek.

There was a clattering, and Acantha's voice came from a distance amid a chorus of crying. "Oh now, there's a love, you're all right. Don't step there, let Granny—Pru, what do you—"

The phone went dead.

"I'll give her a ring tomorrow," Pru said.

As they pulled into the drive at Greenoak, Pru looked for Danny's car. "If he came back and we weren't here, I wonder if he might've gone to the Blackbird."

Christopher made the loop of the drive and pulled back out into the lane.

It was a quiet late Sunday afternoon at the pub and they found Danny where he'd been Saturday evening, on a stool at the end of the bar. This time, he had a pint as well as his sketchbook.

"All right there?" Christopher asked him.

Danny looked up. "Yeah, thanks. I stopped by and you weren't there, so I thought I'd wait and try again in a bit. I need to get my bag. Ellis wants me to stay at his house."

"Does he?" Pru asked, the question stalling for time as she tried to decipher Danny's mood from the wooden look on his face. She glanced at Christopher.

"Why don't you two take a table," he said, "and I'll get us drinks. Same again, Danny?"

"Thanks."

"Wine for me, please," Pru said.

Pru led Danny to a table by the fire, its afternoon blaze reduced to a pile of embers giving off delicious warmth.

"Were you doing a sketch of the pub just now?" Pru asked.

"Yeah. It's not much."

"May I see?"

He opened to a drawing that looked down the bar, with shelves of bottles lined up against the mirror and the cask handles standing at attention. He'd caught Ursula Whycher looking over her shoulder in midlaugh as she stood at the optics with a glass in hand.

"It's amazing how your drawings convey the feel of a place."

"Oh, I don't know. Er, thanks."

"I showed your sketch of the kitchen to the friend of mine who's an artist," Pru said, "and she was quite impressed. She'd love to talk with you. She lives in Winchester." Although, God knows where she was at that moment. "She can do the same thing with her paintings—make you feel as if you're right there."

Danny held his own drawing out at arm's length and peered at it. "I do it for a lark. I've never talked to a real artist about it."

Pru took that as yes, he would like to meet Sabine, and so moved on to the next subject. "So, you and Ellis had a chat."

Danny offered only a shrug.

"It was nice of him to ask you to stay," she said.

"I suppose," Danny said with not an ounce of enthusiasm. "He said Mum had been banging on about having me come back here and move in with them and that I'd said I would. He told me it was one of the last things she'd said to him." He looked down into his empty pint glass. "She never said that to me. Not like that. I mean, you know, she was my mum and would say wouldn't it be nice, but ..."

Pru saw red—actually red, as anger rose inside her. Here was Danny grieving his mother's death, and Ellis attempts to guilt him into moving to a house that had never been his home.

Christopher arrived with the drinks, pausing for a moment when he saw Pru's face.

She took a deep breath before speaking. "I remember that

you and your mum talked often. When was the last time you saw her?"

Danny's eyes were on Pru, but he seemed to be looking at something else, remembering. "It was June last year. She said why don't we meet at Annamarie's, and so I took a few days off." He smiled. "Mum had been taking piano lessons—she was always starting something new—and Annamarie has this piano in the big sitting room at the home. None of the old people ever touched it. Mum went through all the music and found a song-book from *Cats*, and sat down and started playing. That lasted about a minute before one of the old fellows came over and said, 'Here now, love, shift yourself and let me put us out of our misery.' And he sat down and played, and he's really good. Annamarie says he plays every afternoon now, but no one would ever have known he could if Mum hadn't tried and made a dog's breakfast of it."

Danny laughed, but his eyes were sparkling with tears.

Pru dug in her bag for a tissue—for herself—and shot Christopher a look.

"Danny," she said, "we'd love it if you stayed at Greenoak instead of going to Ellis's. But only if you want to. It should be your choice, and no one should try to make you feel bad one way or the other."

The young man's smile faded. "It's an awful house," he said. "She hated it."

That settled it. When they returned to Greenoak, Danny went upstairs to phone Ellis and explain he would be staying put for the time being. Christopher started the fire in the library, and Pru rummaged in the freezer and discovered a heretofore-overlooked container of chicken korma. She popped it into a hot oven and cooked rice. Later, when Danny came back to the kitchen, he said nothing about Ellis, only reporting that Zoe Bagshaw had rung to remind him about the reading of the will at ten the next morning.

Conversation was sparse round the kitchen table at dinner. Pru imagined Danny stewing about Ellis—or perhaps he was thinking of his mother or his girlfriend. What about Christopher? Had his thoughts returned to his old mentor, John? Pru's brain couldn't decide what to worry about—her thoughts were a jumble of murder, Claudia's will, a million pounds, John and Sabine, and, just because she didn't have enough on her mind, frozen soil. She had to examine her thought process to find out why she'd added that last concern, and decided it was because she and Simon had hoped to transplant several hebes over the winter, and they certainly couldn't do it now. Even if they managed to pop the roots out of the soil, the plants would never settle again and that would be the end of the shrubs.

The next morning, Pru made certain to be downstairs first, and surprised herself by getting there before even Evelyn arrived. A half hour later, Pru, at the table with a cup of tea, heard the gravel crunching in the drive. Peachey's van, she thought, although in a bigger hurry than usual.

Evelyn came in blustering, unbuttoning her coat and trying to take it off before she'd removed her handbag from her arm.

"Peachey had a puncture bringing me over," she said, breathing heavily. "And his spare was flat. Can you imagine? Well, it's put me off my schedule, and that's a fact, because now he'll be late with the shopping."

"Would you like me to do the shopping this morning?" Pru asked.

Evelyn seemed to consider it for a moment, but then said, "No, that won't be necessary. I just need to calm down."

"I'll put the kettle on," Pru said.

By the time Christopher came in, the cook had caught her breath and was sitting at the table with her own cup of tea.

"I've just been telling Ev about Danny," Pru said.

"Poor sausage," Evelyn said. "To lose his mum like that. You were right to bring him here—who else has he got?"

"He's got quite a few people interested in him," Christopher said, "but we're neutral territory, and so I think he feels safe."

Evelyn got to work, and Pru joined Christopher for breakfast. After he'd left for the station in Winchester, she lingered over another cup of tea, waiting for Danny.

There was a crash at the sink, and Evelyn swore, causing Pru's teacup to stop halfway to her mouth. Evelyn never swore.

"Look at that—when was the last time I broke a cup?" she asked. "First Peachey's flat and now this. What'll be next?"

"Next?" Pru asked.

"You know what they say—things come in threes."

They do say that—at least someone had said that to Pru, and quite recently. Who?

The swing door opened a few inches. Danny edged in and waited just inside the kitchen. He'd smartened himself up for his morning appointment—no tie, but a smoky-blue jacket, a fresh shirt, and trousers with a crease.

"Very nice," Pru said. "I like the jacket."

He tugged at the sleeves. "It's not mine. Belongs to Libby's brother."

"Well, it suits you." Pru introduced him to Evelyn.

"Pleased to meet you," Danny said, still standing.

"And I'm happy to meet you," Evelyn said. "Now, you sit down and let me cook you breakfast. Scrambled eggs all right? I hear you work in a café in Inverness. That must give you a lot of experience."

"Just with fry-ups," Danny said. "Otts always has a big pot of some thick stew at the back of the stove, but he's the only one who knows what's in it. That was your chicken korma we ate last night, wasn't it? I might like to take that recipe back. You're a good cook." He turned to Pru. "And you, too."

Pru laughed, but, fair play to them, neither Danny nor Evelyn joined in.

"Danny's an artist." Pru went to her bag, retrieved his drawing of the kitchen, and held it up to Evelyn. "Look at this."

"I could do you another, if you like," Danny said.

"We'd love it," Pru said, tucking the sketch behind one of the plate rails on the Welsh dresser. "So, Evelyn, all right for your shopping?"

"Oh yes, it's fine. Peachey'll be by later, and that's plenty of time to simmer the beef."

Good—with Evelyn back on schedule, perhaps that would keep the superstition of three at bay. Then, Pru remembered who else had mentioned it. Tabby. She had said that Claudia's death was the second bad thing to happen at the Temple household—the first, according to the neighbor, was that they had lost a pet.

"Danny," she said, "did your mum have a dog or a cat?"

He looked up from buttering a slice of toast. "No. Ellis said he was allergic to animals."

The mudroom door banged, and Simon called, "'Morning, all."

Danny left in time for the ten o'clock reading of his mother's will at the offices of Bagshaw & Churchill. Pru and her brother lingered indoors discussing how early the peas could be planted out, and before they knew it, it was time for elevenses. Eventually, cold or no, they layered up and went out. Pru stopped in the potting shed to fill her coat pockets with a few general purpose items: a trowel, snips, a ball of twine, a few wooden plant labels, and a permanent marker. The contents of her murder room—sheets of paper and a heap of pink sticky notes—sat on top of the seed cabinet. She would get back to them soon, but now she followed her brother to the Mediterranean garden at the southeast corner of the terrace. It was frigid, but sunny, and they stood there, hands in the pockets of their coats, contemplating the scene.

Simon picked up on a discussion from the previous week. "I thought we were going to mark their places with sticks."

"We did, I'm sure of it," Pru said. "Maybe a fox stole them."

Simon cut his eyes at her. "We don't know how many have survived. I don't think we should try replanting."

"They bring good color in summer," Pru said. "We can't give up on them." Besides, she had just been bragging about their agapanthus to Tabby.

"We've lost that lot at the corner already," Simon said. "I don't see the point in trying again."

"We planted those just before that bout of heavy rain last year, and they drowned," she said. "I think if we improve the drainage in that entire area, we'll—"

Simon looked over Pru's shoulder and lifted his chin, pointing up the terrace walk from the front of the house. She turned and squinted in the bright sunlight, at first seeing only a figure—tall, wearing a russet-brown cashmere coat and carrying gloves in one hand. When his thick hair came into focus, she realized it was Ellis Temple.

CHAPTER 16

Pru's first thought upon recognizing Ellis Temple was that he and Claudia must've made a striking couple.

"Ms. Parke," Temple said as he neared, "I'm terribly sorry to disturb you while you're working."

Not only was she stunned to see him, but also a bit surprised that he'd remembered her name. He'd been distraught the two other times she'd encountered him, and had referred to her as *you there*. Was he here to lodge a formal protest about his stepson staying at Greenoak?

"Good morning," Pru said. "Simon, this is Ellis Temple. Mr. Temple, my brother Simon Parke."

She said no more. He couldn't be looking for Danny, because he'd just seen him at the reading of Claudia's will. Temple had also seen Christopher and now must know Pru was married to the detective inspector on his wife's murder enquiry.

"How do you do?" Temple nodded to Simon, and turned back to Pru. "I wonder if I could have a word with you."

There was a calmness about him—almost penitence. Here was an Ellis Temple Pru had not seen before.

"Of course. Let's go indoors. Is that all right?" she asked her brother.

"Sure," he said. "I'll finish up here."

She grinned at him. They hadn't actually been doing any work. "Don't stay outdoors too long."

Pru led Temple not the way he'd come, but instead down the terrace and round the other side of the house, thinking she would deposit the contents of her pockets in the potting shed as they passed. But she abandoned that idea when they reached the corner and she saw that several of the sticky notes had followed her out of her failed murder room and were scattered over the ground, like pink breadcrumbs leading the way to …

She was close enough to recognize first one—*Claudia's money?*—and then another—*What is his alibi?* What would Ellis think of her attempt at solving Claudia's murder? Surely, he was too far away to read them. Nevertheless, Pru hurried him round the corner.

Continuing past the mudroom, they made the circuit of the house and arrived at the front, where Temple's red Jag sat at the U-bend in the drive. Pru led them in Greenoak the proper way, through the front door, just as her phone rang.

Without thinking, she pulled it out of her pocket and looked at the screen. Acantha.

Ellis saw it, too, she felt sure he did. Pru stashed the phone back in her pocket where it continued to ring. She feared Ellis would break out into another rant about medievalists and their herbal potions, but Evelyn popped out of the kitchen and saved the moment.

"Oh, good, Mr. Temple has found you. Shall I take coffee into the sitting room?" Evelyn asked, sounding a bit too below-stairs for Pru's taste. Is this the sort of reaction Ellis Temple prompted in people—kowtowing to his posh presence?

"Thanks, Ev," she said. "I'll help—I need to wash up, anyway." Pru showed Ellis the way and then went back through the kitchen to the mudroom, where she shed her coat and washed her hands while Evelyn arranged the coffee tray.

"He's the husband?" she whispered, as if the walls had ears.

"He is," Pru said. "He must've just come from the reading of the will."

"What's he doing here?"

"He probably wants to talk about Danny."

"He won't try to take him away, will he?"

Pru smiled at this. Evelyn had met Danny only that morning, but she could mother-hen with the best of them.

"As Danny is an adult," Pru said, "it's his decision where to stay." Pru picked up the tray and turned to push the swing door open with her bum, adding, "But if Ellis Temple wants a fight about it, we'll be ready, won't we?"

In the sitting room, Temple stood at the French doors, where, down the terrace to the right, lay the Mediterranean garden, now empty.

She set the tray on the coffee table between the two facing sofas, and Ellis sat across from her. She poured out the coffee and gestured to the milk and sugar. Ellis picked out two sugar cubes—one at a time—and dropped them in.

"Daniel tells me he'd prefer to stay here instead of coming home," Temple said, adding milk to his coffee.

"Danny's a fine young man, and this is a difficult time for him. We're happy to have him here," Pru said, hoping that would put an end to the topic. "How are you doing, Mr. Temple?"

"Ms. Parke, I'm afraid I've come off in rather a bad light," he said, his brow slightly furrowed. "I've come to apologize for my previous behavior. I've only just realized that you have little to do with these medievalists who promote the use of dangerous plants and treatments."

"A medieval herb garden doesn't promote the use of dangerous plants," Pru said, adding milk to her coffee, stirring fiercely, and sloshing it into the saucer. She set the coffee down.

"Not any more than the poison garden at Alnwick in Northumberland promotes the use of poison. A replica of a walled medieval herb garden at the Hospital of St. Cross will help to illustrate how people lived and worked at the time. It's a part of history. I support the work of the group, and I may even join the board." *Was that still on the table?*

"Someone lured Claudia into thinking she could drink that … that poison I found there on our kitchen table, believing it would look as if she did that to herself. I know Claudia could be easily swayed, but she would never have done that. So, they made a mistake, didn't they?"

Pru didn't speak, remembering that Ellis was the first one to assume suicide and clung to that assumption longer than anyone else.

"I understand what the police are after," he continued. "They think perhaps with Claudia's history of changing her mind, those people thought they'd better act fast before she decided to give the money to some group trying to find the Loch Ness monster." He clicked his tongue. "Those people were using her, just like others have in the past. Hartfield, obviously, continues to try. I suppose he could've done this to her—God knows what sorts of drugs he can get his hands on. It was his behavior that led to Claudia being in the state she was when we first met—without purpose, and Daniel without any structure. What sort of a life was that?"

That Claudia may have been easily taken in, Pru would concede. But Danny was another matter.

"Danny seems to have a good view of life."

"He's drifting with no goals."

"He's happy."

"He's delusional, just like his mother. What sort of success will he find where he is now? Godforsaken Scotland, dirty little café catering to fishermen. No, I want him to get a proper job. I want him to come and work with me."

"You want him to sell cars?"

"Well-crafted British motors are among the finest automobiles in the world," Ellis said, and then waved a hand as if brushing the topic aside. "It's what I can do to make up for ... I wanted us to be a family. But Claudia and I married when Daniel was at an awkward age, and I understand he wasn't able to see that to get ahead in life you need structure and discipline."

"Perhaps it was best that he went to live with his grandfather," Pru suggested, only because she could think of nothing else to say. She stared down at her coffee, but her gaze flickered up to Ellis.

His face turned gray and grim. "This is all down to me, isn't it? You can see why I've lashed out at others, blaming them for Claudia's death. But even if it were the medievalists who murdered her or Hartfield wanting the money he never got before, I blame myself. Because if I had been paying more attention, I wouldn't have let her be coerced into drinking the foul liquid that killed her. If I had been there, she'd be alive today. Yes, Ms. Parke, it's my fault."

Evelyn appeared in the doorway.

"Sorry to disturb," she said, her cheeks flaming, "but your phone rang, Pru, and I answered. Would you like to take the call, or shall I say you'll ring back later?"

It was no wonder Evelyn look flustered—she never answered someone else's phone. "Well, I—" Pru started, trying not to look eager at this reprieve.

"I'm sorry to have kept you," Ellis said, standing. "I must be on my way. Would you ... would you tell Daniel that I ... I'm sorry."

Evelyn saw Temple out, and Pru went to the kitchen. Her phone lay on the table, and Christopher was on the line.

"Hi," she said.

"Is he gone?"

"Yes. So that's why Ev answered my phone—she saw it was you and thought I needed rescuing."

"Did you?" Christopher asked.

"Well, I didn't mind the visit being cut short, I'll tell you that."

"What did he want?"

"It's hard to say," Pru said. "He's feeling guilty about leaving Claudia alone. Also, he wanted to make a case for Danny to stay on in Winchester and sell cars." She allowed herself a snort. "How was the reading of the will—who was there?"

"Danny, Hartfield, Temple, Finley Martin, and Rollo Westcott. Things got off to a rousing start when Hartfield and Temple got into it trying to outdo each other as Father of the Year. It was brief—Zoe Bagshaw saw to that. It turns out Claudia had more than that million pounds that's been tossed about—nearly two million, all told."

"So it wasn't all going to the dormice or the garden or Arlo," Pru said. "That is, the field cow-wheat."

"Now it all goes to Danny," Christopher said. "What's left after death duties, of course. That'll bring it down to about that same million."

"How did he take it?"

"He looked resigned."

Imagine not wanting a million pounds. Imagine receiving a million pounds with all the baggage Claudia's money came with.

"He'll be back here?"

"He will. Now, I wanted to let you know, John is at work."

"How is he?"

"I don't know—he won't see me."

Pru quashed an urge to speed to the Winchester police station and march into the detective superintendent's office and give John Upstone a piece—another piece—of her mind.

"I haven't heard from Sabine," she said. "I don't want to ring, but I might drive past their house to see if she's home. That story of the gallery in Somerset sounded bogus to me."

"Why don't we leave them to it?" Christopher asked. "They'll sort it out."

Silence.

"Pru?"

"Yes, of course," she said. "Leave them to it. Even though I will be in Winchester today—to see Acantha. Bye now."

She ended the call as Evelyn returned with the coffee tray, both Pru's and Ellis's cups full and untouched.

"Sorry, Ev," she said. "That's a waste of good coffee."

"Never you mind," Evelyn said. "Sometimes all that pouring and stirring and milk and sugar is just something to do."

"You're right there." Her phone rang, and when she saw the screen, she answered it with "Oh, sorry—I was just about to ring you back."

"Forgive me for being so persistent," Acantha said, "but I thought it best to try you again. I've the children arriving any minute, and I'm not sure how I'll get any work done."

"I don't need to stop by today, then," Pru said. "We'll make it another afternoon."

"No, please, I'd rather you did. Any time this afternoon. Just ring the bell."

"Yes, all right," Pru said.

"Wait! Don't ring the bell—in case the baby is asleep. Text me."

"A text upon arrival. See you later."

Her phone rang again. Pru, never a social butterfly, considered silencing the ring so she could ignore any other calls. But perhaps not in the middle of a murder enquiry. Here was Zoe Bagshaw.

"I feel as if we've lost touch with you," the solicitor said. "There's so much gone on. Would you have time for a chat today?"

Her Winchester dance card was filling rapidly.

"Yes, certainly," Pru replied.

"Lovely," Zoe said. "Shall we say three o'clock?"

"Three o'clock," Pru repeated, ended the call, and turned to Evelyn. "That's me away."

"But what about lunch?" Evelyn asked.

"I'll get something while I'm out," Pru replied. "Before I see Zoe. Or after."

Could she fit in a stop at Tabby's first? The neighbor might have more to tell about Claudia's friends and associates who stopped by regularly. Pru knew that a good and observant neighbor was worth her weight in gold. And, there remained that unremembered thing Pru had wanted to see. Or was it a question she needed to ask Tabby? Whatever it was, it continued to elude her. She needed her memory jogged.

But instead of Tabby or lunch or Acantha—and before her appointment at the offices of Bagshaw & Churchill—Pru found herself pulling up in front of Orchard House.

Sabine's old Citroen van was not parked out front. Instead, John's dark metallic-gray BMW sat at the curb. Pru left the engine of her Mini idling as she stared at the house. Christopher said John had been at work that morning, and so what was the car doing here? Lunch? Possibly. Regardless, there was no need to hang about. She had just put her car in gear when a text *pinged* on her phone. It was from John.

You may as well come in.

Yes, she may as well.

He opened the door as Pru walked up, and she had a chance to take in his appearance. He was certainly dressed for work—proper dark suit and tie—but even though his clothes were not wrinkled, he gave off the impression that he'd slept in his car. Or not slept at all.

Pru hesitated in the entry as the door was closed behind her. "Hello, John. Are you all right?"

"Where is Sabine?" he asked.

She was struck by his flat, defeated tone, but she felt no sympathy.

"Have you tried phoning her?" Pru asked. "She tried phoning you."

He exhaled in a huff and looked round. "I want her to know she can keep the house. There's no reason for her to move."

John walked off toward the kitchen, and Pru was behind him like a goose nipping at his heels.

"She can *what*? That's it—you're leaving her? What was all this for, John? Marriage, moving to Winchester—what was the point if you're turning right round and putting an end to it?"

He pulled up at the kitchen counter, and Pru almost ran into him. "I thought it would be all right," he said. "I thought I'd be allowed a bit of happiness at last, but I made a mistake. I've hurt her, and it's better to end it now than go on like this."

"Why does it have to be like this? You were happy," Pru said, needing to hear this confirmed. "Weren't you and Sabine happy?"

John looked at her with dark eyes, as if sizing her up. "Has Pearse ever told you how Molly died?"

Molly, Molly, Molly. Would the woman have wanted to be raised to sainthood?

"She had a heart attack."

John turned away from Pru and stared out the window and down to the two old apple trees. "That morning, she didn't feel well. I was in a hurry and said to her, 'Ah, it's just the flu.' I'd had a callout first thing to the scene of a murder, you see—a woman shot by her boyfriend. I told Molly to take a couple of paracetamol and go to bed, that I'd ring her at lunch. But I didn't. It was a messy scene—he'd used a shotgun, close range, and he was still volatile. He'd taken his own child as a hostage and locked the two of them up in the attic. The thing lasted all day. We couldn't even move the body until evening. Police on one side of a door, him on the other. We got the child out, but not before he'd shot one of my officers, too. It was after seven when I finally rang Molly, but she didn't answer. I went home, and there she was in bed. She'd died ten hours earlier—not long after I'd left."

Here was the story not even Christopher had heard.

"I'm so sorry, John, but you can't think it was your fault?" she asked.

"Don't you see the irony? I had spent the entire day with a dead woman only to go home and find another one waiting for me." He choked out the last part. "I told her I'd ring at lunch."

"She was already dead by lunch. You couldn't've done anything." He didn't answer. Pru tried to imagine the weight of eleven years' worth of guilt. "But why now, John? Why does all this matter now?"

"When I met Sabine ... Well, what she saw in a crusty old police officer I can't tell you. But I know I felt—as if I could breathe again. We both have ghosts in our pasts, but she showed me it was possible to look forward instead of back. We made plans. Winchester was a fresh start. I knew you and Pearse were nearby, and I had intended to get in touch, but we were busy at the beginning. Then the middle of December, it hit me. I'd forgotten Molly's birthday. Third of December and it had passed without me even thinking of her. I'd left her alone up there in York, moved away, and carried on with my life. How could I have done that to her? Was I so shallow that our years together had meant nothing?"

The guilt of the living—but hadn't John Upstone carried it a bit too far? Pru held back from telling him so.

"Does Sabine mean nothing to you?"

He whirled round on her. "Sabine means the world to me. She means life."

"Tell her."

"What good would it do? I've botched everything—she's seen me for what I am now." He drummed his fingers on the kitchen counter, tapping out empty time. "Do you know where she is?"

At that moment, Pru could've shaken him till his teeth rattled. "We aren't in fifth grade, John," she said. "You want to know, ring her yourself."

He was quiet for a moment, and then, glancing at Pru, he said, "Fifth grade. Is that an American thing?"

She saw it in his eyes—the tiniest spark—and left him to it.

Pru crept up to the front door of Acantha's building as if her footsteps might be heard two floors and several brick walls away and wake the baby. She sent a text and waited only a moment before the lock clicked. She walked in the building and took the stairs.

The door to Acantha's flat opened a few inches, and two pairs of eyes only waist-high to Pru appeared.

"Hello," she said.

One pair vanished, and Pru heard *"Granny!"* in a whisper-shriek.

"Yes, thank you, Nina," Acantha said in a quiet voice. She opened the door, and Pru saw the woman in a new light—a rather disheveled one. She wore leggings and a shapeless aqua sweatshirt that hung down to her knees and had a few spots on the shoulders. She had on sneakers that may have been put through the wash one time too many and from which the laces had been removed. Atop it all, Acantha's sleek, black bun was pierced with not one, but two pencils and a crayon.

Acantha looked down on the boy and girl who had glued

themselves to their granny's legs and were now staring up at Pru.

"Off you go now, children," their granny said. "Remember our arrangement?"

One more child—a boy a bit taller than the others—looked into the entry from the living room. "If we don't disturb you, and the baby has a proper sleep, then it's a run in the park followed by pizza for tea."

"And who is it that decides if these demands are met?" Acantha asked.

"You do," the three said in a sad chorus.

"Right. Pru, cuppa?"

As Acantha led the way, the children returned to books and dolls and a legion of tiny figures that looked to be aliens.

In the kitchen, the kettle switched off. Acantha poured up the tea and set the pot on top of the microwave while Pru stood, hesitant to shift any of the piles of papers and books that covered the table.

Acantha snapped shut a laptop that sat perched on volume three of *Herbs in the Medieval Kitchen*. "I hope you don't mind me asking you round again. It's only that I wanted to talk more about this dwale."

"There's something else the police should know?" Pru asked.

"It isn't that," Acantha said, holding the jug over two mugs. "Milk?" she asked.

"Yes, thanks."

Acantha continued. "It's more about the history and what was used and things I thought you might want to know but would probably bore your husband. The inspector."

"I did run across more about dwale online," Pru said, who had done one quick search since hearing the word, but hadn't read much of what she'd found.

"It's only recently—that is, recently in the world of medieval studies—that scholars have realized dwale was here in Britain at all. The mixture was quite far ahead for its time, if you think that there was nothing else to dull the pain of surgery. Biscuit?"

"No, thank you."

"But the recipes are fairly wide ranging. I mentioned before about bryony being an English addition, and that belladonna was often added."

"That would certainly be a toxic mix," Pru said.

"Possibly. Doesn't it also depend on the strength of the plants, though? Here in the Northern Hemisphere, something like henbane or hemlock might not have as high a level of toxins as plants grown in warmer climates."

Pru knew heat and light played a part in a plant's flowering. A tree that might flower in shady conditions in a hot climate could be shy to produce flowers in the shade of cooler regions. So, it made sense that heat during the growing season could change the strength of chemicals in the plant.

"So you're saying that the person who mixed this dwale didn't know what he was doing?"

"It would be a risky business," Acantha said. "But there's something else. The amounts in recipes for dwale are measured in spoonfuls. 'Three spoonfuls of hemlock juice,' 'three spoonfuls of wild neep'—that's the bryony. Did the person who made this dwale actually have access to the liquid, or did he boil up the plants himself? And if he did, he had to have strained the liquid and then ..."

"Dispose of the leftovers," Pru said. "But where would they be?"

"I don't suppose police searched everyone's rubbish bin?" Acantha asked.

"Or compost heap. Although, I don't suppose it would matter now."

"Well, regardless," Acantha said, "I wanted to share the information. I realize the police may consider me the most likely person to cook up a pot of dwale, but I wouldn't. And why would I tell you all this if I had been the one to do it?"

Because you've now had plenty of time to remove all traces of dwale from your own kitchen? Pru glanced round at the myriad of jars and old wooden spice boxes. Did she keep such stuff here? Should police carry out a search?

"Granny," said a quiet voice in the kitchen doorway. It was the smaller of the two boys. "May we have a ginger nut each? It's a long time till our tea."

"Yes, love, you may. Get them yourself."

The boy dashed round the table to a stack of tins at the end of the counter. He removed two, popped the lid on the third, and grabbed two handfuls of biscuits.

"Three," Acantha said without looking behind her. "One each."

Clunk went the extras back in the tin. "Three," he confirmed.

Pru would've dearly loved to stop for a bite of lunch, but she'd told Zoe Bagshaw three o'clock. She hadn't left Acantha's flat until quarter to, and that meant she could make it just in time. She turned into the church car park, dropped her two-pound coin in the box, and scurried across the road to the entry of Bagshaw & Churchill with its black-and-white-checkerboard stonework and ziggurat plinths. She rang the bell and, assuming the camera on Zoe's laptop would show who it was, smiled. She was buzzed in.

Still no one in reception, and so Pru continued to the door of the inner office, which had been left ajar. She heard voices, and so hesitated, only peeking in to make her presence known.

Zoe was alone and on a call, with her phone on speaker. She lifted her chin to nod Pru in, put a finger to her lips, and gestured to a chair. A man was on the line. Pru thought the voice was Finley's.

"... Just some indication of what Danny plans to do, that's all I want," he said.

"You know I can't disclose my client's wishes until he allows me to," she said. "I don't know why you're even asking."

"Oh, give over, Zoe," Finley said. "He doesn't want the money—you know that, I know that. So, it's got to go somewhere. I don't give a fig where that is as long as I can be the one to deliver it. You owe me this."

"The books are closed on our account, Finley. I owe you nothing." Zoe sighed—a great heaving sound that was sure to be heard on the other end of the conversation. "I'll see what I can find out. No promises! Bye now, Fin-Fin."

"Don't call me—"

The rest of Finley's request was cut short when Zoe ended the call. She glanced at the screen of her phone, and then up at Pru.

"That's Finley Martin for you," she said, raising two perfectly arched and filled-in eyebrows. "Always looking out for Number One."

"Yes, well," Pru said, unable to come up with any other comment. "Sorry I'm a bit late."

"Absolutely no need to be sorry," Zoe said. "Coffee?"

"No, thank you."

"Well, Pru, to the reason I've asked you here. I really only wanted to check in about Danny. Your husband—that is, the detective inspector—told me he was staying with you out in—"

"Ratley. The other side of Romsey."

"Yes, yes, that's it." Zoe smiled. "As clients go, Claudia was one of the better ones. True, she bounced from idea to idea and that could make her a bit difficult to track, but she was always eager to learn things—anything, really. But regardless of her inability to focus, the one constant in her life was her son. He was her world, really. Danny's quite down to earth with a lot of common sense—which was not one of Claudia's strong suits. But he's thoughtful and generous, and in that way, I see a great deal of her in Danny. Don't you think?"

"I met her only the once," Pru said. "But, yes, Danny is a fine young man."

"A fine young man who will end up inheriting a million pounds after death duties. I don't believe he knows what to do with it. Finley doesn't care where the money goes—you heard him say as much. Medieval gardens have no particular place in his heart. No, most of Finley's heart is filled with admiration for himself. But if Danny decides to give the money away, Finley wants to be the one to orchestrate it. There's a great deal of prestige in the charity world, and he believes brokering a deal—that is, setting up a sizeable donation—will lead him to managing larger and larger gifts. I believe he hopes to work his way up to the Duchy of Cornwall." Zoe chuckled.

"And Finley is asking you to tell him what Danny wants to do with the money? Is that what Finley meant, that you owed him 'this'?"

"I owe him nothing. Our divorce settlement was clear—I got his half of this practice. The fact that now he rues the day he made the agreement has no bearing on anything other than Finley's petty mind." Zoe sniffed and shifted her phone from one corner of the desk to the other. "I don't suppose Danny has said anything to you about what he's considering?"

"No," Pru said and, to put a stop to Zoe's fishing expedition, asked, "What happened between Arlo and Ellis this morning?"

"Oh, you heard about that, did you? It was nothing, really. Arlo voiced his concern over the way Ellis is trying to insinuate his way back into Danny's life. Ellis took exception and … well, it was over before it started. Helped, I've no doubt, by the fact that there was a police presence, so you can thank your husband for that. No, Ellis is full of this expansion to Temple Motors, and he can't see anything else. He's quite taken with the idea of Danny coming into the firm."

"Hasn't Arlo asked Danny to get involved with The Guard's revival?" Pru asked.

Zoe lifted her chin and looked down her nose at Pru.

"Arlo has owned up to his mistakes. He isn't asking for anything from Danny."

Except a bit of cash to fund the band's reunion.

"I hadn't heard about Ellis's expansion," Pru said.

"Vintage luxury cars. Why own any old Bentley when you can own a 1952 R Type something or other." She shrugged. "We had a lecture on it this morning fortunately cut short by the arrival of your husband."

Sounds like a jolly gathering, Pru thought. But had the reading of the will got them any closer to finding out who murdered Claudia?

"I'm breaking no confidences," Zoe said, "when I tell you that upon their marriage, Claudia gave Ellis five hundred thousand pounds to help start his motor company. It was money from an aunt of hers." Zoe gave Pru a sly look. "A good start in business, wouldn't you say?"

This was news to Pru. Did Christopher know, or was this Zoe's way of telling him? "That was generous of her."

"Yes, it was. Claudia had a generous spirit. She led a simple life, and you can see that reflected in Danny, can't you? I'm sure if she hadn't died, that this million pounds floating about would've landed somewhere eventually."

Pru rang Christopher while sitting in the church car park.

"I've had no lunch," she said. "But I do have information. Are you free?"

He waited for her on the pavement outside the café at the

bottom of the hill from the police station, his breath coming out like smoke.

"Quick, now," she said, giving him a kiss, "inside before we freeze." The warm, delicious aromas wrapped round her, and for a moment Pru forgot about everything but food. She checked the daily menu board. "Cauliflower soup with chili oil—perfect. That'll warm me up."

They ordered and took a table before Christopher said, "What did Zoe Bagshaw want to tell you?"

Pru put a finger up. "Hold onto that thought. Before I went to see Zoe, I . . ." John Upstone first? No, stick to the enquiry for the moment. "I went to see Acantha. Remember she rang yesterday. She wanted to explain to me that the person who made dwale would've had to strain off the liquid and discard the plant material."

"And?"

"I suppose she thought you might've searched people's houses and looked in their rubbish bins."

"Not without probable cause we couldn't," Christopher said. "She's waited awhile to tell you that."

"I know what you're thinking—it points to Acantha." Their food arrived, and Pru took a moment to lean over the bowl of soup, breathe deeply, and take a spoonful before continuing. "Her kitchen is an herbalist's dream, I'm sure, and it would be quite easy to hide all sorts of things in there, but she couldn't. She wouldn't—her grandchildren have free rein, and I don't believe she'd ever put anything dangerous within their grasp."

Pru went back to her soup, and Christopher ate his sandwich, but she knew he was watching her.

"What's her alibi for that night?" Pru asked him.

"Didn't she tell you?" he asked.

"That's not my remit, is it? I'm on herbs, not timing."

He conceded with a nod. "She says she spent the night at her daughter's with the grandchildren, because both parents were working."

"There you are, then—she wouldn't leave four little ones alone to go off and drug Claudia and … she wouldn't."

"Right, so," Christopher said. "Next, Zoe Bagshaw."

"It seemed as if she had several points to make—probably hoping I would repeat everything to you," Pru said. "And so I will." She told him about overhearing Finley on the phone, and then how Zoe seemed to want to paint a picture that put Arlo in a good light and Ellis in a bad one. "Claudia got his business started after they married by giving him half a million pounds. Did you know that?"

"The financials of all concerned were so completely without note, I've asked Sophie to have another go at them," Christopher said. "She's finished with the GBH, and I'm glad she's back."

"When Ellis stopped at Greenoak this morning," Pru said, "he made it sound as if Claudia and Danny had needed rescuing. But in a way, Claudia had rescued him. Too bad he's got an alibi. What about Arlo?"

"Hartfield was with Zoe Bagshaw the night Claudia was murdered," Christopher said. "So they are each other's alibi."

"Is that allowed?" Pru asked.

"It's convenient, I'll say that," he replied. "We've got them on CCTV at the corner near her office and flat. She's walking her dog, at just after one o'clock, and Arlo joins her along the way. That doesn't entirely rule him out."

Pru scraped down the sides of her soup bowl, licked the spoon, and sat back. "There's just one more thing. Before I went to Zoe's office and before I went to Acantha's flat, I decided to drive by and see if Sabine was home. Just to know—I wasn't going to ring the bell or anything. She wasn't there, but I had paused long enough for John to notice me, and he invited me in."

"Invited you?" Christopher asked.

"So to speak. He told me about the day Molly died." Pru repeated John's story.

"I've never heard those details," Christopher said. "His team would've known what had happened, of course, but they would never have discussed their boss's emotional state no matter how many drinks at the pub."

"Sabine said when they first met, John had talked about Molly, but she doesn't know that it was John forgetting Molly's birthday at the beginning of December—just a few weeks ago—that caused him to clam up. It's as if he's held vigil for Molly all these years. Perhaps that's why he hasn't retired yet. Still trying to make up for her death."

She spoke cautiously, knowing Christopher still kept the memory of his father's early death in his heart. Were all police officers trying to save someone from their past?

"He should've been honest with her from the start," Christopher said.

"Maybe he'll tell her now." This was no happy ending, but Pru sensed something in Upstone had cracked and broken open, and it might lead to better times. "I have hope."

Christopher took her hand across the table. "You can always see the best possible outcome."

"That's me," she said, "Pollyanna to the core." Pru had carried that label with her throughout her life, and, although for years it had annoyed her, she no longer minded.

"It's gone four o'clock," Evelyn said by way of a greeting when Pru walked into the mudroom.

"Sorry we didn't wait tea for you," Polly said, her mouth full of what Pru suspected was ginger cake, although she knew that only by the aroma, because the plate was empty apart from a smattering of crumbs.

Regardless of missing tea, Pru smiled at the scene: Evelyn setting out containers on the counter to await the pensioners' dinners; Polly and Bernadette across the table from each other; and in the chair at the end, Danny.

"Here now," Evelyn said, "I've put the kettle on. And look in that other tin there, and you'll find shortbread."

"Thank goodness," Pru said, forgetting she'd just had a bowl of soup as she popped the lid off the tin. "Otherwise, I'm sure I would starve. Well, what have I missed?"

"Danny says that his girlfriend, Libby, has never been to England," Polly offered.

"And that led us to talking about whisky," Bernadette said. "Because Libby's family owns a small distillery in the Highlands."

"Too small to export," Danny said, "but they do a good coach trade. I'm sorry I didn't bring you a bottle, but"—he shrugged—"I didn't know."

"Perhaps next visit," Pru said, happy that their teatime conversation didn't seem to have included any mention of murder or money. She joined them and Danny talked at ease about Inverness, Libby, the café and Otts, the owner. When asked, he reached over and pulled his sketchbook from atop the Welsh dresser, flipping through to show them drawings from Scotland and Winchester, too.

"Oh, look," Bernadette said. "It's the Hospital of St. Cross—that's the Porter's Lodge, isn't it?"

"Yeah," Danny said, "I went over to see the place, because Mum talked so much about it. She said they still give out bread and a drink to anyone who asks, and have done for ..."

"For centuries," the vicar said.

"Yeah. She really liked the garden idea. History for today, she said."

"There now," Evelyn said, drying her hands on a tea towel. "Your evening meal is beef and Guinness pie. It's a large one—I daresay it would feed quite a few of you, especially with a bit of mash to go along."

Pru turned to the two women. "Can you stay? Polly, ring Simon."

"Wish we could," Polly said, looking as if she meant it, "but we're meeting one of my client's for dinner. Chumley's Chimneys."

"I've a parish council meeting," Bernadette said, checking the time. "In an hour. And they can drag on forever."

There was a sharp knock at the front door and a sharp stab of apprehension in Pru's stomach. Please don't let it be Ellis again.

"I'll go," she said, and hurried out to the entry. When she pulled open the door, a blast of freezing air hit her, stunning her as much as did the sight of Arlo Hartfield, wearing an open sheepskin coat over his usual tight black uniform.

"Hello, Pru," he said. "I hope you don't mind me stopping. I'd've got here earlier, but I had a bit of trouble with the satnav and had to look in at the pub to ask where you were. They all know you round here—I like that about a village. Good-looking pub, too, nice woman behind the bar."

"Hello, Mr. Hartfield," Pru said.

"Oh no, please, none of this *Mister* business—it's Arlo. Look, I've come about Danny. Is my boy here?"

CHAPTER 17

"Come in." Pru opened the door wide and stood back. "Come through to the library, and I'll go see if Danny is"—Danny is what? Up for entertaining a visitor who has come begging? —"able to join us."

Lame, but Arlo nodded as if understanding what she had really meant. Pru took him to the library and switched on a few lamps.

"I'm sorry the fire isn't lit yet," she said.

"'Sarright," Arlo said. "I don't feel the cold." As if to prove it, he took off his coat and Pru saw he'd made one concession to the weather—he wore a long-sleeved T-shirt. Still black, but this one with the field cow-wheat one side and on the other, the news that *The Guard Is Back!*

Pru took his coat away to the kitchen.

"It's Arlo," she said to Danny. "I've put him in the library."

Polly and Bernadette sat up, but Evelyn paid no attention as Peachey had arrived and they were loading the pensioners' meals for delivery.

"Do you want to see him?" Pru asked Danny. "We could ask

him to stay to dinner, or I can send him on his way. Whichever you want—I don't mind."

"No, he can stay," Danny said. "Otherwise he'll just … you know."

Keep pestering you. "Okay, good," Pru said.

They went out to the library together, and found Arlo standing at the mantel and looking down at the fire as it flickered, cracked, and popped.

"I hope you don't mind me getting it going," Arlo said, nodding to the nascent blaze.

"Not at all, thanks," Pru said. "So, Arlo, I hope you can stay to dinner."

Hartfield looked from Pru to Danny, who shrugged and said, "Yeah, stay if you want."

Arlo's craggy face broke into a smile. "That's very kind of you. Thanks, I will."

Pru left them to it, but kept the library door ajar so it would be easy to come back and listen to make sure things were not getting out of hand—such as, if she heard Arlo asking for money. She went back to the kitchen, where she found Evelyn and Peachey gone, and Polly and Bernadette on their phones.

"But Simon," Polly said, "it's Arlo Hartfield. I'll ring Chumley —he won't mind being saved the price of a dinner, I can tell you."

"Just as well, then, Nate," Bernadette said into her phone, "especially as you're packing for your winter holiday. We'll be finished before you know it."

"Right, love," Polly said, "I'll nip over and collect you."

"That's grand," Bernadette said, "it'll be the fastest parish council meeting ever, won't it? Bye now."

They ended their calls, both smiling.

"Looks like three more for dinner," Polly said.

The two women left, promising to return within the hour. Pru thought she should start the mashed potatoes—how hard could that be? But the only time she'd tried it by herself, the result was a watery, pasty mixture, which flummoxed her, as she was sure she'd done a proper job of draining the pot. Perhaps she'd peel the potatoes and let Polly take over from there. But before she got stuck in, she'd check on Danny and Arlo.

She crept close to the library and stopped outside, unseen, to gauge the situation.

"You think I should've talked Mum into that?" Danny said with heat.

Pru's hand moved slowly to the door.

"No, of course not," Arlo said. "That's what I'm saying, that I wouldn't use you that way."

Pru withdrew her hand, but stayed listening.

"I'm not leaving Inverness," Danny said.

"Why should you?" Arlo said. "But this is all a shock—your mum dying that way, and suddenly you're lumbered with a pile of money. I'm only saying if you need someone to help you sort out what to do—"

Danny cut his father off. "You'd be happy to advise me?"

Pru pushed the door open and smelled the tension like the air during an electrical storm. Arlo had remained at the mantel, and Danny stood halfway across the room, by the reading table, his hands at his sides, his fists clenched.

"I'm just in the kitchen if you need anything," she said brightly. "Anyone want a drink?" She heard the crunch of gravel on the drive. "That sounds like Christopher. I tell you what, I'll send him straight in to see what you'd like and I'll get back to the kitchen."

"Do you need help?" Danny asked. He looked hopeful.

"No," Pru replied. "I'm only going to peel the potatoes."

"I can do that," Danny said, and shot past her.

Pru smiled at Arlo. "You won't be alone long."

~

She followed Danny to the kitchen. He had pushed up his sleeves, and was tying on Evelyn's pinny.

"I'll put the pie in the oven," he said. "It'll take at least an hour."

"Yes, good," Pru said as Christopher emerged from the mudroom and took in the scene.

"We've company for dinner, and Danny is helping," she said. She took Christopher's arm, drew him out to the entry and, in a whisper, apprised him of the situation, ending with, "And, so, Arlo is in the library now."

"I'll go in and keep him company," Christopher said. "I'm sure he'll be delighted to see me."

Pru squeezed his arm and returned to the kitchen to join Danny peeling potatoes. "Bernadette, Polly, and Simon have managed to change their plans, and they'll be here for dinner. Is it too much for you, all this?"

"No," Danny said. *Plonk* went a potato into the pot. "It's better. I know I should … I know he's trying. Mum said he wanted to make up for how it was."

"They were in touch?" Pru asked, dropping in a spud.

"Yeah. Mum said it was Ms. Bagshaw that did that—got them talking. I'm not sure Arlo is all that interested in field cow-wheat. Ms. Bagshaw said he got hold of the idea a few years ago once he was a functioning member of society again." He laughed. "She said that, I didn't."

The water was coming to a boil just as Danny tossed in the last potato. He put the lid on and said, "I'll keep an eye on it for you."

Headlights flashed in the yard—the rest of the dinner party.

"No, you go on to the library. I'll bring you back in for the mashing, how's that?" A young arm would do better with the vat of potatoes they had on to cook.

She waited for Bernadette, Polly, and Simon, and took them

into the library where Christopher and Arlo bookended the mantel, the former looking serene and the latter, nervous.

She introduced Arlo, after which drink orders were placed and distributed—gin and tonics, glasses of whisky, and, for Arlo, tonic only, with a slice of lime.

Pru loved a good gathering for dinner, but admitted to herself that this was the second in a row in which the undercurrents might prove more interesting than any idle chatter.

But the meal went off without any flare-ups. Danny had provided the muscle for the mash, and Pru remembered just in time there were leftover roasted vegetables and put them in the oven when the pie came out. The dinner-table conversation stayed off the topic of murder and money, but couldn't avoid The Guard—especially as there were two star-struck fans at the table.

"Are you writing new songs for the reunion?" Polly asked.

"Oh," Arlo said, "I've noodled with one or two tunes, but it's the lyrics that come to me first. Sort of like a message sent from —" His gaze darted to Bernadette and then away. "Well, you know."

"Oh, I do know," Bernadette said. "I've used your lyrics in a sermon or two—'Your love is etched onto my heart' and 'Don't say goodbye when *au revoir* will do.' "

Pru heard Polly humming. Bernadette joined in, and they finished by singing aloud.

"Where were you two ladies when I was hiring backup singers?" Arlo asked. Polly and Bernadette giggled.

Bernadette had the forethought to provide for their afters by bringing along a large box of fine chocolates that a parishioner had given her for Christmas. The box had remained unopened these few weeks by, according to the vicar, "some miracle."

The chocolates, coffee, and brandy—Arlo had seconds on coffee—and the fire, revitalized by another log, turned the atmosphere mellow.

"How did you celebrate your birthday this year?" Arlo asked Danny.

The question seemed to startle Danny, but he answered readily. "Otts made a cake—it was as big as a table—and anyone coming into the caf that day got a slice. Next day, too."

"When was your birthday?" Pru asked.

"Tenth of January," Arlo said. "There's a day seared into my memory." He smiled at his son.

"I was born at one of The Guard's concerts," Danny told them.

"At the concert and *on* the stage," Arlo said. "We were playing a gig in a dingy hall in Ripon. Freezing cold it was, in the dead of winter." He looked into the fire. "That's the circuit we were on there toward the end—the band. Claudia had come along on the tour. It wasn't easy and we weren't staying in the best of places, and there she was as big as a house but still beautiful as ever. Part of me wished she hadn't come with, but . . . " He shook his head. "But most of me was glad she did, because I got to be there when Danny was born."

"Mum always said she went into labor at the start of the concert, but didn't want to interrupt."

"She stood at the back," Arlo said. "It wasn't a large room and there weren't all that many people in it, but I would've seen her no matter the crowd. It was the same the first time I laid eyes on her. At the end of this night, she came up to the stage and said, 'I think this is it.'"

"You were born actually *on* the stage?" Bernadette asked.

"She said it was Arlo's last number that did it," Danny said.

Arlo burst out laughing "'Come On, Baby, Show Me Your Good Side.'"

"I love that one," Polly said, and immediately The Guard's new backup singers offered a few bars.

"How do you remember all those words?" Simon asked and Polly rolled her eyes.

"Good thing there was a nurse in the audience that night. You were one loud little bugger," Arlo said to his son. "Redfaced and squealing your head off."

Danny, redfaced again, dropped his head. Was his dad embarrassing him? Pru couldn't be sure, but if so, she saw that as a good sign.

The evening ended with Arlo and his groupies singing a few bars of The Guard's "Letter in a Box" and Simon having a last rummage in the greatly diminished box of chocolates.

In the entry, as coats were buttoned and cautions about icy roads were offered, Arlo asked Danny about Claudia's funeral.

"Dunno, do I?" Danny replied. "Ellis has got something on for Wednesday morning at a funeral home. Catered do at his house after."

A look of distaste crossed Arlo's face, as if he'd taken a swallow of sour milk. "Git," he muttered, loud enough for everyone to hear.

Tuesday morning dawned a more normal winter's day, what with the temperature creeping up above freezing. Pru and Simon took that as a good sign, and went out to the parterre garden to discuss if they'd taken enough penstemon cuttings last year to fill in any holes in the corner beds. This led to bickering about how many of which color they had put in two years ago and how many of those had died. When they couldn't agree, Simon retrieved his garden journal for proof that they'd planted fifteen Garnets and all had survived their first year. By the time the question had been settled, it was time for coffee.

Pru was halfway through a cinnamon bun when she, Simon, and Evelyn—soup ladle in hand—paused and listened to a muffled ring.

"Yours," Simon said. Pru went in search of her phone and found it at the bottom of her bag in the mudroom.

"Pru Parke, this is Tabby," the scratchy voice said.

"Hello, Tabby, how are you?"

"Well and good, thanks. Now, I've done what you asked and I've made a list of the visitors Mrs. Temple had. You know, the regular ones I remembered."

"That's great," Pru said. "Perhaps I'll drop round and collect it. Would that be all right?"

"Grand," Tabby replied. "I was that scared you would ask me to send it on email, and I'd have to tell you it's only a piece of paper."

"I'll be there within the hour."

"You quitting for the day?" Simon asked when she'd ended the call.

"We were finished, weren't we?" Pru asked, sorting through her pile of shoes in the mudroom in search of a decent pair. "Unless you'd like to get a start on resetting the stone pavers under the kitchen garden gate?"

"I believe I'll wait until we've hired that assistant."

"Will you be back before Danny?" Evelyn asked.

Danny had gone off soon after Christopher, saying he had tracked down an old friend and perhaps he might stop in at the Royal Oak, because Arlo wanted to give him a proper tour of the place. Pru had dug out a spare key to the mudroom door for him. "Just in case we're gone when you return," she had said.

"Probably, I will," Pru said to Evelyn. "But at least he can come in and make himself at home."

"It's good to have a young person round the place," Ev replied. Pru agreed.

~

There was no red Jaguar parked in front of the white monolith when Pru arrived. Next door, Tabby had the kettle on and a plate of biscuits on the table. Pru would need some of what she called "serious food" before long, but now accepted the cup and took a custard cream. Perhaps Christopher would be free for lunch later.

"You see," Tabby said, pushing the paper across the table, "I've organized it by day and the time, and then the car. It's easy for me to remember time of day, because of what I was doing at that moment. I've always had a good mind for details."

Pru scanned the information, which dated back a couple of weeks and had been written in pencil on notebook paper that had a ragged edge where it had been torn out. She could identify the people by their name, description, or make of car—Arlo, Acantha, Finley. She saw that Claudia had left with Finley on Wednesday morning and returned that evening—off to the herb nursery north of Bristol, Finley said. The overall comings and goings fit with Tabby's description of Claudia's quiet life being punctuated by bursts of activity.

"What's this highlighted bit down here?" Pru asked. The yellow marker had smeared the penciled words.

"Oh, I forgot that the fellow in the little blue car came twice that day, so I made a note of it down there."

That day was Thursday, the day before Claudia was found dead. Finley had driven her to and from the meeting at the garden site, then gone back that evening to collect the signed papers, which had gone missing. She pointed to a scratched-out line. "What was this?"

"That's Mr. Temple."

Pru squinted, trying to read behind the crosshatching. "Why did you cross him off?"

"Because I wasn't asked about him, only about visitors."

"You mean, he came and went twice on ..."

"Wednesday," Tabby said. "Mrs. Temple was away from late morning on to evening. Probably too sad to stay home, because that's the day I told you about, when they lost their little dog."

Pru looked up from her tea. "I'm not sure they had a dog," she said.

"Cat?"

"No," Pru said. "Danny—Claudia's son—said they had no pets."

"Well, then, what was Mr. Temple burying out there in the back garden?"

CHAPTER 18

Pru leapt up from Tabby's table and went to the window. The brick wall that ran down between the houses was low enough for Pru to see over it and into the Temple back garden. The oval-shaped lawn next door was ringed by a planting bed that was deeper at the back than on the sides. On her brief visit inside the white monolith, Pru had viewed the back garden from the open-plan kitchen and living area. She remembered the one plant that had caught her eye—an Asian mahonia, a striking evergreen shrub known for its upright stature and horizontal, prickly branches. The specimen in the Temple back garden had been different. Instead of growing straight up, it listed to the right, its branches pointing in the air or at the ground. Just as it might look if it had been dug up and couldn't settle back in the frozen soil.

Was it still there? Pru couldn't see it from her vantage point looking out Tabby's kitchen window, because a narrow yew was in her line of sight. Pru shifted to one side before she could spot her target.

Yes, still there, rising from the low, mounded forms around it. It still leaned, looking a bit like a wonky windmill. And now, staring at it, Pru thought the leaves were turning black, as it would if its roots had been exposed and the plant was dying slowly.

"There?" she asked, pointing. "Is that where he was digging?"

"Yes," Tabby said, joining her at the window. "But why else would he be digging in frozen soil if he hadn't needed to?"

"I don't know, but I think I'd like to take a closer look."

"You want to go over there, into their garden?" Tabby asked.

"Yes, because ..." Pru couldn't quite say why—the words hadn't formed in her mind yet. "I'm sure it's nothing. But there's a problem with that mahonia, and you know how it is, you hate to see a plant in distress."

"I don't think Mr. Temple is home at the moment," Tabby said.

"That might be for the best," Pru replied.

The two women looked at each other for a moment, neither speaking, then Tabby turned and led Pru out to the entry.

"Right," Tabby said, wrapping a scarf round her neck and pulling her knit hat down to her eyebrows so that her apple-red cheeks pooched out. She donned her coat and picked up her rocking stool. "You just be careful. I'll plant myself on the pavement to keep an eye out. You'll have to go into the garden through the front—we don't have a common gate. If you hear me do this—" she stuck her forefingers in her mouth and whistled two short bursts so loud Pru blinked "—means he's here. You won't have time to get out the way you go in, so you'll have to climb over the wall or hide back in the corner to keep from being seen."

A nervous giggle erupted from Pru's throat. This was ridiculous—covert operations to check on the health of a plant? Still, what did she have to tell Christopher otherwise? *There's something nefarious under the mahonia, so you'd best send SOCO.* No, she needed more concrete information. At least it wasn't a dead body. Probably.

Pru and Tabby walked out as if they were on a casual stroll of the neighborhood. At the pavement, Tabby plopped down on her stool and then nodded Pru on her way. Pru continued to amble until she'd made it halfway up the Temple front walk, and then hurried to the metal gate at the side of the house that led to the back garden. Good, it wasn't locked. She went in and closed it behind her, glancing out to the pavement where Tabby, rocking on her garden stool, gave her a thumbs-up.

Even though the house stood empty, Pru skirted the lawn as if staying out of someone's line of sight. She was careful to keep her feet on the grass, because just inside the planting bed was a wide band of crocus in bloom, looking like a thick lilac necklace.

She approached the mahonia carefully. Even though the shrub was further back into the mixed planting than she had realized, she could see its leaves were indeed turning black and the spiny tips beginning to curl under. If this place had anything to do with Claudia's death, then she knew better than to destroy evidence, and so she remained on the grass and gazed into the border to get an idea of what had happened.

A shrubby mugo pine blocked her view of the ground at the base of the mahonia. Pru moved to the side and dropped to her knees in the grass. She put her hands on her thighs and leaned into the border. Yes—there she spotted the telltale sign that the plant had been disturbed. The wood and roots of a mahonia are bright yellow, easy to spot, and she could see them sticking out of the soil as if they'd been cut or hacked through when the plant had been dug up. The mahonia had been dropped back into its hole, but the hard, frozen ground had not been accommodating, and the result was that the shrub sat askew. Was there something underneath the loosened root ball? She leaned in a bit further.

Two sharp blasts of Tabby's whistle sent a shock wave through Pru. She lost her balance and toppled headfirst into the bed. At the last second, she put her hands out, saving herself from landing face-first in a low, twiggy barberry, but flattening crocus as she did so. The barberry's thorns grazed her chin and caught on her scarf, but she barely noticed as she scrambled up with one thought: Ellis Temple was home and she must flee.

Instead, she stood frozen.

She'd never make it out through the gate in time—he was sure to see her. She'd have to climb the brick wall and drop into Tabby's garden. No, that wasn't an option, either. When had she ever been able to scale a five-foot-high wall? These thoughts came to her in the moment after Tabby's alarm, as Pru's heart beat a rapid-fire rhythm. She was one second away from flinging herself into the bed and hiding behind a rangy rhododendron, when she heard a single, longer whistle blast.

"Sorry—false alarm!" Tabby called from the gate. She'd tucked her plastic stool under an arm and stood, puffing like a steam engine. "I saw something red and panicked. It's only Sameer and his Royal Mail van."

The adrenaline drained from Pru's body in an instant, and she almost collapsed on the spot. On wobbly legs, she made for the gate.

"Did you see anything?" Tabby asked.

Pru shook her head and then nodded. She cleared her throat, trying to find her voice. "I'm not sure I know what I was looking for. I'm going to tell Christopher."

Pru argued with herself on the short drive to the police station. So Ellis had dug up a plant—what of it? He hadn't been burying a body, obviously. Not even one for a pet. But he'd come home during the day while his wife was out. He'd gone into the dim light of a frigid winter afternoon, and dug in the garden. He had, most probably, murdered that mahonia.

Perhaps she could ask Christopher to arrest him for that? She giggled and then got hold of herself—she mustn't sound crazy. *Think, Pru.*

If not a body, what would Ellis Temple have buried? What might he have needed to get rid of?

Who had cooked up the dwale that Claudia drank? Acantha said the concoction would've been strained and the resulting dregs of plant material must've been disposed of.

Kitchen scraps at Greenoak were put in the compost to break down and be put back into the garden as mulch. Even in freezing weather, their compost piles were large enough to be hot at the center, and that's where they would bury what needed to break down. But dumping something barely under the soil surface in this weather? It wouldn't break down, that's for certain. It would be the same as putting it in the deep freeze.

As she pulled her Mini into the car park and switched off the engine, Pru burst the bubble of her rising excitement by reminding herself that Ellis Temple had been in Oxford all day and night Thursday, returning home Friday morning to find his wife hanging from the first-floor landing. His movements—or lack thereof—were on the hotel's CCTV. Could he have had an accomplice?

Her story would probably amount to nothing, but regardless, Pru would tell it in a sober manner to the detective inspector running the enquiry. Better too much information than not enough, yes?

In the station as she relinquished her pruners, Pru looked at the grimy palms of her hands and only then noticed that the knees of her trousers were damp and muddy.

"Been at it, have you?" the desk sergeant said pleasantly. "I'll let him know you're here." He nodded over to the seating area, occupied by only one other person, a woman whose sleek chestnut hair hung in the sort of manageable layers Pru always dreamed about and who wore one of those suits that appeared both casual and businesslike at the same time. Pru took a seat across from her and attempted a smile.

The woman glanced at the desk sergeant, at Pru, and then away. She sat poised on the edge of the chair and fixed her eyes on the door that led further into the station, her hands clutching a shapeless bag of soft leather. She looked as if she were about to run for a bus.

"I've learned to turn them in first thing," Pru said, just as a matter of conversation, "although I've never considered secateurs to be a weapon."

The woman tore her gaze away from the door and looked at Pru as if replaying the comment. She breathed and then smiled. "I don't know. I've sliced a slug or two in half with mine."

Pru laughed. "Yes, well, you're right there. Nothing like waking up one morning to find your hostas looking like Swiss cheese. You're a gardener?"

"Can't help myself, can I?" the woman asked. She released the grip on her bag, drew out a slim, engraved case, and offered a card. "It's my business—of sorts. I sell garden ornaments, you see. Direct and retail. We often use my garden for photo shoots."

Pru looked at the card—Art in the Hedges. Garden ornaments. Hadn't she only just been talking with someone about this?

"We don't deal in your fake antique Romulus-and-Remus imports from Italy," the woman continued, beginning to sound like a sales brochure. "We specialize in bespoke pieces—hand carved here in Britain from Portland stone. They give that quiet beauty we're known for and they will last for centuries, of course."

A light bulb went off in Pru's head—a light bulb bright enough to illuminate an entire ballroom. She knew who this woman was. She began an excavation of her own bag.

"I'd love to have a chat with you," Pru said, coming up with her card case, open and empty. She continued the search. "My brother and I are head gardeners at Greenoak. We're just the other side of Romsey. It's the parterre garden, you see. We need some solid stonework to carry it through the year." At last she brought out a battered card and presented it to the woman.

The desk sergeant called out over the counter, "Detective Inspector Pearse is on his way out."

The woman shot out of her chair.

"I'm sorry," she said, "I must be on my way now."

"But ma'am," the sergeant said, "you asked for him."

"Yes, well," the woman said over her shoulder as she grabbed her coat and made for the door, "I've changed my mind. That is, it's not important."

Pru hurried after her, catching the door as it was about to close. "Do you have time for a coffee?" she asked. "Please—I'd really like to talk with you. Can't you wait? You don't have to wait in here—look, see the café at the bottom of the hill? I'll meet you there."

The woman backed up a step, her gaze darting over Pru's shoulder, into the station. "Well, I don't know—"

"Please," Pru said. "We desperately need some sort of statue for the garden. The children dressed as the four seasons or something. Right? I won't be two ticks."

Before she could refuse, Pru turned back into the station as Christopher came out into the lobby.

"Sorry, sir," the desk sergeant said. "You've lost one of them —the one who wouldn't give her name."

"I know who she is," Pru said. She looked down at the business card in her hand, and then up at her husband. "Laura Quigley."

Christopher glanced round the lobby. "Where's she gone?"

"She was nervous," Pru said, looking to the desk sergeant for confirmation.

"She was that," he agreed. "I've seen 'em like that, ready to leg it if they get a fright. I'm surprised you kept her here as long as you did, Ms. Parke."

"Not long enough, though," Pru said, turning back to Christopher. "She's one of them, isn't she? A member of Ellis Temple's business consortium?"

"Yes," he said.

"Had you asked her here?"

"No—but I was intending to question her again."

Pru looked out the door and down the hill. Laura Quigley was nowhere to be seen. "Well, I'm meeting her for coffee—at least I hope I am—and maybe I can find out what she wanted to tell you."

"Don't you think I should be the one asking her?"

"Will you go down to the café," Pru said, "and force her back to the station to sit in an interview room?"

"If she's come here about the enquiry," Christopher said, "I may have to do just that."

"But she's expecting me," Pru said. "We're going to talk about garden ornaments. You see—it's perfect."

"Does she know who you are?" Christopher asked.

"No," Pru said, "she thinks I want to buy a statue. And I do. Simon and I have talked about something for the parterre garden. But, maybe after a bit, I could work the conversation round to …"

"Murder?"

Put that way, it didn't sound likely.

"Do you want to come along?" she asked.

Christopher thought for a moment. "No, you go on. I'll follow in a few minutes. Wait now." He took Pru's hands, turned them over, and saw them streaked with mud. He looked at her knees—trousers still soggy—and lifted her chin, examining the small scratches. "What have you been doing?"

Her hand flew to her face. "Oh, I forgot. I have something to offer. But it can wait—I'd better go before she chickens out."

~

Laura Quigley sat at a small round table in the back of the tiny café, with a coffee in front of her that looked untouched. She didn't appear poised to flee, but neither did she look at ease.

"Thanks so much for waiting," Pru said. "Isn't it funny how you meet just the person you need to in the most unusual places."

"Yes, well …" Laura picked up her coffee spoon and gave it a puzzled look as if she wasn't sure what to do with it.

"I'll just get my coffee," Pru said. "Won't be a minute."

At the counter, her stomach growled. This should be lunch for her, but she didn't want to be busy with eating when there was a witness—or a person of interest or whatever Laura might be called—on the verge of escape. Pru ordered a small latte.

"Well," she said, settling back at the table, "let me tell you about our parterre garden, and perhaps you'll have some suggestions."

Laura brightened and took a drink of her coffee and they began talking about gardens and art, although Pru kept on alert for any opportunity to turn the conversation to her own purposes.

"Stonework can be both beauty and function, really," Laura said. "A well-carved bench, for example, has its uses. A stone water feature brings such life to a landscape and is good for wildlife. Although for great effect, a large statue can't be beat as a centerpiece or tucked within the border, surprising and delighting visitors when they come across it."

Laura pulled up the company's online catalog on her phone. "You mentioned the statue series of children representing the seasons. We don't carry those at the moment, but I know just the ones you mean, and special commissions are no problem. We do have a lovely lady with a basket—you know the one I mean, don't you? Let me see where that is." She flipped through screens until one image caught Pru's eye and a door opened.

"Oh, look at this one—is that a monk?" The figure wore a long robe tied with a belt and held an armful of plants. "That's a fine rendition. I can even tell what he's holding—rosemary, and those broader leaves are sage, I think. Is he medieval?"

"Yes," Laura said, "or thereabouts. Now if I can just find that lady."

Christopher might walk in any moment, and Pru had hoped to move the conversation further along than it was. Ill-timed though it might be, she took a leap.

"I've become quite interested in medieval gardens lately," Pru said. "That's how I met Claudia Temple."

Laura froze.

"You're part of Ellis Temple's business group, aren't you?" Pru asked.

Laura flushed and glanced round her at the empty seats. "Is this a setup?"

"How can this be a setup? Did someone ask you to come to the Winchester police station today?"

"No one asked me. I came because ..."

"Because you wanted to see the police."

"I didn't lie to that detective," Laura said.

"Of course you didn't," Pru said with unfounded conviction. What did she know of Laura Quigley?

"Are you police?" the woman asked.

"No, but I'm married to Detective Inspector Pearse. He's the one who talked with you."

Laura pointed at her. "You said you were a gardener."

"And I am. I became interested in the medieval garden before Claudia died, and then Christopher took on the enquiry. We both want to find out what happened to Claudia, but from different perspectives. Had you ever met her?"

Laura's face reddened, but she didn't look as if she were

about to take flight, so that had to be a good thing. Instead, she stared at the table. Pru waited. The screen of Laura's phone went dark. Pru kept waiting, stirring her coffee for something to do. The door to the café opened, and it was Christopher.

"Laura, here's Detective Inspector Pearse."

Her head shot up. She threw Pru an accusing look.

"Yes, all right," Pru said, "I did tell him we would be here. But you wanted to talk with him, didn't you?

"Hello, Ms. Quigley," Christopher said when he reached the table.

"Hello," she whispered.

"Would you like another coffee?" he offered.

Laura shook her head. Christopher pulled another chair over and sat.

"You wanted to see me?"

She tucked in her chin and frowned. "What I told you was the truth. It's only, the last few days …"

"You realized there's more?" Christopher suggested. "Something you've only just remembered about Ellis Temple?"

Pru, relieved of duty, sat back with a sigh.

"There's never been anything between Ellis and me," Laura said, keeping her eyes down as she shredded her paper napkin. "Oh, a little harmless flirting over the years, but what of it? I … my husband and I separated before Christmas, and since then, I've been a bit adrift. And then it was time for one of our twice-yearly meetings. We, all of us, look forward to these—they're rather energizing. I come away with good ideas for my company."

"And this time?" Christopher asked.

Laura nodded at the prompt. "After dinner on Thursday, we all had another drink and then the others went to their rooms, and only Ellis and I were left in the bar. He was quite charming as always."

Pru wondered where that charm had gone, because she certainly had seen none of it.

"But this time," Laura continued, "I was vulnerable. I can see that now, but at the time it didn't matter. We went back to my room." She swallowed hard. "This isn't something I'm proud of, and I'd rather it didn't become common knowledge."

So far, this was a story of infidelity—on Ellis's part—and Pru couldn't quite see what it had to do with Claudia's murder.

"And the two of you were together the entire night?" Christopher asked.

Laura nodded once, and then her brows furrowed. "Actually, I'm rather unclear on the rest of the night. We were talking … after … and I suppose it came to me what I'd done, and I said as much. Ellis was very kind and said he would take all the blame, but hadn't we both needed … oh God, I felt such a fool. Humiliated, even. Here he's a married man, and I would never … "

She picked up her coffee and set it down again, the cup rattling in the saucer.

"Take your time," Christopher said.

Pru, rarely on hand to watch Christopher interrogate someone, was fascinated with the proceedings, but at the same time felt a sympathetic pang of humiliation for Laura.

After a deep breath, the woman put a hand to her chest and said, "The consequences of my actions seemed to crush me, and I told Ellis as much. How could I sleep now, I asked him, knowing what I'd done. He said why didn't I take one of my sleeping tablets, and so I did."

"He knew you took sleeping medication?" Christopher asked.

Laura shrugged. "The thing about our group is that we cover all aspects of running a small business, from accounts, to marketing to … more personal struggles. We've discussed my sleep problem, the scarcity of British silk thread for weaving, the worry that Regency bathroom taps will become old hat. Owning your own company is not for the faint of heart."

"Ellis Temple was in bed with you all night?" Christopher asked and Laura flinched.

"Of course," the woman blurted out and then dropped her head, and continued quietly. "Well, he was there when I woke up the next morning. He was ever so kind and repeated what he'd said about how what had happened needn't go any further and … oh, I don't know. I just wanted to forget the entire thing."

"Had Mr. Temple ever talked about his wife's money—the inheritance from her father? That he needed an influx of cash into his company?"

"There was always one or the other of us bemoaning our lack of capital, Inspector. Ellis has opened a vintage line to his business and those old cars are incredibly expensive."

"Was he short of money?"

"He didn't say specifically. He did say that the outlay for his expansion had set him back, but he seemed confident it was a good investment."

"Ms. Quigley, did you leave the hotel with Ellis Temple during the night?"

Pru saw the question startle Laura—it came from nowhere, just as the woman had thought she was on more stable ground, talking business matters.

She took a sharp breath. "I certainly did not! I told you, I took a sleeping tablet and they always knock me out … and …" She blinked as if trying to bring a thought into focus.

"What is it?" Christopher asked.

"I did not leave the hotel, and I have witnesses," Laura said, but sounding not entirely happy about it. "This is what has concerned me since you spoke to me. I checked out quite early that Friday morning, and when I looked at my bill and found a tea service I didn't remember ordering, I asked about it at the desk. The overnight clerk was still on, and he said I had come into reception at half past one o'clock that morning wearing my dressing gown and asked for tea and scones. It's the sort of hotel where they don't say no to a guest. They served me at a table in the reception area, and after, he said, I went back to my room."

"And you didn't remember doing that?" Pru asked.

Laura shrugged. "It's a rare side effect of my sleeping tablet. I may get up in my sleep and … look awake and do things that I don't recall the next morning. I once drove to the all-night shop in our town, bought five Tunnock's caramel wafers, and stood at the counter and ate them. But, really, these things happen so seldom that it's never been, you know, a problem."

"Was Ellis in your room when you went back?"

"I don't know, you see. It isn't that this incident of tea in the wee hours of the morning is hazy in my memory, it's that I have no recollection of it at all. And so, I put it out of my mind, because to me, it was another reminder of my behavior, and nothing I wanted to dwell on."

"You didn't mention it to Temple?" Christopher asked.

Laura's face reddened.

"That's it, isn't it?" she asked. "I did. He was leaving early that morning, too, and I asked did he remember me getting up and leaving the room. He didn't answer at once, but then he said, oh yes, he remembered that I had wanted another drink and went out to the bar and came back in a bit. 'Whisky,' he told me, 'from the taste of it.' Whisky! There's a thing he doesn't know about me—I don't drink whisky. Well, that was that—I didn't want to hear anything else about our night together."

Christopher watched Laura, who now met his eyes. He nodded. "Thank you for coming back to tell me this. You'll need to amend your statement—perhaps you could go back to the station with Pru and see Detective Sergeant Grey."

"Yes," Pru said. "Of course."

Good thing Sophie was back on the enquiry, because Pru wouldn't've wanted to hand Laura over to John Upstone.

Christopher rose and gave a slight nod toward the door.

"I'll be right back," Pru said to Laura. She followed him out of the café and onto the pavement. "Where will you be?"

"Oxford. I need to confirm this latest version of her story and ask a few more questions of my own."

"In person?"

"It isn't as easy to lie to someone face-to-face."

"Someone at the hotel lied to you?"

"That's what I intend to find out. It could be unintentional. People withhold information for all sorts of reasons. Often they like to blame it on the person asking the question. 'I didn't tell you that, because you didn't ask'—that's a favorite excuse. No matter how relevant they think it might be."

"This means Ellis is back on your suspect list."

"He'd never been taken off, but I'd say this moves him up a notch or two." Christopher took her arm. "Will you be all right?"

"Yes," Pru said. "You go—let me know how you get on."

He nodded, then glanced down at her muddy trousers.

"Are you sure you don't want to explain?"

"Later."

When Pru went back into the café, Laura asked if she could stop in the loo. Pru, now in the unusual position of police escort, said yes, but then worried the entire five minutes Laura was out of her sight in case the woman had decided to escape by standing on the toilet and crawling out one of those tiny windows. Then Pru thought she'd perhaps been watching too many police programs on television. Still, she was one second away from marching in to check when Laura reappeared.

They walked up the hill to the station, and Pru said, "Do you always remember to dress when you go out on these nighttime sleeping jaunts?"

Laura gave her a sideways glance.

"It isn't a police question," Pru hastened to add. "I just wondered if when you're asleep like that, you remember to put clothes on."

"There's a part of my subconscious," Laura said, "that must understand propriety. Of course, I'd gone to the shop that time in my nightie and robe, too. The desk clerk at the hotel told me I had no shoes on. I suppose I knew I wasn't going outdoors."

At the station, Pru waited in the lobby as Detective Sergeant Sophie Grey took Laura back for her amended statement.

"Good thing you came back," the desk sergeant said to Pru, as he handed over her pruners.

"Thanks," Pru said. She sat in the lobby and rummaged in her bag, coming up with a peppermint that stuck like glue to its wrapper. Beggars can't be choosers, she thought, peeling off the recalcitrant cellophane and popping the candy in her mouth to calm her growling stomach. She'd taken a chair in direct line of the sad-sack spider plant, and after a few minutes, she could stand it no longer. "Mind if I clean that up a bit?" she asked. "Just snip off the dead leaves, you know."

"Have at it," the desk sergeant replied.

While Pru got to work with her pruners, there was a flurry of activity in the station lobby, as a few uniformed officers and one or two customers came in and went out. Were they called customers? She'd never thought to ask Christopher that and filed it away for later. The spider plant did not take up much of her time—she was long finished a half hour later when Laura emerged, looking startled when she saw Pru.

"You didn't need to wait," she said, the relief of telling her story evident in her easy manner and smile. "I couldn't've escaped."

"I wanted to make sure you knew I'm serious about the garden ornaments," Pru said.

Sophie Grey emerged, too, gave Pru a nod, and spoke to the

desk sergeant.

Laura buttoned up her coat. "This is so unreal," she said. "I can't believe Ellis would do anything to harm his wife, but all these questions"—she shot a look at Sophie—"is that what they think?"

"Is that what you thought? Isn't that why you came to Winchester from Oxford?"

"I suppose it is. Are they going to arrest him?"

Pru shrugged. "I'm not really part of the enquiry."

"Pull the other one, why don't you," Laura said quietly.

"So," Pru said, "you'll give me a quote on the four season statues?"

The subject of business brought a smile to Laura. "Yes, of course I will."

When she'd gone, Sophie said, "Her conscience caught up with her."

"Good thing, too," Pru replied. "Also, it shows you what sort of hotel it is if you can walk into reception at two o'clock in the morning and order tea and scones."

"I doubt they blink an eye," Sophie said, "and only ask 'fruit or plain?'"

"Is this a break in the case?" Pru asked, edging toward that mix of relief and fear and repulsion.

"Not exactly a break," Sophie said, "but interesting. It's taken the boss up to Oxford, and it's led Detective Superintendent Upstone to assign me the task of going over the CCTV from the hotel. Again. There's my evening sorted."

"But there's just the one camera?"

Sophie nodded. "On the drive. So, I hear you're the one who persuaded Laura Quigley to stay and tell her story. Good work."

"Happy to do my part, but it was only because of our garden connection. Which leads me to tell you about something Ellis Temple's neighbor noticed."

Two men walked into the station arguing with each other

about a car being clamped and demanding to see someone from traffic.

Sophie nodded to the door behind the desk sergeant. "Do you want to come back?"

"No, it's not much." Pru explained about the uprooted mahonia. "Claudia was away on Wednesday with Finley Martin. He took her to an herb nursery near Bristol, and they didn't return until that evening. Ellis was due in Oxford, wasn't he? So, what was he burying in the garden? And then there's this. Acantha rang this morning to say that the dwale—the herbal mixture—would've been strained and then there would have been the left-overs to dispose of." Pru frowned. "Ellis doesn't seem the type to cook up his own herbal mixture, but it's worrisome, don't you think?"

"Did you tell the boss?" Sophie asked.

"I didn't have the chance," Pru said. "He was eager to get away to Oxford."

"We'll take care of it. Of course it's all for naught if there's no evidence of Temple leaving the hotel. Especially when we've several suspects so close to hand that night."

"Yes," Pru said. "They all wanted Claudia's money. Not for themselves, but for the garden. It's odd."

"Well," Sophie said, "I'd better get to it. You all right?"

"Yes. See you."

Pru wasn't all right. She felt hollow, as if she'd given all she could and her gas tank was empty. Petrol tank. This was a fanciful thought until she remembered she'd missed lunch and here it was gone four o'clock. She looked out the window of the station to see that it was already dark. She'd had about enough of winter.

After Sophie went back into the station's inner sanctum, Pru remained in the lobby and thought. Christopher's journey to Oxford would be about an hour up and an hour return, plus time for questioning. He could be back in time for dinner.

There was one more thing she wanted to do before she left Winchester, and she had plenty of time. She wanted to talk with Sabine. Was she still somewhere in Somerset? Had she returned to Orchard House? Had she decided to leave for good? Pru sent a text: **Are you home?**

A few moments later, a reply came. **At a gallery near the Cathedral.**

I'm in town. Do you have time to meet?

Twenty minutes? Sabine replied.

Royal Oak is near you.

The long, low pub held a comfortable crowd—groups of people at tables or standing in clusters, and a line of drinkers at the bar. Pru scanned all the faces until she'd reached the back room, where she had talked with Arlo that first day. There, Sabine sat at a table next to Danny, who had his sketchbook out.

"Blind contour drawing," she was saying. "So here, start with a fresh sheet and your pencil at the top. Look at"—Sabine glanced up and saw Pru in front of them. She held her hand palm out, and Pru stopped. "Look at Pru and not at the paper. Let your eye follow her outline, and as you do, let your pencil do the same on the paper."

Pru had never modeled before and wasn't sure if she was allowed to breathe. She kept as still as possible until Danny said, "Okay, can I look?"

"Can I move?" Pru asked.

"Yes and yes," Sabine said. She leaned back against the settle, looking entirely at ease.

Pru broke her pose and leaned over the table to see Danny's work as he began to fill in the sketch. She was surprised to recognize herself in it. "How did you two know to find each other?" she asked, sitting down.

"I noticed someone with a sketchbook and couldn't help being nosy," Sabine said. "It's like you and plants. And when I saw Danny's work, I knew he was the same artist whose work you showed me."

"Artist," Danny said. "I don't know about that."

"Well, this couldn't be more perfect," Pru said. "I'm going up to the bar and order a sandwich—can I get you two anything?"

She left them discussing shading and smudging and charcoal, and returned to the table carrying a tray with her coronation chicken sandwich, several packets of crisps, and three pints of bitter. Danny leapt up and took it from her, all the while asking Sabine about a watercolor wash. Pru left them to it, listening, not understanding, but enjoying the talk.

At a pause in the discussion, she asked, "Is Arlo around?"

"He went off a few minutes ago, but said he'd be back," Danny said, tipping the last of the crisps into his mouth.

Then, the three of them had a good chat wandering through topics of interest but of no great import. Sabine told how she had spent a month in Inverness two years earlier and had done a series of paintings focusing on Urquhart Castle on Loch Ness, but had spent most of her time in an enormous bookshop housed in an old church. Danny said he and Libby had their eye on a garden flat and would have room for a few veg and herbs and asked Pru for recommendations. Pru wanted to know the difference between painting in oil and acrylic and how to tell the media apart when you look at someone's work.

But through it all, Pru reserved a fair portion of her thoughts for worry. Did Sabine look rested and renewed because she and John had reconciled—or was that a steely resolution to go her own way that Pru saw? Was Ellis involved in Claudia's death? Danny had given no indication that he thought so. It seemed he didn't like his stepfather for a host of other reasons, but not murder.

Had Ellis cooked up dwale in the kitchen when Claudia was

out and about with Finley Martin and then buried the dregs in the garden? How had he forced Claudia to drink the stuff? Pru recalled the many times Ellis had done his best to point the finger at Acantha for leaving herbs and mixtures on the doorstep and coercing Claudia to try them.

Had he slept with Laura Quigley in order to have an alibi? How did he get from Oxford to Winchester to kill Claudia and then back again without being seen? Why would he do it? Pru's thoughts wrapped round one another until they were a mass of wriggling red worms in the center of a compost pile. When Arlo approached the table, she swept away her tangle of worries and said, "Can you join us? The pub isn't too busy?"

"Yeah, well, hiya, Pru," he said. "It is picking up, but I've just had a quick dash home and back so that I could show Danny this." He waved a half sheet of paper, limp with age, and then held it against his chest as if he'd just won a school prize.

It was a drawing done with crayons. The setting was the out-of-doors, represented by a large round tree and a border of grass at the bottom. Three people stood with a picnic basket: a man with spiky hair, a woman with a broad smile, and a boy whose features were disguised by a large stuffed bear in his arms.

Danny screwed up his face. "Did I do that?"

"You did—you were five and a half years old," Arlo said, and turned to Sabine. "You can see his talent, can't you, even then? As a lad he was always messing about with drawing. Good, innit?"

"It isn't good," Danny said, his face scarlet.

"But it is," Sabine said. "Your representation is quite developed, and you understood position in space and the relationship among all the parts. What was the bear's name?"

Danny stared at the drawing. "Bear," he said.

"Was he really as big as you?" Pru asked.

"He was," Arlo said. "I remember Bear. I'm sorry to say I

don't remember much else from those years. I was seriously losing the plot about then. Your mum was right to leave." His face lost its animation. "Wonder what's happened to him, your Bear."

"Mum kept him." Danny shut his sketchbook. "I've got to be going."

"Yeah," Arlo said, "all right, son. Look, tomorrow, I want to be there."

"I don't want to think about tomorrow."

The barman called out to the boss.

"Better get back to work," Arlo said. He rubbed his hands on his denims and shrugged. "See ya."

"I'll be on my way, too," Sabine said. "Danny, we'll be in touch, right?"

"Yeah, thanks," Danny said, standing.

"Sabine?" Pru followed her out of the back room, but over her shoulder, said to Danny, "I'll be right back."

Sabine stopped near the bar to pull on her coat. She looked past Pru to Danny, who had opened his sketchbook again.

"I'm glad you wanted me to meet him," Sabine said. "I hope he keeps at the drawing. He's just the age Tom was." She dipped her head, looking into her bag instead of at Pru. "The age Tom will always be."

"I'm sorry if that made it hard for you," Pru said.

"No," Sabine said. "Not hard. At least, not as hard as it used to be."

"How are you?" Pru dared to ask. "How is John? How are the two of you?"

"We're … talking," Sabine said.

"Good. That's good—isn't it?"

Sabine answered with half a shrug. "We'll see."

"While Danny is here, perhaps you and John could come to Greenoak for dinner again. Come early, if you like, and you two artists can spend the afternoon drawing, and Christopher and

John can"—Pru waved her hand vaguely—"go fishing or something."

Sabine laughed as she gave Pru a hug. "Thanks for not giving up."

That fed Pru as much as the sandwich did. She went back to Danny with a warm glow that cooled when she found him staring at the table instead of drawing.

"Will you be going back to Greenoak now?" she asked.

Danny slumped back against the settle. "I've got to stop at Ellis's house first. He says he has some stuff of my mum's to give me."

"I'll go with you," Pru said, perhaps a bit too eager.

"No, it's all right," he said.

"I'd like to, really."

Danny frowned at her, and Pru realized her eagerness might be giving too much away. What could she tell him about Ellis to explain her reluctance at letting the young man walk into that house alone? He didn't need to hear a load of suspicions that she couldn't back up.

"I don't mean go in with you," Pru said, although she would do if he asked. "I'll go and wait outside. For moral support?"

Danny pulled his silver Honda up behind the red Jag, which was parked in front of the monolith. Pru had just enough room behind Danny, and away from the streetlight. As they'd arranged, she would stay in her car and wait until he came out, then they would return to Greenoak. Pru was grateful there were no floodlights or police cars on the street yet, indicating the big dig in the back garden hadn't started. Perhaps they were waiting until morning. She lowered her window when Danny got out of his car.

"Take your time," she said. "I'll wait here. But let me know if you need help carrying anything." Danny gave her a nod.

The lights were on at Tabby's house, the next one up. Pru hoped the neighbor wouldn't notice her arrival on the street, or she'd be out asking for an update on the enquiry. Pru also hoped Danny wouldn't be so long that she would need the loo, but she didn't think he want to spend that much time in Ellis's company, no matter what. She kept the engine idling and the heater on, staying warm and toasty, and checked her phone for messages. At an odd tapping sound, she lifted her head, looked out into the dark, and saw that it had started to rain. How long had it been since they'd had precipitation of any sort? But was that rain? As she squinted at it, the rain turned to snow—actual flakes, bypassing the sleet category altogether. Wait, now it was back to rain. Rain was good. It would warm them up to normal winter temperatures and melt all the—no, there it was snow again.

Pru's phone rang with a call from Christopher.

"Hiya," she said. "I'm glad it's you. Are you on your way back?"

"Just starting," he replied. "Are you home?"

"No, Ellis had some things of Claudia's for Danny to pick up, and I came along."

"Are you inside the house? Is Temple there?"

"I'm in my car waiting," Pru said, a stab of fear freezing her insides. "Why? What did you find out? Should I go in and get Danny?"

"Do not go in the house. Look, I'll have Grey send a car over."

"What is it?"

"Ellis Temple did leave the hotel that night," Christopher said. "The reason we didn't see his Jaguar on the hotel car park's CCTV is because he was driving Laura Quigley's car."

CHAPTER 19

Pru shivered. There it was—Ellis Temple lied about his whereabouts on the night Claudia was murdered. He'd taken Laura Quigley's car to disguise his movements.

"How did you find out?" she asked.

"Grey went through the footage again," Christopher said. "The first time, we were on the lookout for Temple's car, but this second go-round, she had Quigley's car model and number plate. He departed at eleven fifteen and returned at three thirty."

"How many cars come and go from a hotel in the middle of the night?" Pru asked.

"You'd be surprised. And the two cleaners—the fellows that thought so much of Temple because he'd let them drive his Jag—after I had another word with them, they changed their minds about what they saw that night. As it turns out, they do remember that he left."

"But Laura—"

"The desk clerk confirms her story," Christopher said.

A door slammed and Danny stalked out of the house, his head down and carrying a single carton with a large stuffed animal under his arm.

"He's come out, and he has Bear with him," she said, her voice breaking. She lowered her window as Danny approached his car.

"All right, Danny?" she called as a flurry of snow drifted in the window. She shot a nervous glance at the house.

"Berk," Danny said, and then added, "sorry, not you. He thinks he can …"

She didn't hear the rest because he'd popped the hatch on his car and was stowing the box and Bear.

"I'll follow you home," she said. "It's coming down a bit. You'll be careful, won't you?"

Danny slammed the hatch closed as Christopher, still on the phone, said, "Pru?"

Pru put up her window and said, "Danny's right—he is a berk."

"Do you see any sign of Temple?"

She scanned the house. All the lights seemed to be on, but there was no moving shadow within. "No, he's staying put, I guess." Danny pulled out. Pru put her phone on speaker and her Mini in gear. "Here we go."

"I'm staying on the line," Christopher said. "Is it snowing?"

"At the moment," Pru said, "but it changes back and forth, rain, snow."

"Is he heading to the A3090?" Christopher asked.

"Yes, it looks like it."

"Is anyone behind you?"

The question caught her short. She glanced in the rearview mirror and back to the road. "No." She looked again. "No, I don't think—" Her eyes darted to the road and the mirror, back and forth and then she saw them, headlights far behind. "Wait," she said. They disappeared, then reappeared again. Pru broke out in a sweat. "There is a car, but it's a ways back."

"I'm going to let Grey know. How far along are you?"

Pru had driven this road many times lately, but it was dark, and the precipitation had settled on snow, which changed the world round her. "Getting near the Straight Mile, I think."

"Stay on the call, and I'll be right back," Christopher said.

Pru concentrated on the road ahead. She wished Danny would drive a bit slower, but, at the same time, quicker so that they could get away from the car behind. It soon caught up with them, and kept varying its speed, pulling closer and then backing off. Could this be just some random driver who wanted to pass? At a bend in the road, she checked her rearview mirror and got a good look at the car—low, red, and sleek. A Jag.

They all three turned onto the Straight Mile, a road that wasn't all that straight, but had quite a few bends as it wended its way past small clusters of houses and into the countryside. Pru kept her eyes on Danny's taillights, not wanting to get too close. Once or twice, Ellis pulled out as if to overtake Pru, but headlights of an oncoming car stopped him. Otherwise, there was no traffic. The snow fell heavier now, and it felt as if the three of them were the only ones on earth.

"Christopher?" she asked, but he didn't answer. Still on his other call, asking Detective Sergeant Sophie Grey to send assistance.

Ellis sped up and pulled out again, but he did it at the worst time—on another curve in the road. As it passed, the Jag fishtailed in the slush, and Pru pumped the brakes lightly to keep from being hit. Not lightly enough, because the action sent her into a spin. Pru had few memories of bad winter weather and icy roads, and even less experience driving in dicey conditions, and now couldn't remember what her next move should be. She gripped the steering wheel to ride it out.

The spin was like the chase, slow, certainly not much faster than a merry-go-round. On the first circuit, Pru saw Danny's taillights and caught a glimpse of the Jaguar missing the bend and heading for a tree on the other side of the road. An oak, she noted without thinking. On her second full circle, she saw headlights. Had Danny skidded, too, and now faced her, or was this another car stopping to assist? No time to decide, as her Mini then broke from its spin and sailed sideways. Looking out her side window, Pru saw the tree trunk coming closer, closer. Then, the right front tire hit the ditch, pitching her forward at an angle, a second before her driver's-side door slammed into the trunk and the airbags went off in her face.

The entire episode couldn't've lasted longer than a few seconds, but had seemed like forever. Pru broke into action, panting and batting away the airbags as they deflated. Her headlights showed nothing but snowy, watery, muck. She looked across and out the passenger window and saw, not more than twenty feet away, Ellis emerging from the Jag and Danny leaping out of his own car. The Honda's headlights illuminated the road as if it were a theater set with fake snow sifting down from pillowcases and onto the stage.

Pru tried to get out of her car, but the driver's door was snug against the tree trunk. She clambered up and over the console, took the handle of the passenger door, and pushed. It opened only a couple of inches, meeting resistance in a tangle of bare twigs and branches.

She peered out and saw Danny approach Ellis. "You made her life miserable," he shouted.

"Danny!" Pru called through the narrow opening. "Can you help me, please? I'm stuck." Although, she wasn't as much panicked about being stuck in her car as she was about not being able to intervene between Danny and a murderer.

Ellis turned her way, squinting. "Was that you in front of me?" he asked in an accusatory tone. "Why are you here? What does any of this have to do with you?"

"You leave her alone," Danny said as he marched past his stepfather and to the Mini. He thrust his arm through the stems, took hold of the door handle, and gave it a yank. The opening widened another inch.

"Daniel," Ellis said, spreading his arms out, "be reasonable. These are family matters, and I don't like it that you're being influenced by outside parties with their own interests. We need to settle this between us."

Danny whirled round. "You aren't my family!"

"Danny," Pru said, "could you try again, please?" But it seemed nothing could distract the young man now. He advanced on Ellis as Pru began kicking the passenger door hoping for a few more inches so she could squeeze out.

"You've got to think of yourself now, Daniel," Ellis said in a pleading tone. "This is your chance."

"It's all *you* ever did, think of yourself," Danny shouted. "You never cared anything about my mum."

"I tried to sort out her life for her," Ellis snapped, the conciliatory tone gone from his voice. "It was hopeless. You must see that. Her life was one disaster after another."

"You can't say what someone else's life is," Danny said. "You aren't the judge of the world."

"I know chaos when I see it," Ellis shouted. "I did us all a favor."

Pru stopped kicking at the door and listened to the silence.

Danny's voice was low and rough. "What did you say?"

Ellis shook his head.

"I tried to take her in hand and make up for what you never had—that's what I meant."

"Danny?" Pru called. "Danny, I need some help here."

He paid her no attention. He didn't move. He stared at Ellis.

A thought hit Pru—her headlights were still on and the engine still running. The car had power. "Oh my God," she said, and pressed the switch for the passenger-side window, which slid down quietly on command. She crawled out, put a foot straight down into icy water, tripped over a branch, and landed on her hands and knees in the freezing muck.

Trying to catch her breath, Pru looked up at the scene,

backlit by the Honda's headlights. Ellis and Danny both stood stock-still, with great wads of snowflakes swirling round them.

"It was you?" Danny asked, so quietly Pru could barely hear.

"You haven't been served well by the parents you were given, Daniel," Ellis said, drawing himself up. "I mean to make up for that."

"You!"

Danny charged at Ellis, who took one step back, but the young man was quicker. He threw such a punch its impact resounded in the stillness of the night and sent Ellis flying backward. He hit the Jag with a *bam,* sank to the ground, and lay still.

All at once Pru heard a siren—more than one—and a host of blinking blue lights appeared. She wasn't sure where they all came from, and at the moment, she didn't care. Uniformed officers poured out of vehicles as Pru ran to Danny, skidding a bit on the snowy road, and put an arm round him. He hadn't moved from the spot as he stared at Ellis.

"Did I kill him?" he asked her.

Pru cut her eyes at the figure, slumped like a rag doll in the slush, and thought she saw a foot move. "No, of course you didn't," she said. "Are you all right?"

"Pru?"

It was Sophie. She approached them at the same time she motioned the PCs toward Ellis.

"Hello, Danny," Sophie said. "I'm Detective Sergeant Grey. Are you two all right? Look, why don't you come sit in my car, and we'll sort this out. No need to stand in the rain."

It was, indeed, rain again and seemed to have finally made up its mind to stay that way, because it was coming down in buckets. As Sophie led them to her car, the change in the weather caused Pru alarm.

"You might want to look at that mahonia," she said. "If it warms up too quickly, whatever you might find wouldn't be in as good a shape."

"Will do," Sophie said. "So much for our Hampshire deep freeze, right?"

Pru and Danny settled themselves in the backseat of Sophie's car. Pru shivered. The young man stared out the window.

"I'm so sorry, Danny," she said.

"I didn't like him from the start," Danny said. "But I never thought he would …" He drew his coat round him and wiped his nose on the sleeve.

Pru was cold and soaked through and thought Danny was probably the same. Even with the car's heater going full on, it would take awhile to dry out. Pru had mud coating her trousers, and no telling what her face looked like. She pulled the alligator clip out of her hair—it had been hanging by only a few strands—and came away with a handful of twigs and wizened hawthorn berries. She attempted to comb through, but her wet hair resisted. She gave up and stuck the clip in however it would go.

The end of it all brought exhaustion and the after effects of shock. Thoughts of home filled her mind—the library fireplace, a hot drink, an equally hot bath. But there would be an incredible amount to do before she would ever get there. And, of course, that's Christopher's evening sorted—even when he arrived back from Oxford, he would need to go straight to the Winchester police station.

"Oh dear," Pru said, "my phone." She turned to Danny. "I was talking to Christopher—I've left it in my car. I'll be right back."

But when she opened the door, there was Sophie holding it out to her.

"He's still on the line," she said.

"Thanks." Pru took her phone and sank back into the car. "Hiya," she said, trying for chipper and failing. "We're fine. I hope you aren't speeding, because the roads are a mess down here."

What she heard in reply was a sound somewhere between exasperation and relief.

"I'll take care," Christopher replied. "What happened?"

A PC knocked on Danny's window and delivered two cups of sugary tea.

"Well," Pru said, "all three of us got caught on one of the bends on the Straight Mile. It was Ellis's fault—he tried to overtake me. We spun out and ended up shaken and a bit banged up, I guess." Danny's eyes darted to her. Pru wondered what sort of injuries Temple might have suffered from his blow. "But nothing serious. Danny and I are waiting in Sophie's car. Mostly right now, I'd just like a bath."

"When I get there, I'll need to go to the station first," Christopher said.

"Yes, of course. Danny and I will be fine at home. We'll see you later."

Pru sipped the tea and watched the activity, the police officers going back and forth in the rain. She had lost track of the time—dark is dark in winter, and it probably wasn't as late as it felt. At last, after both she and Danny had given their statements, and an ambulance had taken Ellis away, Sophie drove them to Greenoak.

"Is Ellis all right?" Pru asked.

Sophie glanced at her in the rearview mirror. "Yes, he's fine —just precautions. I'm sure he'll be spending the night at the station, not the hospital."

"Good," Pru said, giving Danny a nod. "Good."

CHAPTER 20

On their way to Greenoak, Pru noticed a familiar van pass them. And when they arrived home just before eight o'clock, instead of the house looking cold and dark as it well should with no one at home, there were lights on. Sophie left them and drove off and Pru and Danny went in through the mudroom to be met with the feeling of warmth and the fragrance of soup and the sight of the cook at the hob.

"Evelyn!" Pru squeaked, which was all she was able to get out after a rush of emotion overcame the solid front she'd wanted to show Danny. "Whatever are you doing here?"

"Never you mind about that," Evelyn replied, wiping her hands on her pinny. "Look at the state of the both of you. You, young man"—she pointed at Danny, who looked cautiously at her finger—"upstairs to your room for a bath."

"Yes, ma'am," Danny said, peeling off his wet coat.

"You can leave those shoes here, too," Evelyn added and then turned to Pru. "You as well."

"Yes, Ev."

Upstairs, Pru tiptoed through her bedroom to keep from shaking any mud off. In the large tiled bathroom, she stood in the corner to strip off her clothes and then rolled them into a bundle. Still, she made a terrible mess. As the tub filled, she added a few drops of honeysuckle-scented oil and poured herself a brandy, setting it within easy reach before she climbed into the bath. The steam rose round her as she stretched out. She sighed, feeling a bit guilty at her pleasure when Christopher had a long evening of work ahead.

When she went downstairs again, Pru heard Danny's voice in the library. She put her ear to the door and listened.

"Yeah, I'm okay," he said, "but I miss you. England isn't such a bad place—you might like it here."

Pru decided she should head for the kitchen, where she found Evelyn bent over the open oven door. The cook glanced over her shoulder and said, "Don't you look better, now."

"I feel better, too," Pru replied, but still she thought that sitting was better than standing. She sank into a chair. On the table in front of her was a tray with soup mugs.

"Ev, did I see Peachey's van on the road when Sophie brought us home?"

"You did. Christopher rang and asked if I could come over and be here when you arrived. I said it was no bother. He asked if Peachey could go see to your car and to Danny's. No point in me just sitting here waiting, so I sorted out a bite of supper for you."

"Did Christopher explain what happened?" Pru asked.

"I'm sure he didn't tell me everything, but he explained enough," Ev replied. Then, the swing door opened, and there was Danny at the same time a *beep* came from the drive.

"That'll be Albert," Evelyn said.

Albert Peachey came into the mudroom carrying a carton and a stuffed animal.

"'Evening, Pru. 'Evening, Danny," he said. "Ev taking care of you, is she?"

"She is," Pru said. "I see you've rescued Bear. Do you have a report on our cars?"

"Yes, I've been seeing to them. Didn't want to leave this fellow all on his own though."

Peachey held Bear out to Danny, who took the stuffed animal and dropped him in a chair as if it were nothing more than an old coat, but Pru noticed he give Bear a scratch behind an ear.

"Police will take care of the Jaguar," Peachey continued. "It hit that tree smack on and bent the front end so that it looks like the car tried to suck on a lemon. That Honda, Danny, is fine and I'll have it back to you here tomorrow morning. But yours, Pru, didn't fare well running into that hedge. It'll need a bit of work."

"Better the car than you," Evelyn said. "Right, Albert—we'd best be on our way."

"Thanks, Peachey," Danny said.

Peachey grinned. "You're very welcome."

"Now you two," Evelyn said, "take your supper out to the library—the fire's already going."

Evelyn and Peachey left, Pru filled the tray, and Danny carried it out. They settled at the fireside with mugs of tomato soup and toasted cheese sandwiches, cut into soldiers and perfect for dipping.

They ate in silence, but after Danny had finished off the last of the sandwiches, he asked, "Did you know he did it?"

Here it was. "I … suspected, but only because of what I learned this afternoon. Look, Danny, I can tell you my bits and pieces, which I will certainly do if you want, but Christopher will have the whole story. I don't know when he'll be home, but I'd say he'd be willing to tell you."

Danny nodded. After a moment, he asked, "Why did you come to England?"

Pru was happy that they could talk of things other than

murder—at least for a while—although a little voice in the back of her mind wondered if Danny were asking because he thought she was one of those old people who told good stories. Well, so what if she was—she told him hers.

"Simon's your brother," Danny said at the end, "but he's English?"

"Yes. He stayed here and grew up with relatives. Did you grow up in Winchester?"

"Yeah. Mum and I lived in a house that had been converted to flats. There were two on the top floor, but only one kitchen between them, so we shared with the woman next door. Jagoda, that was her name. She'd been a Polish refugee during the war—came over when she was only five. She looked after me when Mum went to work."

"Where did she work?"

"Here and there," Danny said. "I remember she worked in a bakery, because she'd bring home the broken cakes and the like. Then she got on in the billing department at a car-hire company. That's where she met Ellis."

He poked at the fire and added a piece of wood as they fell silent again. Pru had a great many questions—probably the same as Danny—but no one to answer them. They would have to wait until tomorrow, when Christopher would explain just how Ellis had managed to carry out his murderous scheme.

Danny looked up from the flames. "I should ring my dad. Would that be all right?"

Pru reined in her delight at hearing this. "Yes, yes, what a good idea. Look, I'll take these things in." When Danny rose, she added, "No, you stay, I can wash up this time."

~

She was rinsing the mugs when Christopher came in the door. Grabbing a tea towel to dry her hands, she got to the mudroom before he'd taken off his coat and threw her arms round him.

"You're earlier than I thought. I'm very glad."

He slipped his arms round her waist and kissed her, long and lingering. His lips were warm and his face only chilly—a good gauge of the rise in temperature outside. After another kiss, and then just one more, he leaned back and looked at her.

"How are you?" he asked.

"No worse for wear," she said. "Barely a bump or bruise, and that was from the airbags."

"And Danny?"

Pru looked over her shoulder in the direction of the library. "He seems peaceful, and yet still a bit on edge. Does that make sense?"

"It does." Christopher buried his nose in her hair. "I'm sorry I missed your bath," he said.

"You'd be sorrier if you'd seen me just before. Have you wrapped everything up already?"

"Enough for tonight. Is Danny still awake?"

"Yes. He wanted to phone Arlo and tell him what happened —as much as he knows, at least. I thought that was a good sign. Perhaps after all this, he'll end up with a real father. About Ellis ... can you explain to Danny?"

"I can do, yes," Christopher said as he took off his coat.

"Good," Pru said, "because I already said you would." She rushed on. "Have you eaten? There's soup left. Oh, and thanks for asking Ev to come over and meet us."

"She didn't have to be asked twice. I ate a sandwich in the car on the way back."

"I'm sure that was lovely," Pru said.

"I don't even remember what it was now," Christopher said as they walked into the library.

Danny stood.

"How are you?" Christopher asked.

"Fine, sir. Well, you know."

"Would you like a drink? Whisky or brandy?" Christopher asked.

"Whisky, sir. Thanks."

"Pru?"

"Brandy, please."

Christopher took the drinks over to the fireplace, and for a moment, the three of them stood there, as if offering a silent toast to Claudia. Pru sat, and then so did the two men.

Danny took a sip of his whisky and said, "Did he confess?"

"He did," Christopher said, sounding mildly surprised. "He was questioned, gave his statement, and signed it. His solicitor was present."

"Will you tell me?" Danny asked. "How he did it? Everything?"

"Son, you don't need to—"

"I want to know. I have a right to know, don't I?"

Christopher watched him for a moment, and when Danny didn't flinch under that intense gaze, said, "Yes, you do."

So, he told him, and Pru listened just as carefully as Danny. Some of the things she knew or had guessed. At first it was odd to her that Ellis had admitted to the crime, but then she heard his voice again as he argued with Danny on the road—Temple had sounded proud of what he'd done. He thought he'd saved Danny from ... what? Having a loving, if slightly scatterbrained, mother?

Christopher explained how Ellis was able to drive from Oxford and back that night without looking as if he'd left the hotel at all by going in Laura Quigley's car—and the blind eye turned by a couple of the hotel employees. "We might not have known for a long time, except Pru intercepted the woman who owns the car and encouraged her to tell us."

"He drugged Mum?"

"It was a poorly made medieval recipe that, centuries ago, was used as an anesthetic. I'm sure it was as dangerous then as it is today. He didn't realize the mixture's potency. Your mother died fairly quickly, and according to the medical examiner, probably just fell asleep."

"Too clever for his own good," Danny said thickly.

"Temple said it was no trouble to persuade your mother to drink it after he told her that Acantha Morris had left the jar for her, claiming it was some herbal mixture. Claudia held Ms. Morris in great esteem, and drank it down. This way, Temple thought it would show that in theory if not in fact, her death was the fault of the medieval herbalist all along."

"He's good at pointing fingers," Danny said. "Always has been. Nothing sticks to Ellis."

"That seems to be what he believed. Even now that he's admitted to what he's done, he contends that the real guilty parties are those that tried to talk your mother out of her money."

"He poisoned her," Danny said quietly, as if to himself, "and she died. And then he took her and he …" He swallowed hard, leapt up, and paced in front of the fire, back and forth, then stopped suddenly and sat down again.

Christopher waited a moment before continuing. "The rosemary and lavender in your mother's pocket are common plants and it wasn't difficult to find myrrh, but there was more to his plan when it came to making the dwale."

"What's in it?" Danny asked.

"Herbs, some quite potent," Christopher said.

"Henbane and hemlock are poisonous," Pru said.

"How did he find that stuff?" Danny asked.

"He'd ordered live plants online, just as Ms. Morris suggested someone could've done."

"Greenhouse grown this time of year," Pru added. "But there's nothing illegal about them."

"On the first pass looking at financial information, we hadn't caught these purchases," Christopher said. "He used a credit card he'd taken out in Claudia's name and the address of his business. The internet is full of various recipes for dwale, but Temple substituted where he had to. He apparently wasn't willing to go so far as to buy opium."

"It has opium in it?" Danny asked.

"Temple's substitution was to use an old prescription of your mother's for hydrocodone."

Danny frowned. "She never … yeah, I remember she had back trouble, and she got those tablets. But she never took any."

"He cooked up this mixture as he thought he should, but then had to strain it. He disposed of the material by burying it in the back garden. We found that out, because Pru spotted something wrong with one of the plants. He'd shredded the documents for the donation that your mother had signed and he buried them, too, thinking that they'd disintegrate before anyone found them."

"Shows what he knows about soil biology," Pru said, "if he thought all that would break down in freezing weather. And also, had it never occurred to him that someone might see him digging in the garden and wonder why? If he'd taken the time to get to know his neighbor, he'd've realized nothing slips past Tabby. Except when he went back that night, she didn't notice, because he wasn't driving his red Jag."

"He's in debt," Christopher said. "Your mother gave Temple five hundred thousand pounds to start his business, but now he's expanded, going into vintage-car sales. He did this regardless of the fact that the original business wasn't doing well. He's like a gambler who thinks one more bet will solve all his problems. He'd mortgaged the house and hidden his debts well, I'll say that for him."

"That bloody house," Danny said, "and the way he lived. The world had to be perfect for him. To think he planned that whole thing to make it look as if Mum killed herself. To get her money."

"You'll inherit what's in your mother's name," Christopher said, "but it'll take a solicitor to sort it all out."

"Ms. Bagshaw can take care of it," Danny said. "Get rid of that house, for one thing. Good riddance to it. Good riddance to him, too."

They fell quiet, the only sound in the room a rustling sigh as a piece of wood in the fire collapsed and embers crumbled through the grate. For a brief moment, Pru thought about another brandy, but then realized she'd just as soon crawl into bed at this point. Christopher looked weary, too, and Danny sat slumped in the chair, his empty glass loose in his hands.

"Did you talk with your dad?" she asked.

Danny looked up and a bit of life returned. "Yeah. I didn't tell him much—didn't have much to tell, did I? But it's just as well, he was that angry. I did say I don't want that funeral tomorrow—it isn't right. And he said he'd take care of canceling it."

"Good," she said. "But, perhaps you would like a service of some sort? A small gathering to remember your mum?"

"Dunno." Danny frowned. "Maybe. But it would have to be something that would've suited her, you know."

"I could talk with Bernadette," Pru offered. "Remember, she's our vicar. I believe she'd be happy to help. You could have the service at St. Mary's."

"Yeah, she's all right." Danny managed a smile. "Arlo'd love that, wouldn't he?"

They all stood. Pru and Christopher moved toward the library door, but Danny hesitated.

"I punched him," he said. "Ellis. I hit him pretty hard." He worked his right hand, stretching the fingers out as if remembering how that had felt. "He fell back and hit his car. Is he injured? Will I be charged with something?"

"Did you?" Christopher asked with an innocent tone—

feigned, Pru thought. "He did have a mild concussion from hitting the back of his head on the car, but he said he'd slipped on the icy road."

In their bedroom, Pru turned to Christopher. "Danny did hit him."

"Yes, I thought as much. Temple had quite a bruise on his jaw. It was swollen, and he kept worrying a back tooth—I believe it was loose." Christopher sat on the chair in the corner and took off his shoes. "In Temple's mind, he did all this to save Danny. After he'd admitted everything, he contended that Danny needed a good example set for him. As if Temple believed he could murder Claudia and still be an upstanding citizen."

"He was deluding himself," Pru said. "I don't believe Ellis could see past his own nose." She pulled her sweater off over her head, and then added, "Danny probably wishes Claudia had been able to give the money away. Now what's he going to do with it?"

CHAPTER 21

Libby arrived on Wednesday evening, having taken the train from Inverness to Edinburgh, Edinburgh to London, and London to Eastleigh, where she could've got another train to Romsey, but instead Danny drove over to collect her.

Libby was a wide-eyed strawberry blonde, her eyes made wider still by this being her first time ever in England. She arrived with a bottle of her family's whisky for Pru and Christopher, another one to open on the spot, and tales to tell of her journey south. Throughout dinner—at the table in the kitchen—Danny said little, only watched her with shining eyes. Her thick Scottish accent and rate of speech meant Pru got about half of what she was saying and needed a moment to translate the rest. She reacted to Libby's anecdotes a bit later than others, like a laugh track out of sync.

The difficulties with accents went both ways. As they were clearing the table, Libby said to Pru, "Danny's not told me much what with all that's going on, but he's loved staying here, and kept saying to me oh wait until I meet you and how much I'd love it here. And really, aren't you grand for putting us up?

You're that welcoming it's as if you're Scottish, but of course you aren't." Plates in hand, she looked at Pru. "Are you English?"

"No," Pru said, "I'm American. I moved here from Texas."

"Oh," Libby replied and nodded. "That's why I cannae quite sort out your accent. I knew you sounded different, but I thought perhaps you came from Cornwall."

On Friday morning, Pru and Christopher, dressed in their Sunday best, met Danny and Libby downstairs at the front door. Pru had spent Thursday harvesting fresh cuttings from the garden and replacing all the flowers in St. Mary's from the large vases in the front of the church to the small ones in each of the windows. The weather had warmed to normal winter temperatures, the gray skies flashed occasional patches of blue, and at any time throughout the day, you could be caught in a short sharp shower. Pru would take wet over frozen any day of the week.

Evelyn had spent the day before baking and making tiny sandwiches, because after the service for Claudia, people were invited back to Greenoak. Pru had returned from her flower guild duties to find Libby and Danny both lending a hand with food, and so she got to work herself counting cups, saucers, stacking small plates, and making sure everything matched.

Come ten o'clock on Friday, Reverend Bernadette Freemantle welcomed everyone to St. Mary's and conducted the service with love and care. Danny, Libby, Arlo, and Zoe Bagshaw sat in the front pew, and the rest of the people were scattered behind them in the small church. Members of the Winchester Medieval Garden Society board attended, plus Rollo's husband, Ken. Terry Reed was there—Danny had made a point of phoning and inviting him. Polly and Simon sat with

Christopher and Pru. Two pews held people Pru didn't know but later learned were neighbors of the Temples. They had been invited on Danny's request by Tabby Collier who had arrived wearing a beret and a tartan woolen coat that stayed buttoned up to her chin—the church, as all British churches are in winter and often summer, was chilly. She had on tartan woolen tights, too. Not the same tartan, but no matter.

John Upstone and Sabine were there. They sat across the aisle and one pew back, forcing Pru to casually swivel her head round to get a sense of how things were going between them. Sabine gave a small wave, but John, sitting directly behind Tabby, seemed intent on studying her beret to which she had attached a collection of lapel pins, the sort you get for supporting badgers or hedgehogs or hazel dormice. John appeared relaxed, but Pru couldn't say for sure if they had put on their best faces for the day, or if things between them had improved.

When Bernadette asked if anyone would like to speak, Danny rose, tugged on the jacket—the one he'd borrowed from Libby's brother—and stood in front next to the urn of Claudia's ashes. He shared memories growing up with a loving mother and told a few anecdotes. He finished a bit teary, and when he went back to the front pew and sat beside Libby, she put her arm round his shoulder. Zoe went next, and she spoke of Claudia's determination to make a difference in the world. After that, Arlo rose.

Pru was a bit worried that Arlo would start talking up The Guard's reunion concert, but he kept on topic and shared what he remembered of Claudia's love of life and of their son. Pru noticed Danny bow his head. She'd been fine until then, but at that point had to open the packet of tissues in her hand.

Danny and Arlo stood with Bernadette at the door as people filed out. Pru waited a bit further down the church walk with a reminder that everyone was invited to Greenoak. Then, she rushed off to help Evelyn, in case there was something to do at the last-minute, which there wasn't, of course. When people arrived, she collected coats and then began circulating through the sitting room with a tray of drinks and encouraging people to have a go at the table of food, which looked as if they'd expected a hundred people and not twenty.

This roaming about the room suited Pru, because she got to listen in on and occasionally join many different conversations.

"Sherry? Wine?" she asked when she came across Danny talking with Terry Reed. "Or something from the bar?"

"Christopher works with the badger people," Danny to Reed. "Isn't that right, Pru?"

"He does, yes."

Terry nodded. "There's a great deal to do for our countryside all the way round. Don't you have the Scottish wildcat to look after, Danny?"

She continued her rounds, hoping to catch either Sabine or John free so that she could stick her nose in business that was not hers, but they were continually engaged in one conversation after another—Sabine with Tabby and John with Christopher, then John and Acantha and Sabine with Zoe.

On Pru's next swing through the room, she noticed someone out on the terrace. It was Tabby, and so Pru set down her tray, went through to the library, and out the French doors to join her.

"Oh now," Tabby said, "isn't this a lovely place? Even here in winter, you can see this garden has good bones."

Pru was one second away from telling Tabby that the garden had indeed had bones in it at one time, but Simon popped out of the library. Brother and sister seemed to have some internal radar system that told them when there was a visitor to the garden.

"Here's my brother, Simon—he's been head gardener here at

Greenoak for donkey's years. Simon, Tabby has a lovely garden next door to where Claudia lived."

"I saw you taking a look at those pittosporum," Simon said to Tabby, nodding to three short, round shrubs with wavy-edged leaves. "We've a good contrast with hebes and pittosporum in the parterre garden. Would you like to see?"

Simon and Tabby set off for the garden in the front of the house. It was rather hidden by a high yew hedge, and visitors loved it. Pru would've gone with them, but knew her duty lay indoors, so retraced her steps through the library to the door of the sitting room, where she spotted—across the room—Rollo talking with John Upstone. Something in their body language told Pru the conversation was almost over—yes, there, they were shaking hands. Here was her chance. Pru grabbed her tray from where she'd left it and headed for them, automatically murmuring to people as she did, "Sherry? Wine?" but not giving them a chance to reply.

She was five feet away from John when Libby walked up to him. Foiled again! Pru veered off to the next nearest conversation—Christopher and Arlo—and thought she might listen in on Detective Superintendent Upstone to make sure he wasn't sounding like a bear.

"Sherry? Wine?" she muttered to Christopher and Arlo, even though they each had whisky and fizzy water in their respective hands. Pru cocked her head for better reception on John and Libby's conversation.

"I hear Danny may try for art school," John said. "My wife is an artist, and she's offered to help him find a place. She says he has talent. She has an eye for that sort of thing, of course, being an exceptional artist herself."

Over her shoulder, Pru flashed Upstone a smile, then turned back to Christopher. "Did you hear that?" she asked. "He said 'my wife.' Not that I was eavesdropping, of course, but don't you think that's progress?"

"Remind me not to assign you any undercover work," a strong voice from behind Pru said. She whipped round as John Upstone continued. "You realize you're circulating with an empty tray?"

~

Supper was a quiet affair that evening. It consisted mostly of leftovers from the reception and was eaten at the kitchen table. Arlo and Zoe stayed, and by the time they'd moved into the library with coffee, Pru had learned a great deal about rock bands and discovered that the solicitor was a musician in her own right.

"Flute," Zoe said, settling onto the sofa, "not drums. Not that he hasn't tried talking me into it." She patted Arlo on the knee. "You'll find your drummer, don't worry."

Danny cleared his throat. "I've worked out what to do about the money," he said, as if a million pounds was one of those irritations in life.

Christopher and Pru took chairs on either side of the fireplace, Libby sat next to Zoe, and Danny remained standing by the mantel.

"Well, let's hear it, son," Arlo said.

"You already know," Danny said to him, and to the others, "Arlo refused to take any of it. Stubborn old ..."

Zoe laughed, but Arlo said, "Ah now, I didn't refuse, did I? What I said was that the lads—the other band members—and I can pay for our own reunion, and that Danny can give it away to others, but he should take at least some of the money and do what he wants with it."

"And what have you decided?" Christopher asked.

"I'm giving the dormice some of it," Danny said. "I talked to that fellow, and Libby and I looked stuff up and—"

"They're the sweetest wee things," Libby said, "and they live down here in England, did you know that?"

"Mum was concerned," Danny said, "and it wasn't that she gave up on dormice, it's only that this medieval business caught her interest, and so they'll get a share. It's not the whole amount, but when I talked with Mr. Martin, he seemed all right with it."

"All right?" Zoe asked. "Finley was thrilled, as are the others. You're very generous, Danny."

"Yeah, well. And some money for Annamarie—she needs a new boiler and a new roof—and bits and bobs to a few others."

"And you?" Arlo reminded him.

"Well, I'll take some art classes—Sabine knows someone local for me to work with. I'm not quitting the caf, though."

"Otts couldn't do it without him," Libby said. "Everyone's missed Danny these few days. But no one more than me." She looked up at him with raised eyebrows, and he grinned.

"Instead of that garden flat," Danny said, "we're going all out to find a bigger place with good light."

"Sabine says the light in Inverness is perfect, and Danny should take advantage," Libby said.

"And we'll have a big room kitted out for Libby's work, too," Danny said.

"I run the distillery's website," Libby explained, "book coach tours, manage the online gift shop, that sort of thing. I can do that from anywhere."

Pru wished the young couple could stay at Greenoak longer—she might absorb some of their endless energy—but they were leaving the next morning.

"We're stopping to see Annamarie on our way back. She was sorry she couldn't be here for Mum's service, but she has the old people."

"We hope you'll all come to Inverness on your summer holidays," Libby said. "And of course, stop at the distillery for the full treatment. Arlo and Zoe, Christopher and Pru, Sabine and Mr. Upstone—who else now?"

"You'll need to open a bloody B and B before you know it," Arlo said.

"Yeah, well," Danny said, "at least I'll know how to cook the breakfasts."

~

Only after Danny and Libby had left on their long trek north did Pru and Christopher discover the little treasures left for them.

On the counter in the kitchen was a sketch of the room itself—the farm table with a half-eaten Bakewell tart on a platter and almond slices scattered about like a series of trails leading to empty plates, giving the suggestion that a tea party had only just ended.

Pru found another drawing on the mantel in the library. In it, the fire blazed. Two people sat on the sofa, although all that could be seen of them was the tops of their heads and their sock feet stretched out toward the warmth. On a nearby low table, a bottle of the Highlands best single malt.

On the Monday when Evelyn went to the first floor to clean, she soon returned and took Pru back up to the guest room where Danny and Libby had stayed. The pair had tidied up, stripped the bed of linens, and thrown the duvet back over the mattress. Perched on a pillow was a drawing of Bear. The stuffed animal sat at a table that held bottles of catsup, vinegar, and brown sauce. In the background could be seen vague figures at a counter. Otts café.

~

Wednesday, Pru rose in the dark—telling herself that it was February and surely the sun would be rising a few seconds earlier than the day before—and went straight out to sweep the terrace walks. That chore under her belt, she settled down at the kitchen table with toast and marmalade and a steaming mug of tea. When she'd finished with her toast, she brushed off the table, washed her hands, and was tying on her pinny just as Evelyn arrived.

"Goodness," Ev said, "aren't you the early riser."

"I thought it best to get the cake made, and then I could dress for the meeting."

The board meeting of the Winchester Medieval Garden Society. At the end of the reception for Claudia at Greenoak, Rollo had glanced longingly at the yew hedge and down the terrace as he and Ken readied to leave. "Your brother has a real eye for balance in the landscape, doesn't he? I'd love to have more time to look round."

It was the heaviest of hints, but Pru hadn't minded and then and there offered to host the board meeting. Making a cake for the meeting was the bigger problem. She had promised Evelyn that she would do it all herself—under supervision.

"Right then," Evelyn said now, hanging her coat and bag on a peg, "we'd best begin."

Christopher came into the kitchen during the delicate "don't overbeat the batter" stage. He said not a word. Evelyn delivered tea and toast to his end of the table, and he'd left for work by the time the cake was out of the oven.

"Now," Ev said, "you've plenty of time to dress."

"Cardamom," Acantha said. "I remember this cake. It's quite lovely. Cardamom, of course, was such a rare spice in medieval

England. It showed a certain amount of wealth to be able to obtain it."

"I'd love the recipe," Rollo said. "That is, Ken would love the recipe—I'd only pass it along."

Rollo, Acantha, Finley, and Zoe had arrived in separate cars, looking like a convoy. Pru asked Simon to lead the garden tour, and they had come indoors only after the light mist had turned heavy. Over coffee, Rollo perused Simon's garden journals—at least a few of them—admiring the recordkeeping that mixed opinion and impression with actual data on every page. "You manage to say so much in so few words," Rollo said. "I can't seem to write anything in a few words."

After Simon left, the business part of the meeting began. Pru had been officially welcomed onto the board, then Finley went over finances. Danny had been generous, donating five hundred thousand pounds to the garden. It was half of what Claudia had promised, but real enough and would pay for everything up to the moment—those bricks, for example—and with enough to hold the sale of the land. The remainder of the meeting was taken up by brainstorming fundraising ideas.

"Actually asking for money is vital," Zoe said, "but you need publicity, too. Getting the word out to as many people as possible can be the only way."

A few assignments were made to chase up facts and figures —Pru volunteered to work on a plant budget, because she knew plants were always the last thing bought.

As the meeting drew to a close, Pru heard a knock at the front door. Evelyn had gone upstairs to clean, and so Pru excused herself and went out to the entry.

She opened the door to find a man who looked to be in his mid- to late thirties in a tight-fitting pale gray suit over his slim build, a wide red tie, and slicked back dark hair. He smiled at her.

"Pru? Pru Parke—it is you, isn't it? Of course I feel as if I know you, even though all we've ever done is speak on the phone."

"Hello," Pru said, then added, "please come in" even though she had no idea who he was and desperately hoped the stranger would identify himself. But he strode past her and into the entry without offering a name.

"Well, it has been a drive, you know, down from London, but I knew that this was the best thing to do because, firstly, we could meet face-to-face, and secondly, I would be able to see your garden. It is your own garden you're writing about, isn't it?"

And then, with the feeling of a lead weight dropping to the pit of her stomach, she knew who this man was. Nate Crispin, editor of *Designs On Your Garden*. The magazine for which she was to write an article. An article due … last week.

"Not that you haven't had anything else to do," Nate said as if replying to her thoughts. "Yes, quite a thing down here with that murder. Say, you wouldn't want to follow up with another article, this one about the medieval garden, would you?"

She could follow up her article with another one only if she'd written the first one. Which she hadn't. It had removed itself from her list of things to do and vanished from her mind altogether. Pru had no article, and she felt sure Nate Crispin knew it. Perhaps he was taking the opportunity to visit in hopes of getting from her what he had wanted in the first place—a gossipy article about murder that only tangentially had anything to do with gardens. Although the entry was not warm, Pru began to sweat.

"Yes, that's an interesting point," she said. Had he made a point? "And the thing is that I have been having a good think about the subject, and I'm not sure if I fully explained to you my idea." Because it was difficult to fully explain something she hadn't given a thought to. She'd better confess. "You see, Mr. Crispin—"

"Nate," he said. "Please call me Nate."

"Yes, Nate. You see, I haven't actually been able to ..."

The door to the library opened, and Rollo Westcott put his head out.

"Pru—I believe we could do with another round of coffee," he said. "Oh, sorry, I didn't mean to disturb you."

"Disturb?" Pru asked. She blinked at Rollo—he seemed to glow with something that might just be a glimmer of hope. She marched over to him and practically dragged him into the entry. "You aren't doing anything of the sort. In fact, you are just the person. Rollo, let me introduce Nate Crispin, editor of the magazine *Designs On Your Garden*. Nate, Rollo is on the board of the Winchester Medieval Garden Society. He's a landscape designer and has written a series of articles on the history of garden design. Haven't you, Rollo?"

The look in Rollo's eyes told Pru he may not understand exactly what was going on, but whatever it was seemed to involve getting not only his heart's desire of being accepted as a respected designer, but also the opportunity to promote the medieval garden.

"Nate," Rollo said, grabbing the man's hand and shaking, "it's good to meet you. Indeed, I have written an article—"

"Series," Pru corrected him.

"A series of articles," Rollo amended, "and I'm happy to say that Pru has worked with me on them to make certain the plant material and horticultural information are correct."

"I knew this is just what you were looking for, Nate," Pru said, calling up every atom of persuasion she could. "And so I may have veered off only a bit from our original agreement." That, Pru recalled, was for her to write an article titled "Death in the Garden." She smiled. "Rollo was actually ready to offer the series to another publication, but I believe I've persuaded him to consider your magazine first. After all, you've already garnered quite a reputation, and could do the entire subject justice." Inwardly, she cringed at how thick she was laying it on.

Nate's initial joviality departed, leaving behind only a small, knowing smile lifting the side of his mouth. "Well, well, doesn't this sound interesting? I confess, Pru, that I was a bit worried you were reluctant to come through for us, but now—tell me more."

"Will do," Pru said. "Rollo, why don't you introduce Nate to the others and tell him all about the medieval herb garden at the Hospital of St. Cross. I'll fix the coffee."

ACKNOWLEDGMENTS

Thanks go to you, fans of Pru Parke and the Potting Shed mysteries, because without you, this book—number eight in the series—wouldn't have made it out into the world.

Thanks to Sue Trowbridge at Interbridge (interbridge.com) for help in formatting and advice on all sorts of publishing matters and to the great cover created by Karen Phillips at Phillips Covers (phillipscovers.com). And to the inimitable writing group of which I am proud to be a part: Kara Pomeroy, Louise Creighton, Sarah Niebuhr Rubin, Tracey Hatton, and Meghana Padakandla.

You can visit the Hospital of St. Cross and Almshouse of Noble Poverty in Winchester (sans medieval garden) and read its fascinating history here: hospitalofstcross.co.uk.

ABOUT THE AUTHOR

Marty Wingate lives in the Pacific Northwest and writes mysteries and historical fiction set in Britain. Marty lectures about gardens and travel and leads garden tours to England and Scotland. She is a member of the Royal Horticultural Society. Marty and her husband (her in-house copy editor) prefer on-the-ground research whenever possible, and so they regularly travel to England and Scotland, where she can be found tracing the steps of her characters, stopping for tea and a slice of Victoria sponge in a café, or enjoying a swift half in a pub.

Learn more at martywingate.com

facebook.com/martywingateauthor
twitter.com/martywingate
bookbub.com/marty-wingate
goodreads.com/453259.Marty_Wingate